ELLORA'S
CAVE

DREAMS
OF
THE OASIS

ELLORA'S CAVE
ROMANTICA PUBLISHING

An Ellora's Cave Romantica Publication

www.ellorascave.com

Ellora's Cavemen: Dreams of the Oasis II

ISBN # 1419954482

Edited by Raelene Gorlinsky.
Cover design by Darrell King.
Photography by Dennis Roliff.

Electronic book Publication June 2006
Trade Paperback Publication June 2006

Warning:

Ellora's Cavemen
Dreams of the Oasis II

Treasure Hunters

Sylvia Day

ๆ

Dedication

ω

This story is dedicated to Tina Engler,
who didn't accept 'no' for an answer.

Acknowledgement

ω

Thanks to author and friend, Renee Luke, who accepted my
Cavemen challenge.

Trademarks Acknowledgement

The author acknowledges the trademarked status and trademark owners of the following wordmarks mentioned in this work of fiction:

eBookman: Franklin Electronic Publishers, Inc.
Romantica: Ellora's Cave Publishing, Inc.

Chapter One

ℭ

If the guy in her office weren't so damn gorgeous she might be able to think properly. But he was yummy. In fact, he was so unbelievably handsome Samantha was staring, something that was brought to her attention by the long, masculine fingers snapping in front of her face.

"Miss Tremain." His deep voice, though soft, was filled with exasperation. "Are you listening to me?"

"Beg your pardon?" She blinked rapidly.

He exhaled and took the seat in front of her desk. Crossing one ankle over the opposite knee, he bared to her view an impressive bulge behind the tightened lacings of his pants.

"Animal," she breathed. The bulge jerked in response.

"Huh?"

Sam coughed into her hand as her face heated. "A-animal skin."

"Yeah. It is." Bright blue eyes flashed briefly before narrowing. "I was told that you're the foremost expert on literary antiquities in this part of the galaxy, Miss Tremain. Is that right or should I be looking for help elsewhere?"

"Mr. Bronson—"

"Rick."

"Oh…" The way he said his own name, like it was a sensual threat, made her shiver. And the way he was dressed, in animal skin and some billowing material for a shirt, made her mouth dry. "Why aren't you wearing a bio-suit?"

A dark brow rose. "You want to talk about my clothes?" He shook his head. "You brainy types are always a little weird."

"Look who's talking," she retorted, stung by his comment, one which she'd heard a thousand times. "You are a twenty-third-century mercenary who dresses in nineteenth-century clothing while tracking down a legendary twenty-first-century treasure. Shouldn't you be doing something else? Killing for hire or something of that nature?"

Blowing a loose tendril of hair from her face, Sam stood and began to pace. As long as she didn't look at that breathtaking face, she could keep her wits about her. His dark hair, tan skin and eyes like the Laruvian Ocean were bad enough. When you added in the broad shoulders, tapered hips and animal skin-covered bulge, she had a living wet dream sitting right in her office.

Rick Bronson chuckled and the warm sound of amusement made her womb clench. "Whatever a mercenary does, he does for credits. Hunting treasure is a hunt for credits. Pretty easy to figure out."

"But why this particular treasure?"

"It's worth a fortune."

"It's *rumored* to be worth a fortune. Just as it's *rumored* to exist. You're most likely wasting your time." She hazarded a side glance and her heart skipped a beat at his soft smile. "It seems an odd treasure for a man to hunt for. Why not the Draken Cup? Or the Sarian Stone? Why the erotic e-books?"

"That's a silly question." The curve of his lips deepened. "You know how much those Romantica stories are worth. Ever since the Conservative Censorship Committee succeeded in banning erotica and erotic romance back in 2015 it's almost impossible to find. All the print books have long since turned into dust, but the remaining e-books that manage to make it to the black market bring in a small fortune. Can you imagine how much a database full of those stories would be worth?"

Sam sighed with longing. "Now that the ban has been revoked, finding those stories would not only return literary treasures to the people, but it would help lift this sexual repression that has stifled us all for so long."

"You sound like a woman who appreciates the erotic," Rick purred. He stood and came toward her, his gait slow and filled with seductive promise. The blaster strapped to one thigh and the laser sword strapped to the other only emphasized how dangerous he was. Against the backdrop of her small office, he was even more intimidating. And tantalizing.

Towering over her, he lifted his hand to touch her hair. Sam could swear she felt that touch all the way to her toes, hitting all her erogenous zones on the way down.

"What is this?" he asked, brushing his hand across the tight bun on top of her head.

"Huh?" Damn, he smelled good, too. Nowadays droids did everything, leaving a lot of men soft. Rick was hard all—

Her gaze dropped.

Yep. Hard all over.

He gave a quick tug and her hair tumbled around her shoulders in a wild mess. "Hey!" she protested, snatching at his hand. He moved too quickly and held her hairpin up high, out of her reach.

"What is this thing you had in your hair?" he repeated, staring at her.

She wrinkled her nose. "The stylus for my eBookman."

His eyes widened. "You have a working eBookman?" His hand dropped and he tucked the stylus in his pocket.

"Give me that back," she snapped, brushing her hair away from her face and twisting it into a coil. "Do you know how hard those things are to find on the black market?"

"You can use your finger to work it, you know," he offered helpfully.

As innocent as his statement was, the fact that it came from a man who looked like he did gave it an added sexual dimension. Sam blushed so hard her face felt like it was on fire.

"Oh…" Both of his black brows flew up to his hairline as he caught on. "You're a naughty librarian. With a secret collection of erotic e-books, I bet. And you're not getting this back." He swatted her grasping hand away. "You'll just stick it in your hair again."

"I can't work with my hair falling in my face!"

"And I can't work with your hair all prim and tied up like that. It's distracting." He walked away.

"Who said I was going to work with you?"

Rick snorted. "You survive on grants for your research. In order to get those grants, you're forced to give speeches and offer some of your precious collection for traveling museum tours. I heard you lost a good portion of your pop culture collection in a raid by antiquity pirates a few months ago."

"I did." She sighed with regret. "It was dreadful. Years of collecting and cataloguing were lost." Shaking her head, she hit the button that opened her desk drawer. It slid outward silently and she dug through the scattered contents.

"Think of the credits you would receive if we found that lost database. Don't you find the thought tempting?"

Looking up, Sam stared at him hard. "Exactly how much would my share be?"

"Half."

"You'd give me half?" Her eyes narrowed suspiciously.

"Sure. You're the brains, I'm the brawn. We'd be a team, therefore you should get just as many credits as I do."

"I could keep my brains to myself and hire brawn elsewhere. Then I could keep more than half. What have you got to offer in return for your share?"

"How about this?" He reached into his shirt and pulled out a chain he wore around his neck. Hanging from that was a small cylindrical data chip. "I was told it's '*the key*', whatever the hell that means. I can't find any details about how to use it, but I did find a lot of references to a key being required to access the databases."

"Where did you get that?" she asked, holding out her hand for it.

His brows rose again. "I won it in a wager. The previous owner gave up trying to do something with it." As he dropped the chain back into the neck of his shirt, Sam caught a glimpse of warm, golden skin. "You can examine it all you want, *if* you agree to help me."

She swallowed hard and returned her attention to the contents of the drawer. "Ha!" she cried triumphantly, holding up a hair clip with mostly broken tines and then using it to pin up her wild tresses. "I'm a born scavenger."

"Why don't you prove it," he challenged, "by assisting me? Think of all the people you'll help if we get those books back on the market. Besides, wouldn't you like a little adventure?"

Adventure. She supposed it would be exciting to do the research up close, instead of through pictures and archaic phrases in books. But that wasn't what decided her mind. It was Rick Bronson who did that. The prospect of spending more time with him was far more exciting than her studies or the possibility of treasure. In her line of work, most of the men she ran across were bookish and slight of build. She'd never met any man as blatantly primitive as the mercenary in her office. He was, quite simply, an erotic e-book hero come to life.

"I'm the keynote speaker at the Retro-bration kickoff on Rashier 6," she said, crossing her arms over her chest. "That's a month from now. So that's all the time you're getting. You do what I say, when I say and we just might get somewhere in that limited amount of time."

"I certainly hope we get somewhere."

The sudden heat of his gaze startled her into gaping. Was that sexual innuendo?

She gave herself a mental kick in the ass. Rick Bronson couldn't be interested in her. She was short and kind of plump, with dark brown hair and plain brown eyes. It was never physical lust that inspired her sexual encounters. No, they were more like *"Hey, I'm tired of studying this. Wanna fuck?"* kinds of encounters. Like an afterthought or just a break from the monotony. Although they were sometimes more boring than painstaking cataloguing.

She wished she were the kind of woman men lusted after. What she wouldn't give to have a full-on alpha male tackle her and fuck her senseless. But that sort of thing only happened in erotic e-books and lamentably, she had only a couple dozen of those to satisfy her.

"Shall we get started then?" he asked, breaking into her musings.

"Yeah, let me gather up a few things and I'll meet you on your ship."

He nodded. "Need my help with anything?"

A screaming orgasm would be nice.

"Uh, no," she said, blushing at her own carnal thoughts. "I can manage."

Reminder to self: Pack sex toys.

It was going to be a long month.

* * * * *

Rick stepped out of Samantha Tremain's book-lined office and adjusted the fit of his pants. Who knew he had a liking for semi-timid librarians? He certainly hadn't. Not until he'd been ignored by a pretty little brunette one.

Lost in her book, Samantha had sat there chewing on her nail and muttering to herself. He'd almost opened his mouth to let her know she wasn't alone, but she'd been so damn adorable with her nose all wrinkled up and her soft brown eyes capped with a frown of concentration. Reluctant to disturb her, he'd just watched her silently until she caught sight of him lounging by the door. Then she'd turned that studious gaze on him, raking him from head to toe, stopping for a long moment at his cock. He knew sexual appreciation when he saw it and surprisingly, he'd been turned on by her almost scientific perusal. Her subsequent dazed inability to speak had been very flattering.

Before approaching her, Rick had done his research into her areas of specialty. He'd seen her picture, read her theories and perused database photos of her collections. None of that was able to convey the woman as she was in the flesh. There was just something about her, an indefinable quality, almost as if she were starving for something. Knowing women like he did, Rick would say she was hungry for a good fucking. He doubted she'd ever been ridden properly.

Most men were sadly ignorant about women like Samantha, thinking they liked a gentle hand. Perhaps most of them did. But there were clues that told him Sam wasn't one of them.

The hair for one.

By the gods, those skeins of chocolate silk had fallen down from that tight bun and he'd grown bone hard in an instant. She wore it up because it got in the way, but she didn't cut it. Why? He'd bet it was because it made her feel sexy. He could easily see her naked, that cascade of dark hair tumbling down her back.

And then there was the obvious giveaway — her expertise in ancient erotic romance. She was considered one of the foremost authorities in the galaxy on the subject. He wondered if any man had been smart enough to tap into all that knowledge. Hell, he'd offer himself up as a research subject any day.

In fact, he planned to do just that.

After the adorable way she'd blushed with her own naughty thoughts, he knew she'd be a handful and the prospect of all the fun he could have with her over the next month was just too good to pass up. The two of them alone on his ship, days passing with nothing to do besides lie in bed and fuck like crazy. He had to pat himself on the back for coming to Samantha

Tremain instead of Professor Terrance Milton of the Tolan University. It hadn't been Rick's intent to get involved in anything personal, but he knew a priceless opportunity when it stared him in the face. And a great ass. He knew one of those when he saw it, too.

Humming to himself, he quickened his pace.

It was going to be a great month.

Chapter Two

🔊

Sam slid the last research text she'd brought with her onto the sloped shelf of the bookcase and nodded her satisfaction. She had everything she needed to translate any foreign writing they came across. Now that she was settled, she could examine the interior of Rick Bronson's deep-space Starwing at her leisure. He'd said she was the brains and he was the brawn, but that wasn't entirely true. He obviously had brains, too.

His entire ship, except for the bridge, was decorated like a nineteenth-century mansion. All the chairs, beds and tables were made of simulated wood. The lighting was replicas of candelabras, tapers and chandeliers. All the materials were lush—rich velvets and satins in dark jewel tones. The books that lined the shelves in the library were like hers, ancient paper and threaded bindings instead of electronic editions that would have taken up far less space.

It would take months, perhaps years of research to reach this level of historical accuracy. Sam couldn't help but wonder at his fascination with this particular time period in Earth's history. What did it represent to him? Why did he like it so much?

"Are you hungry?"

At the sound of Rick's voice, Sam spun quickly. "Guh…"

As smart as she was, she couldn't form one coherent word when he was dressed like he was. Barefooted, with loose-fitting trousers and no shirt, he was a prime example of masculine virility. He looked like he'd just rolled out of bed.

Or was prepared to roll into one.

Her stomach fluttered at the thought.

"Was that a *yes* or a *no*?" His abdomen rippled with muscle as he moved toward her and his lips were curved in a rakish smile.

That was a "damn, you're gorgeous". But she couldn't say that out loud.

"I'm hungry, if you are," she said, clearing her throat. That was as close as she could get to flirting. When his face remained politely indifferent, she sighed despondently and asked, "Are we on our way to Simgen?"

"Yes." Rick caught up her elbow and led her down the hall to the dining room. "Could you tell me why you want to start there first?"

"Well, everyone starts the hunt at Voltaing, right?"

"That's because Voltaing was the site of the largest distributor of e-books."

"Yes, that's true. However, if I had something precious to lose, I would hide it in the least likely place, not the most likely."

Pulling out a chair for her, he waited until she sat down and then moved to the cooking unit cleverly hidden in the sideboard. "Anything in particular you want for dinner?"

She shrugged. "Whatever you're having is fine."

"Good." He turned away and she watched the muscles of his back flex as he typed the menu into the unit. "So you think Simgen is the least likely place?"

"I wrote a research paper on the e-book treasure and—"

"I read it."

Sam blinked. "You did?" It had been published in an obscure scholars' journal. She didn't think anyone read it.

"I sure did. It was great. I loved how your focus stayed firmly on the benefits of erotic romance and not the actual treasure hunt."

"Uh…thanks."

"You did a fantastic job pointing out the physical, emotional and mental benefits of regular orgasms, and how reading erotic stories improved the sex lives between couples. I was most interested in your thoughts on increasing mental acuity with lots of sex." Rick turned to face her and in the process revealed his dinner choice—chocolate, strawberries and whipped cream. "You and I are both going to need sharp minds if we hope to find that treasure before the end of the month."

Something warm and fuzzy blossomed in her chest at the look in his blue eyes. "Oh goddess." She gaped in dawning awareness. "Are you hitting on me? I mean, really. Do you want to fuck me?"

"Yes. Really. I do."

She stood and began to pace. "Wow. It could get weird though, working together, after we fuck. And—"

"Now see," he began, grinning, "I wouldn't have taken you as the type to talk dirty. But I like it. It's damn sexy coming from you."

The mischievous look in his eyes combined with that sexy smile made her heart race.

Reaching the table, Rick set the small platter down on a nearby chair. He caught her as she attempted to walk past him and before she knew what hit her, she was flat on her back on the slick wooden surface. He unclipped her hair and plunged his hands deep into her tresses.

Her eyes widened. "Oh wow, you *are* serious."

"Oh, yes," he purred.

"Are we going to do it right here? On the table?"

"Amongst other places."

She swallowed hard. "That means more than once, right?"

"Definitely more than once. I'm looking forward to finding out all your sexy little secrets."

"Are you sure you want *me*?" Mortified that she'd blurted that out loud, Sam smacked herself on her forehead. Only she would second-guess the once-in-a-lifetime opportunity to screw the hottest man she'd ever seen.

"Yes, I'm sure I want *you*, and don't worry about things getting weird. We're both adults. We can indulge in some no-strings, no-commitment sex."

Afraid to open her mouth again, Sam just nodded. That was the only kind of sex she knew, actually. Besides, she sure as hell wasn't going to say, *No thanks. My vibrator will do.*

He reached for the catch of her silver bio-suit and tugged it all the way down. Holding the hem of each ankle, he watched with a burning gaze as she pulled her legs free, but when she tried to shrug out of the sleeves, he stopped her. "Leave that part on."

"Uh… sure." She didn't know why he wanted her to keep the suit under her, but she wasn't going to complain. He might snap out of it and realize she was just a boring librarian.

"By the gods," he breathed, his calloused fingertips drifting over her stomach. "How did you hide all these curves under your suit?"

She looked down the length of her torso at him and was surprised to find that he looked dead serious. And totally in lust, too.

His fingers brushed between her legs. "You're hairless."

"Yeah… Is that okay?"

"Okay? Fuck, that makes me hot as hell."

"R-really?"

But he couldn't answer because his face was buried between her thighs.

With a startled cry, she arched into his mouth, the slickness of her suit sliding along the wood and pushing her toward him. Rick growled and gripped her hips, spreading her wide, opening her to the foraging licks of his talented tongue.

"Oh man…" She shivered as he found her clit and teased it out of its hood with soft flutters. He stroked over the bundle of nerves, back and forth, the pad of his tongue moving without haste, as if they had all the time in the world.

Closing her eyes, Sam reveled in the moment, wondering if she was dreaming and hoping that if she was, she didn't wake up without having an orgasm first.

"Make me come like this," she begged.

The few times her previous partners had gone down on her, they'd attacked her cunt like ravening beasts, rushing to get past the foreplay and on to the fucking. Rick, however, licked her with remarkable tenderness, moving first in soft laps, using his lips, tongue and teeth to drive her crazy. She writhed beneath him, her skin heating before misting with sweat. Everything ached and burned. Her legs shook as silky strands of his hair brushed along her inner thighs.

Reaching for him, Sam threaded her fingers through the dark locks, pulling him closer, rocking upward to match his leisurely tempo. He hummed softly, his tongue pointed and plunging into the creamy depths of her pussy, in and out, until her heart felt like it would burst.

"Rick!" she cried, near mindless with the need to come.

His groan was low and tormented, the vibration traveling up her body and beading her nipples. They strained upward, aching, and Sam released his head to cup her breasts and squeeze them, trying to ease her torment.

"Let me," he murmured against her slick flesh, pushing her hands aside. He rolled her nipples between expert fingertips, tugging them in a way that made her womb contract desperately. "You just lie there and come."

She was going to, she couldn't stop it, her hips pumping her cunt onto his thrusting tongue, matching his rhythm. "Oh goddess...please..."

Rick surrounded her clit with his lips and sucked firmly. The suction was too much, pulling her into orgasm, racking her body with such stunning force she couldn't breathe, her pussy grasping desperately for him to fill it. Before she could gasp for air he was in her, his cock so hard and thick she could barely take him.

"Shit," he gasped, falling forward, caging her to the table with his powerful body. He held still as her cunt rippled along his length with the aftershocks of her release. "You're so damn tight, Sam. Almost too tight."

With a whimper, she muttered, "It's not me, it's you. You're too big."

More like huge. Enormous. Gigantic.

One large hand pushed her hair tenderly off her face. "Am I hurting you?"

She thought about that for a moment, wiggling her hips. Pleasure spread outward, making her moan. "No."

"Can you take a little more?" Sweat broke out on his skin.

"There's *more*?"

He winced. "Please don't make me stop," he begged in a gravelly voice.

Sam stared up the gorgeous man who waited above her and felt something melt. His dark hair hung around his handsome face. The crests of his cheekbones were flushed and a tiny muscle in his jaw ticced from his clenching. His pecs and biceps were hard and delineated by the effort he exerted to hold his weight from crushing her. He was absolutely beautiful, a work of art. And he was hers for the next few weeks. She'd be damned if a neglected pussy would prevent her from having him.

Shifting again, she spread her legs wider and tilted her hips. With a deep groan of pleasure, Rick sank in to the hilt.

Grateful kisses rained down on her eyebrows and temples. He managed a pained smile, which made her heart skip. "I can't remember the last time I was this hard."

"You're kidding." Though she secretly hoped that was true. If he got any bigger, there would be no way he'd fit.

"I wish I was. I'm afraid to move, I think I'll come."

"Go ahead," she encouraged, wanting that desperately. "I already got mine. You can get yours."

Dropping his head, he captured her mouth. He kissed her softly, sweetly, his tongue brushing along hers, tasting her with deep licks. His lips were firm, his skill apparent. Wanting more, she moaned a protest when he pulled away.

"You're perfect," he murmured.

Her skepticism must have shown on her face.

"You don't believe me?" He pulled his hips back, his heavy cock dragging out of her. She watched, creaming with desire as his stomach muscles laced tight and he worked back inside her.

"No worries," she whispered, her throat clenched tight by the most erotic sight she'd ever seen. "I'm just glad I was around when you got horny."

He growled on the next perfect downstroke. "Fine. Think what you like. In a week your cunt will be shaped to my cock, then you'll believe me."

Her pussy clenched tight at his words. In response, he gripped her shoulders and shafted her harder, his hips lifting and falling tirelessly.

"You like that idea?" His lips touched her ear. His labored breathing made her ache to come all over again. "I'm going to fuck you every moment I'm awake. I'm going to sleep with my cock inside you. I'm going to soak you with my cum until you're dripping with it."

"Rick!"

"Naughty girl," he growled. "You love a side of dirty talk with your fucking, don't you?"

Rising slightly, he gripped her waist and pumped her onto his cock, sliding her body up and down, her bio-suit gliding easily over the polished tabletop. Sam could only hold on to his wrists and watch, crying out and writhing with the brutal pleasure. Rick threw his head back and roared as he came, pumping deep into her, his thighs shaking against hers.

The sight of his climax triggered hers, making her cunt grip his cock so that he shuddered and cursed with the pleasure of it.

When it was over, he gathered her up against his chest, their sweat sticking their bare skin together. He chuckled softly, his cheek resting on top of her head.

It was awesome and intimate, and Sam was so grateful for the experience she wanted to cry.

Too bad the month ahead couldn't last.

Chapter Three

ഇ

"Can you bring that light closer?" Sam asked, obviously exasperated. "The way you're holding it makes it difficult to read this."

Rick stepped nearer and rubbed the back of his neck sheepishly. He hadn't been paying attention to the writing on the stone. He'd been angling the light to get a better view of Sam's ass as she crawled on all fours across the dusty floor. She had a nice butt, rounded and slightly plump, just like the rest of her body. He knew from watching her ration her desserts that she thought she was little too full-figured, but he completely disagreed. He was a big man with a hearty sexual appetite. If she'd been any smaller, he would have been afraid of hurting her. As it was, she was beautifully curved, her thighs pillowing his deep thrusts, her breasts large enough to fill his hands.

By the gods, his dick was so hard it ached something terrible.

Searching for a distraction, he glanced around the narrow stone tunnel they stood in. They'd been on Simgen for a week, but it had taken Sam only a day to find this cave. They were the first visitors this place had seen in a long time and Rick could only admire her skill in getting farther ahead than any other treasure hunter in so short a time.

She had painstakingly explained the thought process that led to this discovery, pulling out books, maps, the key he'd won, and scribbled notes—both hers and those published by others. He loved that she wanted to share her mind with him, as well as her lush body. Because of that, he'd made every effort to pay attention to what she was saying, but then she had bent over the table, her ass swaying from side to side as she reached for items to explain her reasoning.

Unable to help himself, he'd opened his robe, lifted hers and sunk his cock into her. Even now, the memory of her sprawled across her research tools crying out as he fucked her was driving him mad.

"Damn it, Rick!" she complained now. "I can't see anything."

Giving up the fight, he sank to his knees and set the lantern on the floor. He caught her around the waist and dragged her atop him. "Oh, Sam." He groaned as her curves settled into his body. "I want you."

"You're crazy."

"For you, yes."

She laughed and kissed his mouth. "We never get anything done."

He rolled, coming over her, coughing at the dust that billowed around them. "We get a lot done."

"Yeah, well, not much of it has to do with the treasure."

Reaching between her legs, he stroked her pussy through her bio-suit. "Do you mind?" he murmured, his eyelids drooping when she gasped beneath him.

"Not if you don't. Do...do you want to go back to the ship?"

"I can't walk now."

"Are you going to fuck me right here?" she asked breathlessly, her eyes wide.

By the gods, it drove him nuts when she talked like that. That shy librarian's exterior hid a sex maniac. And the way she smelled...

"Yeah, right here. Right now." He couldn't wait. Nearly desperate to be inside her, he pinched the catch of her suit and tugged it down. In the process, he knocked over the book she'd been using to translate. As always, the reminder of how smart she was made his cock even harder.

In addition to his fascination with her figure, he appreciated her mind. Because he wanted her to know that, Rick tried not to drag her to bed more than once every couple hours. Sam, however, couldn't go too long without his hands on her. She'd tracked him down a few times and teased him into taking her. It was almost like she was afraid he'd lose interest if he weren't constantly fucking her. Fact was, he sometimes wished he were a little less interested. He couldn't stop thinking about her.

Lowering his head, he caught her lips in a deep, searching kiss. Her soft moan and welcoming embrace made him shudder. She was always ready for him, always welcoming.

"*Sam?*"

Rick lifted his head at the foreign voice and scowled. "Who the hell is that?"

"*Sam? Are you in here?*"

She stared up at him, blinking. "It sounds like Curt."

"Who the fuck is Curt?"

"He's a professor at Jacian University."

"Oh." Slightly appeased at the title of "*professor*", which meant old and boring, Rick pulled back with a frustrated groan. "What is he doing in our cave?"

"I have no idea," she said, pushing at his shoulders. "But you should probably get off me."

"I suppose," he said reluctantly.

Just then a bright light turned the corner and he got a good look at the man who'd interrupted his fun. "*That's* the professor?" he bit out.

"Ah," Curt said with a leer. "Still like to have a little fun with your work, eh, Sam?"

The *professor* was young, trim and handsome, if you liked the golden god-looking type. And if Sam was into that sort of thing, Rick was in trouble, because he was the dark, hulking mercenary-looking type.

"Yeah, she does, and you're interrupting," he growled.

Curt held up his free hand in a defensive gesture. "I didn't mean to get in the way. Honestly. I just wanted to see if we could discuss a partnership."

"Listen." Rick got to his feet and pulled Sam to hers. He refastened her bio-suit all the way to her throat. "Why don't you tell me what you're doing in our cave before you start trying to bargain with no leverage?"

"I've got plenty of leverage, trust me." Curt turned his attention to Sam. "One of my anthropology students found part of an internal memo written the week the database went missing. It's degraded, but with a little elbow grease, we may be able to get something out of it."

Sam looked up from dusting off her pants. "Why share it with me? Why not just do it yourself?"

"You know why," he said, in far too intimate a tone of voice. "You're a lot better at forensic research than I am."

"And in return?" She arched a brow.

"I want thirty-three percent."

"Fuck no," Rick barked. Sam's hand on his arm didn't make him feel better. It just pissed him off further. She couldn't be considering this guy's proposal...

Curt shrugged. "Suit yourself. I'll see you on Rashier 6 in three weeks. Maybe you'll have changed your mind by then."

Rick's hands clenched into fists. The thought of this guy with Sam after his month was over made his blood boil. "Mind telling me how you found us?"

"Those of us who are experts in literary antiquities comprise a very small group," Curt said smugly. "Word spreads fast in our community."

"What he's trying to say is that he's been spying on me," Sam corrected dryly.

"Play nice, Sam," Curt chastised. "Let me e-mail you a small sample of the recovered text, just enough so you can see I'm not trying to cheat you. If you end up wanting what I've got, you'll know where to find me."

"All right." She sighed. "I'll take a look. But I'm not making any promises. This doesn't constitute any kind of agreement."

Nodding his satisfaction, the professor left them.

"Please tell me you didn't screw him," Rick muttered, studying her.

Sam blushed to the roots of her hair.

"You've got to be kidding me." What did she see in a guy like that?

Then his stomach dropped. *Still like to have a little fun with your work, eh, Sam?*

She'd written that paper on how orgasms increased mental acuity. Was that all he meant to her? A recharging of her brain?

"Don't look at me like that." She crossed her arms. "You weren't a virgin when I met you."

"Yeah, well, at least I don't use people to further my research."

"What's that supposed to mean?"

"It means my cock isn't a powercell for your brain."

Sam took a step back, her eyes wide and filled with confusion.

His jaw clenched. "Deny it."

"I don't know what's gotten into you."

"I know what's gotten into you," he said lewdly, "but maybe one cock is as good as another as far as mental acuity goes?"

"Fuck you." She turned on her heel and walked away.

* * * * *

29

Sam tried not to cry as she packed her bags, but it was a losing battle. Every time she reached for a book, the sight of the case of historical books made her throat ache. She remembered sitting on Rick's lap, her head resting on his shoulder while she listened to his explanation of his love for such things.

"I like tactile comforts," he'd said. "The feel of silk and velvet, satins and lace. I like the warmth of wood and the glow of candlelight. Metal is too cold and sterile for my tastes." He'd kissed her forehead and whispered, "I especially like the feel of your skin. That's my favorite comfort at the moment."

Her heart had melted. For such a big tough guy, he could be remarkably sweet and tender.

And a jerk.

She sniffled and took down another volume. She hadn't spent one night in this room. Every night, she'd slept with Rick—warm and content in his arms.

"You're leaving?" he asked from the doorway, making her jump in surprise. She didn't turn around.

"I left some papers for you in the library. They'll tell you everything you need to know. If you have any trouble, there are quite a few experts who can help you out."

He was quiet for a long time, watching her. "How are you getting home?" he asked tightly. "With *the professor*?"

"No." She shoved her book roughly into the duffel. "I told him to use his own elbow grease. That was always my intention anyway, I was just curious about what he had or I would have told him off in the cave."

"So you're just going to quit? What about the e-books?"

The fact that the e-books were the only reason they'd been together at all made her throat tight.

"You can send me my share. Just go away now, Rick. Don't say anything to make me regret what happened between us, okay? Just leave it alone."

He stepped into her room and the door slid shut behind him. "What did happen between us?"

"I wore out my welcome, apparently." She shrugged and made every effort to hide her teary face, but her voice cracked a little. She only hoped he would pretend not to notice.

"If that were true," he said softly, "it wouldn't be tearing me up that you're leaving."

She stilled.

"I shouldn't have talked to you the way I did, Sam. I freely admit I'm an asshole."

He came to stand directly behind her, making every nerve ending in her body flare with awareness and sensual heat. She inhaled sharply, and was inundated with the scent of his skin—skin she'd touched and kissed every inch of. She grew hot, her pussy damp.

"I'm coarse and have a tendency to swear," he murmured in a deep rumble that made her nipples ache. "I'm nowhere near as smart as you are and I lose my temper too easily. There's absolutely no reason for you to even give me the time of day. But you did more than that and this last week has been the best of my life."

Sam heard the remorse in Rick's tone and told herself she really needed to go home, before she sank in any deeper. If she left now, she'd be all right again in a week or two. Or several. If she stayed longer, maybe she wouldn't ever get over missing him, and she had to get over him.

"I got jealous."

His grumbled statement startled her enough to spin around.

"Of Curt?" She stared up at the handsomest guy she'd ever seen and saw a wary vulnerability in his blue eyes that made it hard to breathe. "Why the hell would you be jealous of him?"

Rick gave a self-conscious shrug of his broad shoulders. "He's smart, he specializes in the same thing you do, he's okay-looking, he's—"

Sam laughed at "*okay-looking*". Curt was good-looking, no doubt about it. But… "He never got me off."

Rick blinked. "Huh?"

"He never gave me an orgasm."

He gaped. "*Never?*"

"Well, we only did it a couple times, but yeah, not ever." She tapped her chin with her finger and pretended to think about it. "It might be because his dick is awfully small. And honestly, he didn't know how to use it."

Snorting back a laugh, Rick caught her face in his large hands. "I'm glad he's a lousy lover and I'm sorry for being an ass. I'll make it up to you if you stay."

"With your big dick and an orgasm?"

His lips twitched with repressed humor. "You're killing me. Yes, with my big dick and my hands and my mouth, which will apologize profusely until you believe me. I've got no excuses, I simply suck and don't deserve you. I'm prepared to beg you to stay."

"Okay, that all sounds good, but what about the orgasms?" She gasped as he sank to his knees. "I thought you were kidding about the begging."

This totally could not be happening. Hot guys did not grovel at her feet.

But then he wasn't groveling. He was mouthing her pussy through her bio-suit. The heat of his breath burned through to her skin and she shivered in longing for his talented tongue. "Rick?"

"Mmm…?"

"Is this the apology or the orgasm?"

"Both."

He pulled her to the floor and apologized properly.

Chapter Four

✑

"You know, baby," Rick said, his eyes riveted to the full, swaying ass in front of him as they hiked up the rough gravel path. He had to pat himself on the back for the tiny vid recorder he wore attached to his collar. The plan had been to record the possible discovery of the e-books. Now he could play this back and ogle Sam's luscious butt whenever he liked. "I totally admire you for finding this place. You explained everything to me perfectly and I still can't wrap my mind around how you figured it all out in three weeks."

"We haven't found anything yet."

"But we will. With you in charge, there's no way we can fail."

"You're just trying to flatter me into bed," she retorted, but he heard the pleasure in her tone.

"I have to flatter you into bed now?" He gave a dramatic sigh. "Man, whatever happened to just whipping my dick out?"

Sam paused on the trail and laughed out loud. He was glad to hear the sound. All day she'd been edgy and nervous, like she was preparing for the worst. He knew this search was important to her, so he sympathized. But her happiness was important to him, and seeing her so tense and anxious didn't sit well.

Her dark eyes smiled at him and when she held out her hand, he took it without hesitation. He was not a romantic guy, but Sam brought out what tiny bit of romance he had in him. His mouth quirked in a half-smile. Better face the facts head-on—he'd been tamed by a librarian.

The going got a little tougher as they climbed, but they made good time and before an hour had passed, they'd traveled the distance between his shuttlecraft and the top of the small mountain on the planet Cerridwen.

"Okay," she said when the trail ended. "Now we need to find a rock etched with this symbol." She pulled a folded piece of paper out of the small bag she carried.

"What is that?" He studied the design over her shoulder. "It looks like a circle on top of a cross."

"On Earth it was called an ankh. It means eternal life."

"Huh. Well, that's appropriate for those databases, I guess."

Nodding, Sam handed him the picture and began to peer closely at the rocks in front of her. He did the same. It took almost a half-hour to find the marker, but once they did, things began to move quickly.

Beneath the rock was a switch, which opened a small door in the side of the mountain. Rick led the way, his blaster at the ready, but all they found inside was a lift.

"You trust that thing?" he asked, eyeing it skeptically. "It's been here forever."

"Are you afraid, tough guy?"

"For you, yeah." Leaning over, he looked down the shaft. "Looks like this goes a long way down. I'll go alone and if works without a hitch, I'll come back and get you."

"There's no way you're going without me."

Shooting a scowl over his shoulder, he said, "You're not getting in this thing until I'm sure it's not a total piece of shit."

"Rick."

He hated when she took that cajoling tone of voice with him, he never ended up being able to say no. "Don't do this to me, Sam. Okay? I don't want you getting hurt."

She gave him that soft melting look that made him crazy for her. "Whatever happens, I want you to know that what you've done for me these past weeks has changed my life."

"Huh?" That sounded like the start of a Dear John speech. His scowl deepened.

"Before I met you, I didn't think I'd ever be important to someone. Thank you for making me feel like I was valuable to you."

"Was?"

A throat cleared behind them and they shot each other a knowing look

"Curt," Rick said. "What a surprise."

"This is really touching," Curt said snidely while aiming a blaster at Sam. "But don't you think we should find our treasure now?"

"*Our* treasure?" Sam snapped.

"Yes, ours. I've spent just as many years looking for the e-books as you have."

"So have a lot of other people. So what? We're supposed to divide it amongst everyone who's ever looked for it?"

"No, just me will suffice."

She crossed her arms over her chest. "You're not getting anything, Jerk. Nutbar. Asshole. And put that blaster away before you hurt someone."

Curt fired a warning shot at her feet.

"She gets hurt, you die," Rick growled, his heart thumping madly. He had no idea what this idiot was capable of.

"Get over here, Sam," Curt said softly. "Or lover boy gets blasted."

Sam walked over with hesitant steps, her only thought being to protect Rick in whatever way she could. When she got close enough, Curt caught her by the throat and waved the blaster at Rick. "Call the lift."

"Let Rick go," she said, willing to do whatever was necessary to get Rick out of there.

"Don't be dense," Curt muttered. "He'll notify the authorities."

The tension in the air as they waited for the clanking, whining elevator was palpable.

"What the hell are you going to do, Curt?" Sam asked, her stomach clenched in a knot. She looked across the small space to where Rick waited for an opening to strike. "What's the plan after this?"

"Well, once we find the database, I'll stun you both and take off. You'll wake up in an hour or two, and come find me. Then I'll give you half the credits and you two can split your share. I'll be praised for finding the e-books, you two can run off and make calf-eyes at each other, and we're all happy."

"You know, that might be a great plan if there *was* a database, Stupid. But since there's *not*, you really just succeeded in pissing us off. From what I hear of Rick's reputation, that's not such a smart thing to have done."

Curt stiffened behind her. "What are you talking about?"

"There. Is. No. Database. Get it? Why do you think no one's ever found it? It doesn't exist."

"It doesn't exist?" he cried, shoving her away so he could search her features with his gaze. Rick caught her wrist and jerked her behind him, shielding her with his body.

"No, Dumb Ass," Sam snapped. "You know how much research I've done, how long I've looked, all the places I've excavated. There's nothing to find or someone would have found it by now."

"Then why are you here?" Curt waved the blaster wildly toward Rick. "With him. Why would you be here if there wasn't any treasure?"

She swallowed hard and hazarded a glance up at Rick. His eyes stayed trained on Curt's weapon and his hand at her waist kept her firmly behind him. Looking at the ground at her feet, she said, "Because I wanted to be with him and this was the only way to do that."

"*What?* You're kidding me."

Rick was eerily silent.

"No, I'm not. I knew if I told him the treasure was a myth, he'd send me home."

"Are you serious, Samantha?" Curt gaped at her. "This has all been for nothing?"

"If you want the treasure, then yes, this has all been for nothing, which is no less than you deserve for pulling this lame-o stunt." Her voice lowered. "But for me, I got something out of it. Even if I don't get to keep him."

Curt's eyes narrowed suspiciously and he jerked his chin at the bag by her feet. "What's in the bag? Why bring your tools down here, if there wasn't any need for them?"

Her face suffused in a burning blush. "They're not my tools."

"I don't believe you. Open the bag and prove it."

"Fuck you," Rick said. "Put the blaster away."

"Not until she opens the bag."

Resigned, Sam dropped to a crouch and opened the catch, revealing a variety of sensual accoutrements.

"Sex toys?" Curt cried.

She felt the ripple that went through Rick's powerful frame.

"Jeez, Sam." Curt threw up his hands. "You used to be a literary expert, now you're—"

Rick's fist connected with Curt's jaw with a wince-worthy crack. The professor fell into unconsciousness and slumped at their feet.

"Wow!" Her eyes widened. "That was so cool. I love it when you get all alpha male."

"I'm glad you approve." He shook his head. "I still can't believe you slept with this guy."

"Don't remind me. What do we do with him now?"

"I'm hogtying him and sticking him outside." He turned to face her, his blue eyes dark with predatory alertness. She took a step backward. "Shit-For-Brains can wait until we're done. Then I'll take him and the vid to the authorities."

"You were right on about Curt coming after us."

"Yeah, and you were right on about bringing the vid to prove it. We're a good team."

Sam zipped up the bag and slung it over her shoulder. "Toss him outside and let's go. The lift's here."

He stilled. "Go where?"

"To get the e-books."

"You said you didn't know where they were."

"I wasn't going to tell *him* where they were." She poked Curt softly with the tip of her boot. "So I lied. I knew that would frustrate him enough to slip and give you an opening. It's one of the reasons why he sucks at forensic work. He's had the same information as me, he just couldn't get it together enough to reach the same conclusions. The vid will prove he has no claim to the treasure."

Rick was strangely intent as he stepped toward her. "Was everything you told him a lie?"

"What?"

"Did you lie about everything?"

Backing up warily, Sam tried to figure out what he was up to. And failed. "What are you doing?"

"Asking you a question." He crowded her into the wall, pulling the bag off her shoulder and dropping it to the floor. "Did you tell the truth when you said you wanted to be with me? Or was that part of the lie?"

The way he looked at her told her that *now* was the time to come clean.

"It was the truth," she admitted, staring up at him. "I've known about this place for years, but it didn't do me any good without the key. The moment you showed me this," she reached inside his shirt for the data chip he wore around his neck, "I knew we had the treasure."

He caught her hips in his hands and pulled her into him. The fact that he was fully aroused was not lost on her. "I showed you the key in your office the first day we met."

Sam winced miserably. "I know. I'm a terrible, selfish person. I didn't mean it to go this far. I was going to bring you here earlier, I swear. Then you tackled me on the table and made every one of my fantasies come true."

"Your fantasies?"

"Yes." She chewed nervously on her nail. "And then you said you'd keep making them come true and all of sudden taking you straight to the treasure wasn't looking so good."

Rick caught her wrist and tugged her finger out of her mouth. "You've been crawling around in dusty tunnels for weeks, Sam."

"I had to make it look real, right? If I just hung out in your bed and then one day woke up and said '*Hey! I found out where the treasure is!*' you'd know something was up." Her shoulders slumped. "The truth is I've pretty much lied about everything. Except for when you made love to me. I never lied then."

"Made love," he repeated softly. His look was so intense it stole her breath.

She blushed and looked away quickly. "Sorry. I meant fuck. Really. A slip of the tongue. No pressure. I know we had a deal—no-strings, no-commitment sex. I'm totally okay with that. I'm—"

"I'm not okay with that." He caught up her chin and forced her to look at him.

"You're not?"

"Nope."

"You're giving me The Look." She gaped. "Dear goddess, I can't believe you're giving me The Look after what I just told you."

He bent his head and licked her lower lip. "The get-prepared-because-I'm-going-to-make-love-to-you Look?"

"Make love?" she whispered against his mouth, her heart racing.

"I can't believe all the crazy things you've done just to be with me." Rick pulled her closer and rested his cheek on top of her head. "I'm totally flattered that a woman with your brains would do something so completely off the wall for a guy like me."

She snorted. "It's not every day that a gorgeous mercenary walks into my office and offers to spend a month with me. It would have been dumb to blow the chance to hang out with you. I never thought we'd end up lovers. I just thought I could enjoy looking at you awhile."

The look he gave her when he pulled back was both heated and deeply affectionate.

"Let's get rid of the professor and dig into those toys you brought." He kissed the tip of her nose and then laughed out loud. "Were you planning a seduction here? On the dirt floor? Not that I mind," he assured her quickly.

The fact that he didn't want to jeopardize his chance to play with her made her feel all tingly inside.

"I was planning one last romp with you. I knew when I told you the truth about everything, you'd get really pissed." She blushed. "I was being selfish again."

"When it comes to me, you can be as selfish as you want."

"Really? You're not mad?"

"You can make it up to me." He winked at her. "I still have the vid on."

Sam gaped. "Dear goddess. You want to film us fucking?"

Rick growled and set his hands on the wall on either side of her head. Then he bent his knees so he could rub his cock against her pussy. "Feel how hard it makes me when you talk like that? I want rip that suit off and ride you until you scream."

She cupped his tight ass and rubbed right back. "Bring it on."

"You got it, baby."

As she watched, he made quick work of hogtying Curt and then he carried Dumb Ass's unconscious body outside.

When Rick returned, he was rubbing his hands together. Then he rushed up to her and collected the bag. "Let's go!"

"Jeez, you act like I'm more exciting than the e-books."

He dragged her into the lift and hit the button that started their descent. Before she could gasp, he was stroking her pussy through her bio-suit and she was rocking against his fingers. Licking the shell of her ear, he murmured, "This is the only treasure I'm interested in right now."

Pure heat traveled up her spine and hardened her nipples. Rick nibbled her neck and pressed the steely length of his cock against her thigh. Her ability to think clearly diminished rapidly.

"Here? What if the lift is a piece of shit?"

"Then I'll die a happy man."

He found her clit and rubbed it.

"Wait!" she gasped, reaching for his chain. She wanted to take him to the cave, take her time, love him right. She had a plan, a goal…

One-handed, he pulled the data chip over his head and dropped it around her neck, but he didn't stop manipulating her clit just the way she liked.

Her eyes slid closed as her cunt clenched in anticipation. "Don't stop."

"You just told me to wait."

"No. Don't wait…"

"Do you want to come, Sam?"

She nodded. "Yes…please…make me come."

Rick pulled down the catch of her bio-suit. "Anything for you, baby."

Lowering his head, he caught her nipple in his mouth, caressing it with gentle licks of his tongue. His hand slid inside her suit and then between her legs. Sam moaned, her senses on fire, her legs trembling so violently that he dropped the bag and supported her by the waist.

He parted her lips with a reverent touch, slipping through the slickness of her desire before plunging into her cunt with two fingers. "You're always so wet for me."

Turning her head, she pressed soft kisses to his cheek, her hips moving in time with the pumping inside her. "I can't help it. I want you all the time."

And she did. All the time. She'd been lonely for so long, longing for a man who appreciated the whole package — the brains and the bod.

He took her mouth with a deep, possessive kiss. Against her thigh, his cock was a hot and heavy weight, a tantalizing promise.

"I want you all the time, too," he said against her lips. The pad of his thumb found her clit and rubbed, bumping it repeatedly with every shake of the descending lift. "I want to touch you like this whenever I feel like it. I want to hold you and be with you."

"Oh Rick!" she cried, coming into his hand, her cunt melting with pleasure, her breasts heavy and aching. Knowing her so well, he sucked the hard tips, drawing on them with deep pulls that echoed around his thrusting fingers.

"I need you," he groaned, withdrawing his touch and sinking to the floor of the rattling elevator.

Sam stared down at the beautiful man who waited for her, his large hands opening his pants, his massive cock springing out proudly erect. Hadn't she always wished she was the kind of woman who could arouse a man's lust? She loved the way he was always grabbing her for sex no matter where they were, like he'd die if he couldn't have her. *Right now.* "You always make me feel like I'm the sexiest woman in the universe."

The tip of his cock glistened with lust for her. "To me, Sam, you are."

She shed her suit quickly and straddled his lean hips, holding herself aloft as he positioned the thick head at her drenched slit. Her eyes closed as she sank slowly onto him. This moment was one she always savored, the feel of him stretching her wide, massaging her creamy walls. The undeniable connection.

"By the gods," he said hoarsely, his hands on her thighs gently pushing her downward until he was as deep as he could go.

They held still for long moments, enjoying the closeness. Then he asked, "You ready to watch?"

She nodded, her eyes meeting his. Nothing made her come harder than watching his cock reaming her pussy and he knew it. She leaned forward, setting her hands on his linen-clad shoulders, her chin meeting her chest as she slowly lifted her hips.

"What do you see?" he asked, his view obstructed by her hair.

"Your cock. Hard and thick. Red and kind of angry-looking."

"I'm desperate for you."

"I can tell. Your veins are pulsing and the skin is shiny with my come."

"You're soaked inside." Rick lifted his hips, his cock spearing into her. "It feels so good in you, baby. Hot and tight as hell." He lowered, sliding out of her. "I'm sorry. I don't think I'm going to last long. Fingering you always makes me crazy."

"Don't worry about me. I already got mine." Reaching between them with one hand, Sam spread her lips. "Fuck me now," she breathed, her legs shaking as he bucked upward again, her pussy swallowing him whole. "Oh goddess."

"You like the way it looks?"

"I like the way it feels. You're so big."

Rick quickened his pace, his hips rising and falling, his wonderful cock shafting her cunt with expert rhythmic strokes. She whimpered in pleasure, her hand falling to the metal floor to hold herself up, her entire body shaking with the need to come. The lift jolted to an abrupt stop, but Rick never let up.

"Squeeze me with your pussy," he gritted out. "Ah..." He pistoned faster, moving so quickly she could barely register the sight of it. "I'm...coming..."

She cried out when he spurted, his fingers bruising her thighs, his rasping cry echoing in the lift. He came hard, his cock swelling, his cum hot and filling her up until the delicious pressure pushed her into another orgasm. He groaned and fucked through her spasms.

Sam felt like she was drowning, her body awash in sensual heat and desire, her lust and longing rippling up her spine. She hadn't known it could be like this, had never thought she would find a man who would want her so deeply. Her tears dropped onto his shirt. He pulled her down so he could cradle her to his chest.

They didn't have to say anything out loud. They just knew.

* * * * *

"It's got to be here somewhere," she muttered, her hands skimming slowly along the carved stone.

"Are you sure this is a door?" Rick asked, mimicking her movements beside her.

Sam shot a glance at him and he arched a brow. "Hey, I have to ask. We've been feeling up this wall for almost an hour."

"It's got to be here. I know it."

"I'll look as long as you want," he said solicitously. "But I claim the right for a nooky break if we're here too long."

"You're a sex maniac."

"We never got into the toys!"

She grinned and then laughed, she couldn't help it. She was happier than she'd ever been in her life. "We don't need toys."

"That's true. Damn, I'm a lucky bastard." He stilled. "Wait a minute." Leaning closer to the wall he blew hard at the image of a flower. Sand flew outward, revealing a tiny hole.

"Oh wow." Sam couldn't move. Sure, she'd been cocky and nonchalant about finding the treasure, but that was partly because she was afraid to be wrong. What if this wasn't the place? What if the databases didn't exist? What if she found out that everything she'd worked so hard for was only a myth?

Rick's hand slipped into hers and squeezed. "You want to wait awhile? Think it over some? There's no rush. We've got a week until we need to be on Rashier 6."

Turning her head, she locked gazes with him. *We.* They were in this together.

In tune with her feelings, he tugged her closer and kissed her forehead. "I don't care if we find the treasure. We'll get by without it. If you open this door, do it for you. Not for me. Or don't do it. Whatever. I'll be here for you whatever you decide."

Taking a deep breath, Sam pulled the key chain over her head and stepped closer to the hole in the wall. "Let's do this or we'll wonder forever."

As she slid the key in, he stepped up behind her and put comforting hands on her shoulders.

From a distance, a creak signaled the start of some ancient mechanism. Rattles and groans vibrated through the walls and shook the floor beneath their feet. Rick caught her up by the waist and pulled her back against him, shielding her with his much larger body. Dust and sand billowed around their legs. They both stared, riveted, as the massive stone wall shrank away from them and then slid off to the right, exposing a massive chamber.

Grabbing his blaster from its holster, Rick motioned for her to hang back as he walked cautiously into the dark room.

Suddenly, the space was filled with light as sensors picked up his presence and activated.

"*This* is cool!" Sam breathed, awed as she stepped into the chamber behind him. Spinning slowly, she took in the ancient Earth hieroglyphics that covered the walls. In the center of the room waited three pyramid-shaped databases no bigger than the bag she'd brought with them.

"Oh man...oh goddess... Jeez, Rick. You have any idea how many erotic e-books those databases can hold?"

"Yeah, baby. I think I do. We're filthy rich. And we're going to be heroes. Hey, can you read this stuff?"

She tore her covetous gaze from the black databases and looked at him. "I think so."

He pointed at the arched monoliths that curved up the walls and then across the stone ceiling. On the left, the massive stone was carved in the shape of a man. On the right, a woman. Their backs were to each other and text filled the space between their headdresses. "What's that say?" he asked. "It looks important."

Sam smiled. "It says, '*Ellora's Cave Presents*'."

"Huh?" He frowned. "Wasn't that a twenty-first-century e-publisher?"

"You did your homework!" She beamed with pride. "EC was the largest and most lucrative of many such ventures started during that time period."

"What does it mean?"

"It means they knew what was going to happen, Rick. I don't know how they knew, but they did. EC started planning this in the year 2004."

"How do you know that?" he asked, awed at her deductive reasoning. "How did you know this was here on Cerridwen?"

"It was the twenty-first-century advertisements! No one paid any attention to them. I admit, I disregarded them, too. But in 2004 EC began releasing anthologies called '*Cavemen*'. In each of the print advertisements for those volumes, they embedded symbols. Written in chronological order, the code revealed the location of Cerridwen. Think about it. Ellora's Cave? The very name of the company was a clue."

"How the hell could they know about the Conservative Censorship Committee, so many years ahead of its formation? Intergalactic travel wasn't even possible at that time."

"I honestly don't know." Laughing and crying and spinning with arms wide, Sam was certain her life was perfect. "But look at the treasure their vision created. Look at what they left us to find!"

Rick ducked to avoid her widespread arms and caught her about the waist, lifting her feet from the floor. "We also found each other."

"Yes, my love. And you're the greatest treasure in the universe." Cupping his face, she kissed his nose and asked, "What's next? The Draken Cup? The Sarian Stone?"

His grin was pure carnal wickedness. "The toys."

She rolled her eyes. "What am I going to do with you?"

Hugging her close, he said, "Well, I've got some ideas…"

The End…maybe…

Also by Sylvia Day

ଛ

Kiss of the Night

Misled

Wish List

About the Author

ଛ

Sylvia Day is the bestselling author of highly sensual romantic fiction set in most sub-genres. A wife and mother of two from Southern California, she is a former Russian linguist for the U.S. Army Military Intelligence. Called "up-and-coming" by Romantic Times and "wickedly entertaining" by Booklist, Sylvia is quickly building a name for writing emotional erotic works for the preeminent publishers of erotic romance.

When she's not working on her next book, you can find her chatting with visitors on her weblog, message board and chat loop. Stop by her website to say hi and meet all her bad-boy heroes.

Sylvia welcomes comments from readers. You can find her website and email address on her author bio page at www.ellorascave.com.

Allergic to Love

Anna J. Evans

෯

Dedication

&

To my mom,
the most supportive woman
who might never read this story.

About the Author

&

Anna J. Evans is a multipublished author who thinks romance is sexier with a sense of humor. She loves reading and writing paranormal romantic adventures and is thrilled to hear from fans. You can visit her website, email her, or join her Yahoo group (Anna_Evans_lolsexy-subscribe@yahoogroups.com) for free reads, the latest publishing news, and monthly member-only giveaways.

Anna welcomes comments from readers. You can find her website and email address on her author bio page at www.ellorascave.com.

Chapter One

ဢ

Ella swallowed, but it was hard. Very hard. Almost impossible.

What had he put in there? And was it really worth possibly risking her life to prove that Marcus Ashton was a completely unprofessional and potentially dangerous man who should be fired immediately, do not pass go, do not collect your 401k?

She was a chemist for god's sakes, she should just test the cocoa, find out what he'd used, and turn him in. Why did she feel compelled to drink the damn stuff? Because she was a sick cookie? Perhaps. Or maybe because she knew whatever he'd dumped in her hot chocolate probably wouldn't kill her.

Probably.

"Relax," she whispered to herself, setting her cup down in the section of her lab station reserved for personal effects. She wasn't the sort to risk a spill that might contaminate an experiment.

But you're the type to risk being poisoned? Are you nuts?

"Ella—"

"Shit!" Ella screamed, jumping half a foot as Mandy popped her head into her station.

"You're cussing now? When did this happen?" Mandy asked.

"I'm just a little nervous today," Ella said.

"Maybe you should lay off the hot chocolate," Mandy joked. If she only knew.

"Right!" Ella giggled, somewhat hysterically. Would Mandy think she was totally crazy if she hugged her and begged her to take care of her cat if she mysteriously dropped dead in the next few hours?

Or days. It could be some sort of cumulative toxin.

"All right, you're definitely coming to happy hour today. I was going to ask you to go, but now I'm telling. You need a drink. I'll meet you outside at five-thirty," Mandy said, turning to leave.

"But I—"

"Five-thirty, psycho. No overtime on Thirsty Thursdays," Mandy ordered and then disappeared.

No overtime on Thursdays. If she hadn't been logging overtime yesterday, then she wouldn't be in this mess. Well, she would still be in the mess, but wouldn't know that she was in the mess, wouldn't have, with her very own eyes, seen Mr. Scary doctoring her cocoa mix. Given the choice, Ella supposed she would rather know that she was being poisoned, even if it made her a mass of paranoia nearly incapable of getting anything resembling work accomplished.

"Ella? Can we talk?" came another voice from the entry to her station, a male voice this time. A deep, sexy, lust-inducing male voice that belonged to a certifiable psycho nut job who could be trying to kill her.

"Yeah. Sure. What?" Ella snapped, spinning around to face him, hoping that her eyes weren't as wide and frightened as she thought they were. It was bad enough that her nose started running every time he was in a ten-foot radius, the last thing she needed was to look like a *terrified* snot-nosed kid.

"I wanted to apologize," Marcus said, folding his arms across his incredibly broad chest, his bright blue eyes shining intently down at her. As her entire body tingled with response to his nearness, Ella braced herself for the inevitable sneezing and itching and the migraine that never failed to make a torturous appearance seconds after the Sex God's arrival.

Hurriedly, she reached for a tissue and…

Nothing. Nothing happened. She could still breathe, her head didn't hurt, there was no running nose, no itchiness, nothing, nada. There was absolutely nothing going on in her allergic body to distract her from the rush of raw desire that swept through her every cell. It was crazy, but she felt herself actually tremble as she took him in, symptom free.

Of course, he was ridiculously gorgeous. His nearly black hair was cut close to his head, his eyes passionate and expressive, and all six foot whatever of him composed of pure testosterone-enhanced muscle. He was her dream man—handsome, smart, and just a little bit dangerous. Too bad he made her allergies act up like nobody's business.

And he was trying to kill her or drug her or poison her or something. Mustn't forget that little detail.

"Ella?" he asked.

"What? Um, sorry," she said, blushing furiously as she realized she had missed something, been sucked so entirely into the lust zone that she'd actually turned off her ears.

"I was saying that I think we just got off on the wrong foot. I'd like to start over," he said, stepping even closer until she caught a slightly musky scent, a raw, masculine odor that actually made her nipples tighten against her conservative white dress shirt and a strange aching start up low in her belly.

"Start over," she repeated dumbly, desperately fighting the urge to lean into him, to rest her face against his broad chest and inhale deeply, pulling the lovely smell of him all the way into her soul. So this was what she had been missing while her nose was buried in a tissue.

"I don't know what I've done, but I realize that you're upset with me. So I wanted to say that I was sorry and that I'd like to be friends," he said, reaching up with one of his strong, manly hands to tenderly brush a strand of hair out of her eyes and behind her ear.

Ella felt her eyes close as he touched her, electric shocks of desire burning through every fiber of her being, her pussy beginning to clench inside her black pants as if she would find release simply from the way his fingers slid sensuously over the delicate skin behind her earlobe. By the time his hand pulled away she was trembling, her underwear soaked in her own juices and her hands beginning to reach for the collar of his lab coat, to pull him down to her mouth because she was suddenly ravenously hungry for a taste of Marcus Ashton.

She had to have him, maybe now, maybe right here on the floor of her lab station. If she didn't, she feared she would go mad, driven insane by the need pulsing between her thighs, tightening her nipples, and making her entire body crave to be pressed, skin to skin, against the delicious flesh she knew she'd find beneath his clothes.

"Thirsty Thursday," she gasped, forcing her eyes open and somehow managing to snatch her hands back to her body before she touched him.

"Come to Thirsty Thursday tonight," she hurried on, hoping he would forget that she'd nearly lunged at him, "We all go to The Ballard Inn for the happy hour. Meet us there at around five-thirty?"

"I'd love to," he said with a smile. He looked younger when he smiled, yet somehow even more dangerous if such a thing were possible, like a predator anticipating a particularly tasty meal.

"Great. See you there," she said, forcing herself to take a few steps back, not that she really thought it would help. He'd obviously engineered this reaction and no amount of space between them would ease her craving.

"We'll talk then," he told her. Not asked, told, and then disappeared around the corner. Bossy and psychotic. What a combination.

"Shit," Ella whispered as the air rushed from her lungs. Two curse words in one day, and at work no less. But if any situation deserved a bit of profanity, this would be it.

He wasn't trying to kill her, he was trying to have sex with her. It had to have been some sort of libido-enhancing drug that he'd mixed in with her cocoa. Why else would she be practically fainting at his feet, completely intoxicated by her own rampaging lust? She'd wanted him before, but never lost control, never succumbed to the temptation to try to touch him, taste him, feel how his body would fit against her own.

But evidently, he'd wanted her too, wanted her badly enough to slip an aphrodisiac in her cocoa. The realization floored her, completely blew her mind. It was outrageous, so outrageous that a part of her wanted to stomp off to Mary's office right now and get the bastard fired so fast his beautiful head would swim.

The other part of her, however, wanted to lock herself in the women's bathroom and slide her hand down the front of her pants, slowly stroking herself until she came, until her pussy convulsed as she imagined his hands touching her, his mouth tasting her, his thick cock hovering at her entry, tormenting her for seconds that seemed like hours until he slammed home, filling her completely, stretching her, changing her, owning her with his body thrusting in and out of her own.

"It's just the drug," Ella said, grabbing her cocoa mug and pouring its contents down the drain, trying not to notice that her hands were shaking with the strength of her desire.

Quickly she pulled her lab coat more tightly around her, as if by covering her aching, pebbled nipples she would somehow help staunch the hunger coursing through her body, and raced to the coffee room. Once there she pocketed her green tin of cocoa and carefully made her way back to her station.

Sorry, Chem Pro, but she wasn't going to be working on the company's projects this afternoon. From now until five-thirty, she'd be doing her damnedest to figure out exactly what Marcus had used to drug her. If the chemistry gods were with her, she would have the answer by happy hour and be able to give the man an ultimatum.

Quit tomorrow or she would go to Mary, the boss's boss's boss, on Friday morning and tell her everything. With the cocoa powder as evidence, there was no way that Mary would take Marcus' word over her own. Ella had worked at Chem Pro for five years and was technically Marcus' superior. She had no reason to lie.

"He'll be gone by Monday," Ella muttered soothingly to herself as she began to mix a fresh set of test baths.

As she mixed and measured and sampled, she tried not to ask herself why she was going to give Marcus the chance to leave Chem Pro with his reputation intact. After what he'd done he certainly didn't deserve such a magnanimous gesture, and the fact that he had actually tried to drug a woman into having sex with him was beyond the pale. He didn't deserve a second chance of any kind, he deserved to be fired and slapped with a lawsuit.

But deep down, Ella had to admit that she might have invited this in some sick sort of way. She'd lusted after him since the second she had seen him loading his personal belongings into his locker four months ago. Despite the allergic reactions that she'd eventually realized were being caused by the gorgeous dog owner, she had still ached to be close to him, to discover what it would feel like to have those hands on her body, that mouth teasing her flesh, pulling her breast deep into his mouth as he fucked her like no one else ever had.

She'd known he would be like no one else, that he would fulfill fantasies she didn't even know she had yet. Something deep within her, something primal, had longed for him, ached to be possessed by him, despite the fact that he frightened her. And he did frighten her.

It wasn't his dark and dangerous good looks or his intense aura, she wasn't exactly sure what it was, but her gut told her that Marcus was more man than she could handle. She knew she'd never be able to let him go, would cling to him no matter what he chose to do with her. She would be helpless, weak, and completely at his mercy.

That's why she'd run from him, avoided him from the very start. The allergic reactions were a convenient excuse, but the real reason lay in her mind not her body.

Ella Bradley refused to be used and abused and thrown away again. Her ex-fiancé Carl had been one of those beautiful, dangerous types and look how that had turned out. She'd had to call the police to get him out of her apartment and been forced to come to work for three days wearing glasses to hide the black eye he'd given her after one too many bourbons.

She couldn't let herself fall in love or in bed with another man like that. Ella knew she was smarter than that even if her pussy wasn't.

"Bingo," she muttered to herself, leaning closer to observe the reaction in the last test tube. She was on the right track. A few more tests and Marcus would be on his way out of her life.

She was glad. It was the answer to her prayers.

So why did she suddenly feel like she was going to lose her best friend?

Chapter Two

ଛ

Marcus spotted her instantly. Even in the filled-to-capacity barroom of the local bed-and-breakfast, his eyes were drawn to her. She seemed to shine, filled with more life than any of the other yuppies guzzling down the two-for-one drinks as fast as their tolerance and a modicum of decency would allow. It wasn't just the outrageously beautiful body or the almost waist-length brown hair, it was something more, something purely, perfectly Ella.

He was across the room in a few seconds, maneuvering through the crowd with an ease that wasn't quite human. But then he wasn't quite human, was he? He wondered if Ella would care. He wondered if he would be brave enough to tell her.

"Hello," he whispered into her hair, placing his hands on the bar at either side of her own and leaning forward to press his full length against her back. He was here for more than friendship and it would be best if she knew it from the very start.

"Hi," she breathed, her body leaning back into his for a moment and her ass arching slightly. He was instantly erect, aroused, and ready to claim her as his own right there in the middle of happy hour.

Marcus shook his head slightly and forced himself away from her, away from her heat and her unbelievably arousing scent. He had to get a grip on his desire, otherwise it was entirely possibly that he'd do something dangerous. He had never wanted anyone the way he wanted Ella. His entire being craved her, body and soul, wolf and man. She was his mate, he'd bet his life on it. Although he hoped he wouldn't have to, since his kind became more than a little unpredictable when they finally found the female who would be theirs for life.

He had heard the stories of Weres who had completely succumbed to their baser natures, kidnapping women, attacking them on the street, tearing at their clothes and mating with them wherever they happened to find themselves when the scent of their mate met their nostrils. It was shameful, unforgivable, and uncivilized, to say the least. It was also illegal and punishable by death. The top secret Were Council didn't like anything that drew attention to the shapeshifter community. Humans didn't believe things like Werewolves existed and they wanted to keep it that way.

But with or without the threat of the Council, Marcus had sworn to himself he would be nothing but a gentleman when he finally found the woman meant to be his. Of course he hadn't bargained on how violent his need would be, how desperately he would crave her, how difficult it would be to restrain himself. He wanted her, here and now, and it was going to be hell forcing himself to keep his hands off her, to keep from pulling up the hem of the little brown dress she wore and touching her where she was already wet and aching for him.

And she was wet and more than ready. He could smell it.

"Glad you came," she said, turning around to face him. Great. Now her breasts were only inches from his chest. And her nipples were hard, just like they'd been earlier in the afternoon when he'd first realized that she wanted him as badly as he wanted her. He wanted to taste them, right now, wanted to tease and stroke her puckered tips with his tongue, wanted to pull her into his mouth and drag his teeth along her sensitive flesh until she wanted him even more, until she was even wetter, hungrier, needier.

"Me too. It's good to see you out of your lab coat," he said, thinking he'd like to see her out of even more of her clothing before the night was much older.

"You too," she said, looking up at him through her eyelashes, her dark brown eyes filled with hunger and more than a trace of confusion.

Hell, he would be confused too if he didn't know the need between them was perfectly natural, the textbook reaction of two mates who had finally found each other. Of course, not being a Were by birth, she wouldn't realize that, wouldn't have a clue that something in her genetic make-up called them to each other, would continue to drive them into a frenzy of sexual desire until they consummated their union.

"Ella, I—"

"I'm sorry, Marcus. I can't do this. I just can't. I don't know why you did what you did, why you didn't just offer me the allergy medication, but I don't care anymore. I can't stay here. I have to go," she said in one long breath before she slammed her unfinished beer down on the bar and began to shove through the crowd, struggling toward the exit like a swimmer who'd been underwater too long, a woman in desperate need of oxygen.

She knew. Somehow she knew what he'd done. Shit.

"Ella," he called after her, bursting through the door that led out of the bar seconds after she did, catching up with her before she'd made any progress toward the grove of trees that hid the parking lot from the bed-and-breakfast.

"Go away, Marcus," she said, sounding as if she were on the verge of tears and refusing to look his direction.

"Listen, I'm sorry," he said, still trying to catch her eye.

"I can't do this," she said, now almost running toward the parking lot. He had to stop her, had to somehow save this evening and their future.

"I just wanted to make you feel better. I heard you talking about how I gave you a allergic reaction and—"

"You heard me in the coffee room?" she asked, spinning to face him.

"I was in the supply closet," he admitted, deciding he might as well get all his dirty secrets out in the open. Spying on Ella and her friend Mandy hadn't been one of his better moments, but he couldn't say he was sorry. At least he'd finally found out why she'd been avoiding him for months.

"You were spying on me? Hiding out in the closet?" she yelled, clearly shocked and repulsed. So much for the truth setting him free.

"I was getting more sugar, but yes I stayed in there when I saw you come in. Good thing I did. It's always nice to know when a coworker is plotting to get you fired. For no reason!" he yelled back, finally starting to get angry himself.

"You drugged my hot chocolate!"

"Not yet I hadn't! You wanted me gone because I gave you a runny nose."

"Well, if you had bothered to wash your clothes—"

"Spare me. You were being a selfish little bitch and you know it," he snapped.

"Fuck you," she yelled, clearly shocked that the words had come out of her mouth. He'd never heard Ella curse, wouldn't have believed she'd say shit if she had mouth full of it until earlier in the afternoon. Clearly he was affecting her. Not quite the effect he'd hoped for, but he'd take anger if he could get it. At least anger was passionate and he wanted her passionate.

"That's not a very nice thing to say," he whispered, advancing on her steadily.

"Stop," she ordered, backing away from him, emitting a small yelp of surprise as she bumped into one of the large sycamore trees that lined the parking lot. She started to circle around the tree, started to turn to run toward her car, but he was on her before she could move more than two inches.

He pressed his body into her, pinned her against the tree, his entire being crying out with need as her breasts flattened against his chest and his erection throbbed against the soft flesh of her hip. Marcus felt his breath start to grow erratic, let his hands move to grip the delicious swells of her ass and force her even closer to his aching cock, closing his eyes and willing her to feel how desperately he'd wanted her, how long he'd waited to feel her so close.

"Get off me," she said, her voice firm, but her body already weakening. Her hands were gripping his biceps and pulling him closer, her breasts were arching into him and he knew her hips would soon follow. She wanted him as badly as he wanted her, he could feel the throbbing of her sex through her clothes, smell her feminine hunger.

"You want me, Ella, don't lie to me," he struggled to squeeze out through his clenched jaw, still managing to fight the primal urge to take her that very second, to pull up her dress, rip off her panties and fuck her until she came, screaming and clawing at his skin, the walls of her pussy milking his cock until there was nothing left inside him but profound peace and satisfaction.

But no matter how much he wanted to act on the desire he felt rolling off her in waves, he couldn't ignore her words. No matter how much her body said yes, if her mouth said no he would have to control himself. He wasn't an animal. Shit, he was an animal, but he was a human first.

"It has to be a drug. It can't just be fucking allergy medicine," she panted, her eyes closing and a small moan slipping from her mouth as her hips began to circle against him, her clit bumping against the hard ridge of his erection.

"You think you desire me because I drugged you?" Marcus asked, shocked almost enough to pull away from the erotic little grinding pattern she was tracing up and down the length of his cock. Almost.

"It was an anti-allergen, Ella. Nothing more. I wanted you to be able to smell me, taste me, without anything to get in our way," he continued, gently gripping her chin and tilting her face up to his own. "Open your eyes, sweetheart. Look at my face and tell me you know I'm telling you the truth."

"Sweetheart?" she asked, opening her eyes and flicking her gaze from his mouth to his eyes and back again until finally she smiled, a beautiful hint of a grin that made his heart hurt. It was so perfect. She was so perfect.

"You don't like sweetheart?" he asked, grinning down at her, the urge to claim her lips warring with the need to keep looking at that smile.

"I like it okay. But I still don't understand," she said, her eyes fluttering closed again as he started to trace slow circles around her pebbled nipples with his knuckles.

"You don't understand what?" he asked, his erection becoming almost painful as he eased his hand inside the v-neck of her dress and brushed over her bare flesh, rolling one nipple gently between his fingers and thumb. She inhaled sharply at his slightest touch, moaning softly and trembling against him, her hands sliding up the sleeves of his t-shirt to dig into his shoulders.

"Why I want you so much," she confessed, eyes opening and lips parting, giving him an invitation he couldn't refuse.

He claimed her lips with his own, thrusting his tongue into her sweet mouth, tasting the beer she'd been drinking and the unique essence of Ella, an indescribable flavor that he knew he wanted to taste again and again for the rest of his life. She was his, his mate, his heart, closer to him than his own skin even though he barely knew her. But how could he explain that to her, how could he make her understand something so strange, so beyond the realm of the average human experience?

He couldn't. He couldn't tell her, he could only show her, claim her, take her where they were both destined to go.

With a sound very like a growl, Marcus moved his hands back to her ass, roughly griping the luscious mounds and lifting her, urging her thighs to either side of his hips, pressing his cock into even more intimate contact with her pussy through their clothes.

"Marcus," she gasped, her eyes flying open to search the area around them, "someone will see."

"This is why you want me, Ella," he breathed into her neck, beyond caring what human eyes might observe them.

Without conscious thought, he felt his canines lengthen in his mouth even as he reached down and tore away the silky underwear that covered her mound, that kept her pussy from him, kept him from feeling the weeping center of her desire.

"No, Marcus, wait. We can't, we can't," she panted, wiggling against him in a way that only drove him onward.

His cock was free in seconds, springing through the opening in his boxers and jeans, straining toward her swollen lips, his tip already beaded with cum. He was so close, seconds from exploding simply from the blissful torture of being so near to claiming his mate, his woman, his love.

"Marcus, no. No," she said, her words turning into a moan as he spread her pussy with his hands and penetrated her in one smooth thrust.

As his cock tunneled into her center, stretching her, filling her, pulsing inside her creamy heat, he made the mark, dragging his teeth over the flesh of her throat just enough to draw blood, just enough to cement them for life, but not enough to hurt her, not enough to spill the amount of blood that would transform him into a predator against his will, turning lust to bloodlust.

"Marcus," she hissed, her body tensing as the sting of his bite coursed through her body.

But then his mouth was on hers, canines nearly back to normal size as he swept her mouth, circled her tongue with his own, felt her respond with all the passion he had dreamed of and more. His thrusts began to quicken against his will, the urge to come stronger than ever before as her tight sheath gripped him.

Thank god she was close too. He could feel her now in a way that he couldn't before, attuned to her with an intimacy that wasn't human. Soon she'd be able to feel it too, would sense his moods, his desires, his fears, would know him as well as, if not better than, he knew himself.

"Come, Ella," he begged, moving his thumb down to press and circle against her clit, easily holding her against the tree with one hand.

"Marcus," she moaned, nails clawing into his arms, shaking and fighting her orgasm, struggling against him even as she met him thrust for thrust.

Something was wrong. She wasn't supposed to fight it, wasn't supposed to even realize the transformation had begun for at least another ten to twelve hours.

"Let go, Ella. Relax, sweetheart," he whispered.

"No," she panted, trembling, sweat starting to bead on her upper lip.

"Please," he begged, knowing he was going to lose control in seconds and not wanting to end their first mating without her release. It wasn't only a blow to his pride, but bad luck for their future.

It was a superstition among Weres, similar to the human ban against the groom seeing the bride in her wedding dress before the ceremony. If the female didn't orgasm after the first bite to seal the mating ceremony, there was going to be trouble ahead. Marcus didn't want trouble, refused to let there be trouble.

With gritted teeth, he forced himself to slow his thrusts, stilling his cock completely inside her though his fingers continued to pluck at her clit, rolling the slick, sensitive nub in slow circles.

"Come, Ella," he whispered, kissing her neck, her jaw, and her trembling mouth.

"Marcus, what's happening?" she asked, shivering and shaking, her body still struggling against release.

"Come on my cock," he ordered, slowly smoothing his other hand down to where their bodies met, caressing the flesh around her entry, where his throbbing erection disappeared into her slick center.

There would be time for explanations later. Right now she would come, she would come or he would die trying.

"Marcus," she said, his name somewhere between a prayer and a curse as he began to tease the entry of her anus with his now slick finger.

"Come, Ella, I want to feel your pussy coming on me," Marcus insisted, slowly penetrating her the slightest bit with his ring finger, knowing the exact second that it was too much for her resistance to take.

It was all too much, his thick length inside her, his finger in her ass, his hand plucking at her clit. She couldn't fight any longer. She gave in, surrendered, and came with a primal scream that was by far the sweetest sound he'd ever heard.

"Yes, yes," he moaned as he began to pound inside her, his cock shooting deep into her womb only seconds later.

He came hard, harder than he'd believed possible, his vision blurring and knees threatening to buckle, his entire body continuing to throb and spasm and throb long after he should have been finished with his orgasm.

And she was trembling right along with him, riding him, milking him with her pussy, gripping and pulling and clenching around him until the waves of pleasure finally started to fade, slowly easing in intensity before the taste of bliss that they'd just experienced became too much for mere mortals—or Weres—to handle.

"Put me down," she said, her voice nearly emotionless.

He did as she asked, gently smoothing her dress down around her thighs before he tucked his cock back into his pants and turned to look over his shoulder. No one. There was no one outside the inn and the windows of the bar faced the other direction, looking out over a peaceful lake. The parking lot was also empty, no cars having departed or arrived during their interlude by the trees.

They hadn't been observed, no thanks to his self-control, of course. He'd been as crazed and animal as any other Were, continuing to press onward even when he'd heard her say "no". Marcus felt shame begin to wash over him as he searched Ella's downturned face, praying that she would forgive him. He'd brought her pleasure and they were destined for each other. Surely she would understand that he hadn't meant to hurt her, would die before he would hurt her.

"Ella?" he asked, gently smoothing her hair behind her ear when the prolonged silence became more than he could bear.

"Don't touch me," she said, jerking away from his touch and finally lifting anger-filled eyes to his face.

"Please, Ella. I can explain," he begged, letting her dart under his arm and head toward her car. God, how he wanted to restrain her, hold her close until she understood how he loved her, how she was the most important thing in his life. But he'd already used more force than he could stomach. He had to let her go if she wanted to go, had to trust that his words would be enough to hold her.

"Don't bother," she said, wiping at the beads of sweat that had formed on her face with a trembling hand.

"I love you, Ella. I want to be with you, to care for you, to do anything in my power to make you happy," he said, feeling like a fool even though the words were true.

He'd never said anything like this before. His kind didn't speak words of love unless they were true and they were only true with a man's mate. Marcus had fucked more than his share of women, human and Were, but Ella was the only woman who would ever hear these words whether she decided to give him a chance at her heart or not.

"You didn't ask, Marcus. You took," she said, pausing with her key in the door of her car to throw him a hard look. "I've had enough of men like you. More than enough."

"You don't understand—"

"I understand perfectly. Clear out your lab station and be gone by Monday morning, Marcus, or I'll do whatever it takes to have you fired," she said with horrible finality before she closed the car door in his face and started the engine.

She was pulling out of the lot before Marcus could think of what to do, before he could explain his actions, let alone the other information she desperately needed to know. He wanted to scream, to howl at the darkening sky, furious and hurt and already missing Ella like a piece of his own skin.

He had to follow her, no matter what she'd said, no matter what he'd promised himself. He had to at least try to make things right between them and even if she still refused him as her mate, he would stay with her through her first transformation. It was his duty, would have been his greatest pleasure.

"Now it's going to be the lowest moment of your life," he muttered to himself as he slowly began to shed his clothing, preparing for the change.

He would be able to track Ella more easily as the wolf and as the wolf maybe he would be able to escape this horrible pain for at least a little while. In his animal form, he didn't think nearly as much and the last thing he wanted to do right now was think about anything. He didn't want to think about what a mess he'd made of what should have been the best night of both of their lives, didn't want to think about how weak and out of control he had been, didn't want to admit that he might have lost his one chance at love.

Chapter Three

ဢ

"Kill me now, Whiskers," Ella moaned to her cat from her position on the bathroom floor. She was still trembling from her last round of vomiting and lacked the energy to crawl back to her bedroom. Besides, the cold bathroom tiles felt good against her feverish face.

Food poisoning. It was food poisoning, right? She had made salmon for dinner the night before and it had been a little raw in the center. She liked her food a little raw, especially fish. Still, it wasn't the smartest thing to do. A batch of bad fish could make you wish you'd never been born.

Or it could be the drug, the "anti-allergen" Marcus slipped in your cocoa.

Ella closed her eyes against the thought. She didn't want to think about Marcus at all, didn't want to remember the painful pleasure of his cock inside her, the joy that had filled her entire being when he'd coaxed her body into the best orgasm of her life, or the hint of something beyond passion that she'd seen in his eyes. It had looked like love, not that she'd seen it in a man's gaze before, but that's what it had looked like.

But he couldn't love her. He barely knew her, had drugged her, pounced on her in public, bitten her neck hard enough to break the skin, screwed her senseless against a tree even after she'd asked him to stop, and then he'd let her go. He had just stood there in the parking lot and let her go. Not that she'd wanted him to chase her…well, maybe a part of her had. Maybe most of her had.

She was definitely a sick cookie. There was no doubt in her mind about that now. She actually wanted to be tailed home by a man who thought biting during sex was acceptable foreplay.

Even stranger than that, she had actually enjoyed the bite, wasn't completely averse to being bitten again, and wondered how it would feel to return the favor. She was sick, in the sense of the word that had nothing to do with bodily infection.

"Proweow?" Whiskers asked. People who thought cats only meowed were crazy, Whiskers had at least twenty-five words in her vocabulary.

"No, I'm not okay. I should probably call an ambulance," Ella sighed to her cat, trying to get up the energy to get to the phone before another round of vomiting forced her to cling to the toilet for dear life.

Whatever or whoever was responsible for this horrible feeling, she couldn't just sit here anymore and wait for it to pass. She'd been sick for over four hours and her entire body hurt and burned and ached with what she guessed was at least a 105-degree temperature. She was starting to get dangerously ill.

"Reow!" Whiskers suddenly yelled, hissing and arching and spitting before turning tail and fleeing into Ella's bedroom.

"Whiskers?" Ella asked, wishing she'd kept her mouth shut when she heard the front door being carefully closed, almost quietly enough that she wouldn't have noticed. Almost.

"Who's there?" Ella asked, praying that it was someone to whom she had given the key.

The only answer was a low growling sound, an entirely unexpected rumbling that chilled her down to her bones. Not only was she allergic to dogs, she was deathly afraid of anything canine. She'd been chased and bitten by more dogs than she could count. Dogs hated her at first sight and she hated them right back. And now one had apparently found its way into her apartment. Great.

The dog growled again as it came around the corner and stuck its furry muzzle into her bathroom. There it stopped, staring down at her with gray eyes that were curiously human. She might have been intrigued by the eyes, sucked into their expressive depths, if her entire body weren't screaming for her to run for it because that sure as hell wasn't a dog. It was a wolf, a bona fide, howl at the moon wolf.

"Get out of my house," she managed to breathe. She'd meant to scream at the thing, but simply didn't have the strength. Between the vomiting and the fear, she was doing pretty well not to pass out right there on the floor.

"Ms. Bradley, I'm so sorry to come into your home uninvited," a gray-haired older man with glasses suddenly said, sticking his head into the bathroom and prompting a small yelp from her throat. That would have been a scream too, but once again feeling near death was interfering with her girlish displays of fear and surprise.

"Marcus came to me for help and thank god he did or you'd both be doomed. Of course, without his discoveries there would be no way to help you and we still can't be sure the medication will remedy the problem," the man said, pulling a giant syringe out from behind his back and crouching down beside her.

"What are you doing?" Ella squeaked, somehow managing to scuttle a few inches away from the lethal-looking needle.

"I'm hopefully giving you the antidote. Marcus created it to keep half-Werewolf, half-*Homo sapiens* children from rejecting their canine genes and in the process bringing about their own death. It seems very effective in lab tests, but we have no idea what will happen when the drug is administered to living subjects or what effect it will have on a half-Werecat who has been mate-claimed by a Werewolf. Frankly, I've never even heard of such a thing, but this is the best hope of survival for you both. The Werecat and Werewolf within you will continue to fight until both they and your human DNA are completely destroyed. Marcus has already been dosed with the—"

"Where is Marcus, what have you done to him?" she asked, knowing that she would try to kill this crazy creep if he'd hurt Marcus. She probably wouldn't succeed and she couldn't rationally explain the anger that surged through her, but she suddenly knew that she'd do anything to keep Marcus safe. She might slap him senseless herself, but no one else had better lay a hand on him if they wanted to live.

"This is Marcus," the man said, motioning to the wolf and looking surprised that she didn't know that his pet was her boyfriend.

Whoa. Did she want Marcus to be her boyfriend? It was weird, but she kind of thought that she did. Of course, it was even weirder that she was thinking about whether or not she wanted a man to be her steady when she was seconds away from death by lethal injection administered by a psycho who thought Marcus was a wolf.

"I'm calling the police," she said, narrowing her eyes and trying to look as scary as possible while still huddled on the bathroom floor. Don't show fear and never let them know you were out of options. She knew how to deal with psychos, she'd been raised by one, after all.

"You knew my mother, didn't you?" Ella continued, all the pieces suddenly falling into place. She'd been a fool not to realize the truth sooner. Canine phobias and fever aside, she still should have made the connection the first time he started talking Werecats and wolves. That particular brand of madness had landed her mother in an institution where she'd raved until the day she died about the "creatures" that lived among the human population.

"No, I'm sorry I didn't," the mad scientist said, blinking his eyes in confusion. Confusion, her ass. She was going to see this guy locked behind bars and then she'd find out who had released her mother's files and there would be hell to pay.

Ella gathered all of her strength and struggled to pull herself off the floor, but then the wolf moaned low in its throat and walked over to lick her bare foot. The shock of its rough tongue against her skin was enough to make her fall back to the tiles. Few humans and no dog had ever touched her with such affection. It was crazy and almost enough to make her wonder if she might have missed something, if maybe she should give the man in front of her a chance to explain himself a little more thoroughly.

If he hadn't been coming at her with that big scary needle again, she honestly thought she would have taken a second to wonder how Marcus could have somehow turned furry. Good thing fear distracted her from such kooky ideas.

"No, don't," Ella pleaded as he lowered the needle toward her arm. She was going to die, the certainty of it chilled her down to the depths of her being.

"Ms. Bradley, without this injection, you're already dead," he said, plunging the needle into her skin and depressing.

She felt nothing for a few seconds, holding her breath as she prayed that somehow she would wake up and this would all be a bad dream. But then the world started to fade to black, her entire body melting, relaxing, moving beyond pain until she couldn't seem to think clearly anymore. And then she stopped thinking altogether.

* * * * *

"Wake up, Ella, please wake up," a soft voice whispered in her ear and she felt herself smile. The morning sun was warm on the bed and the sheets were perfectly cool and the naked male body next to her was by far the most amazing thing she'd felt in ages. She stretched and smiled again, knowing that life didn't get much better than this.

"What the hell!" she screamed, bolting upright and clutching the sheet over her breasts when she realized that she was nude. And there was Marcus, stretched out beside her, naked as the day he was born, looking more handsome than any human had the right to, and staring at her with eyes filled with equal parts desire and anxiety.

"How do you feel?" he asked, sitting up beside her and reaching out to cup her cheek in his hand. She tried to pull away, but found she couldn't. Just the smell of his skin was enough to make her want to lunge at him, to smash her mouth down on his, to push him back onto the sheets and impale herself on the cock that she could see was already more than ready for her.

"I feel like I've been tripping my balls off," she said, licking her dry lips and struggling against her desire, beyond wondering exactly where in the hell she'd pulled that little comment. So she was developing a bit of a potty mouth. At the moment it seemed to be the least of her worries.

"You haven't been tripping your balls off, you've been recovering from rejection. I called in sick to work for both of us. I said that you had food poisoning and I had been up with you all night at the hospital," he explained, nuzzling his face into her neck, his breath amazingly sweet for a man who hadn't yet brushed his teeth...or his fangs.

"Get back, wolf boy," Ella said, pulling away from him, knowing her eyes were growing ridiculously wide as she remembered the last few minutes before she'd blacked out.

Holy shit a brick. It couldn't be real, had to be some sort of drug-induced hallucination. It was too crazy, too perfectly crazy, some sick twisted perversion of what she'd heard her mother rave about as a child. Ella was ready to dismiss the experience entirely and demand Marcus tell her what really happened when she saw the little bandage taped at the crook of her elbow, right where the big scary needle had pierced her skin.

"This can't be real," she whispered, feeling her stomach clamp down around its own emptiness.

"I can explain everything. I'm sorry I couldn't last night, but I couldn't change back to my human form. The medication stalled everything out and I was stuck. To tell you the truth I thought I might be stuck forever," Marcus said with a nervous laugh and then reached for her again before he remembered she'd asked him to back off and dropped his arms. By the shaking of his hands and the look in his eyes, he was having as hard a time as she was resisting the strange sexual pull between them.

"You were the wolf in the bathroom?" she asked, trying to sound incredulous, but somehow knowing that he was telling the truth. It was absolutely insane, but he was telling the truth.

"I was. The man who helped us was my uncle, he's a chemist too, and a Werewolf of course —"

"Of course."

"You're not going to make this easy on me, are you?" he asked, smiling at her with eyes that begged her to give him a chance.

"I'm half-Werecat," she said calmly, trying to get used to the idea. Stranger things had happened, right? Maybe not to her personally, but she was sure stranger things had happened.

The hysterical laughter that had been threatening since she first woke up started to bubble up and out of Ella's throat, bursting past the hand she pressed against her mouth. She was losing her mind. That's what was happening. She was going crazy, just like her mother.

"I don't see that it's funny, we both almost died. Why in the hell didn't you say something sooner?" Marcus asked, actually having the nerve to look angry with her.

"Like you told me you were a Werewolf?" she asked. He was crazy too. Why did she have to go and fall for a total head case? Probably because she was a head case.

"That's different. You should have been able to scent me. I couldn't scent you because you're only half Were."

"You're serious, aren't you?" Ella asked, a shred of doubt starting to penetrate her shock. He wasn't lying. He really believed that he was a Werewolf and she was half-Werecat.

Her mother had been telling the truth. Dear god, all those years she'd been telling the truth.

The hysterical laughter rose inside her again, but the sound that came out of her mouth was closer to a sob. Ella shook her head as tears started to gather at the corners of her eyes. Reality as she knew it had ceased to exist and she had to either laugh or cry. Hell, might as well do both.

"You think this is a joke?" he yelled.

"Don't get mad at me. I don't know shit about scenting or Werecatting. I didn't even think it was true. My mom ended up in an institution after my dad died. Nothing she said made much sense, so you'll have to excuse me if I didn't believe that my dad was a Cat Man," Ella snapped, struggling not to get any more emotional than she was already. It was a hard thing to do when thinking about her mom, but she managed. The poor woman. If only she'd lived a little longer Ella could have told her that she believed her, that she finally knew the truth about her father.

"You didn't know? You really didn't know what you were?" Marcus asked, looking completely horrified.

"No, I didn't."

"Ella, I'm so sorry. I had no idea. Don't cry, sweetheart," Marcus said, reaching out to her.

"Don't call me sweetheart," she said, slapping his hands away and swiping at the tears that leaked from her eyes against her will. She didn't like crying in front of other people and liked being comforted by them even less.

"You liked it yesterday," he said, looking hurt.

"I liked you yesterday," she said, wishing she could take the words back as soon as she said them. It was like she'd struck him, wounded him much more deeply than she'd intended.

"I love you, Ella. I'm sorry that I claimed you as my mate without your permission. I'm sorry that I hurt you, that I put your life in danger and...all the rest of it," he said, his face growing expressionless as he moved from the bed and started to dress, pulling on the jeans his uncle must have brought for him last night.

"I'll ask someone from the Council to come speak with you later today, to explain to you our world and your place in it," he continued stiffly.

"Why won't you explain it to me?"

"I have to go," he said.

"So you're leaving? Just like that?" she asked, wondering what it was that kept her from reaching out to him, from pulling him back into her arms as she wanted to so very desperately. He'd said he loved her and she believed him and what was even more strange — she loved him back.

She loved him. The knowledge hit her with equal parts shock and resonance. She did love him, whether they were people or pets, whether it was logical or not, whether anyone else in the world would understand this immediate and passionate affection. But still she sat there, silent and unmoving as he threaded his belt through the loops of his jeans.

Surely she wouldn't let pride or anger keep her from the man she knew she loved. But then again, maybe it wasn't pride. Maybe it was fear, the good old-fashioned fear that she'd felt ever since her family had fallen apart when she was only nine years old. The fear that had prompted her to choose "impossible" men again and again, doing anything and everything to make sure she never had to be vulnerable to love or the pain of loss.

But Marcus wasn't impossible. He loved her, he respected her, and he wanted to be with her, all of her, even the parts she hadn't realized existed. She couldn't let him go, couldn't give up what she knew was her best, if not her only, chance at finding the man she was meant to spend the rest of her life with.

"Wait," Ella said, "don't go."

"You said you didn't like me, Ella. I assume that also means that you don't love me or want to be my mate. I wish I could deal with that and still talk rationally to you about the fucking shapeshifter community, but I can't. I just can't," he said, looking as if he were on the verge of tears.

"Don't curse," she whispered, coming off the bed to stand before him, cupping his wounded face in her hands. How could she ever have thought this man was dangerous?

"You've been cursing lately," he said, his eyes wary but hopeful.

"I know. I just haven't been myself. Or maybe I've been more myself. I hear Werecats are famous for their tempers," she said.

"What do you know about Werecats?" he asked with a small smile as his arms wrapped around her and his hands smoothed down over her bare ass. God she was glad she hadn't put any clothes on.

"Nothing. But I know I don't want anyone else but you to teach me," she said, slowly undoing the belt of his jeans and dragging her fingernails over the bulge beneath the rough fabric. Even touching him through clothing was enough to send an almost painful wave of desire shooting up from her pussy into some place deep inside the center of her being.

"I don't want to be just your teacher," he said, moving one hand to cup her breast, making her gasp as his thumb flicked across her already puckered nipple.

"I know," Ella breathed, closing her eyes and marveling at the unbelievable pleasure coursing through her body. The slightest touch and she was wet and aching for him, dizzy with the strength of her need for him and only him. Maybe not the strongest basis for a lifetime commitment but it certainly was a hell of a start.

"Be my mate, Ella," he pleaded, easing her back onto the bed as he shoved his jeans to the floor, his thick, swollen length springing free from his clothing. Ella reached for him, needing to feel the silken skin of his cock in her hand.

"Do we have to be married in real life too?" she asked.

"I'd prefer it."

"Me too," she said, rolling him underneath her with a strength that surprised her and apparently him as well.

"Shapeshifters are stronger than pure humans," he laughed, a sound that turned into a gasp as she kissed her way down his stomach and took his length in her mouth, suckling and stroking with her tongue as her hands gripped the base of his cock.

He tasted delicious, so delicious she almost wanted to bite him, but assumed he wouldn't really appreciate that, not on such a sensitive area at least. She settled for dragging her teeth slowly, gently, along his velvety skin with just enough pressure for him to feel her teeth. He shivered and his cock twitched in her mouth.

"Easy, tiger, or I'm going to come right now," he growled, his voice thick with need.

"Will I turn into a tiger?" Ella asked, sitting up suddenly. Could she really turn into a cat? What kind of cat and when? Would it hurt? Would she know when it was about to happen? Why hadn't she ever turned into one before? So many questions, so little ability to focus when he was pulling her face up for a kiss she felt all the way down to her toes.

"I have no idea, love, but I'm sure whatever you are you will be beautiful," he said, flipping her onto her back and teasing her nipples with his tongue. She cried out as he pulled a puckered tip deep into his mouth, suckling at her until the pleasure was just short of pain. The knot of desire in her belly grew even tighter, making her lift her hips into him, her body begging for him to claim her again, just as he had the night before.

"I need to be inside you, Ella," he moaned, spreading her thighs and dipping his fingers into her pussy. She knew he'd find her more than ready. She didn't think she'd ever been this wet in her life. He did something to her, something entirely wonderful.

"Condom," she said, reaching toward the bedside table.

"What?"

"Condom. I know we didn't use one last night, but—"

"You're not fertile, I would be able to smell it," he said, looking very sad and pulling away from her slightly, his hands playing through her hair. Who knew fertility could make a wolf so sad?

"What's wrong?"

"We may not be able to have children," he said, searching her face for a clue to how that news might affect her.

"Because I'm a cat and you're a wolf?" she asked. It made sense, in a totally weird "I just found out I'm a shapeshifter" type of way.

"We actually won't know if you will be a Werecat or a Werewolf until you transform for the first time. You clearly responded well to the medication, but whether your body chose your genetic predisposition and became a Werecat or responded to my mark and transformed you into a wolf, I honestly don't know. But if you are a Werecat, you're right, we won't be genetically compatible."

"Will we fight like cats and dogs?"

"Of course not, we're still human first. It isn't—"

"I was kidding, Marcus. Just a little shapeshifter humor," she said, soothing her hands down his back to cup his buttocks and urge him into her. He slid home without a second's more encouragement, his thick cock tunneling into her center until she was completely filled with him and she knew whatever happened it would be all right.

"We'll adopt if we can't have kids," she whispered as he started to slowly move in and out of her in languid thrusts that had her body humming with animal need. She'd never dreamed sex could be like this, so raw and powerful and absolutely perfect.

"I love you, Ella," he said, his mouth on hers, his hands at her hips, his cock moving inside her, every inch of his skin telling her how true his words were, how he would live for her, die for her, do anything it took to make sure they were happy together.

"I love you too, Mr. Scary," she breathed, locking her legs around his waist and pulling him deeper, lifting her hips and clenching her muscles around his thickness, feeling her body start to tremble beneath him.

"I'm not scary," he said softly, the slightest hint of hurt in his eyes.

"I was kidding, Marcus. Besides, I like scary," she said, smiling into his face before she pulled him close and sank her teeth into his shoulder, surprised as hell when she drew blood.

"Shit," he said, jumping slightly before his breath started to come even faster.

"Sorry," Ella moaned.

"Little bitch."

"Marcus!" she said, knowing she would have smacked him if he weren't pumping his cock in and out of her so hard and deep that she couldn't do much more than hang on for the ride and start to come.

She screamed out his name again as the orgasm claimed her, the pleasure almost violent, her skin humming with electricity, her lips numb and tingling, her pussy gripping him so tightly that she knew he'd come any second. And then he did and it was so perfect, so sweet and pure and wonderful to be able to grip his buttocks and pull him as deeply as he could go, feel him spilling his essence inside her.

She'd never had sex without a condom, except for the night before, had never realized how much that little piece of rubber interfered with the intimacy of flesh inside flesh. But then, maybe it was just her newly enhanced animal side that loved the sticky, messy, primal aspects of sex, the fluid, the tastes, the smells.

"You smell so good. I want to eat you," she breathed as he lay heavily on top of her and she licked at the slightly sweaty skin of his shoulder.

"I noticed," he laughed softly, beginning to trail kisses up her neck.

"I said I was sorry."

"I'm not. You're my bitch, now I know for sure."

"I'm assuming you mean in the female dog sense and not the nasty jerk sense?" she asked, finally catching on.

"Only my wolf mate would know to bite my shoulder to complete the second stage of the mate ceremony. Besides, neither of us seems to be feeling sick. If you were still Werecat we'd probably need another dose of the medication," he said, kissing her softly with a tender smile.

"I'm going to be a dog? Will I be allergic to myself?"

"I doubt it, but if you are I'll just dose your cocoa."

"Don't ever dose anything without my knowledge again or I'll tear your heart out and eat it," Ella growled, entirely shocked by her own threat. She meant business, but there was no need to be quite that dramatic about it. Thankfully, Marcus didn't seem overly concerned since he was laughing so hard he had to roll off her onto his back.

"I'm serious. Sort of," she said, forcing herself to frown at him even though his laughter made her want to laugh, to giggle hysterically and roll around on the bed with him like two overgrown puppies.

"I know you are. My mom's going to love you," he said, pulling her on top of him and starting to kiss her again.

She started to ask questions, but then those hands were on her waist, his cock was rising to the occasion against her already fluttering stomach, and Ella realized there was nothing left to say. At least not right now. Question and answer time could wait. For the moment, all she needed was to make love to her mate. Whether he was a cat or a dog or an armadillo didn't seem to matter as long as he was hers.

"I love you, Marcus," she breathed as she straddled him and guided him inside her.

"I love you too."

"I can't remember ever feeling this fucking happy," she laughed, strangely close to tears. This love stuff was crazy.

"Listen to that potty mouth. I knew I'd be good for you," he moaned with a smile.

"Cocky bastard," Ella said as she increased the pace of her hips gliding up and down his cock. But she couldn't really argue because he was good, very, very good.

Eclipse

Denise A. Agnew

ఒ

About the Author

ℬ

Suspenseful, erotic, edgy, thrilling, romantic, adventurous. All these words describe Denise A. Agnew's award-winning novels. Romantic Times BookClub magazine called her romantic suspense novels "top-notch", and her erotic romance PRIMORDIAL received a Top Pick from them. With paranormal, time travel, romantic comedy, contemporary, historical, erotic romance, and romantic suspense novels under her belt, Denise enjoys writing about a diverse range of subjects. The fact she has lived in Colorado, Hawaii, and the United Kingdom has given her a lifetime of ideas. Her experiences with archaeology have crept into her work, as well as numerous travels through England, Ireland, Scotland, and Wales. Denise lives in Arizona with her real-life hero, her husband.

Denise welcomes comments from readers. You can find her website and email address on her author bio page at www.ellorascave.com.

Trademarks Acknowledgement

The author acknowledges the trademarked status and trademark owners of the following wordmarks mentioned in this work of fiction:

BMW: Bayerische Motoren Werke Aktiengesellschaft

Chapter One
New Orleans
Halloween

෨

Dawn Chartrier sat in her parked car and held her breath, certain she might walk into the Den of Wolves tonight and meet her death if things didn't go as planned. Tonight she could discover the mystery of what happened beyond the darkness between death and rebirth.

Dawn looked out at the New Orleans night, with its foggy nuance and mysterious layers. She felt the chill down to her marrow. She'd seen costume-clad revelers around the streets, but once she'd arrived at the club, fundamental change brought a deathly hush over the street. Edginess prickled her skin, her stomach uneasy and her heart throbbing a little too fast. Dawn had never experienced a panic attack, but she fought with rising anxiety to keep her heart steady and her trembling at bay. She'd always been the brave one in the family, willing to take chances. Now that she was here, reluctance dogged at her heels.

What insanity lurked around this single street and caused Halloween partygoers to avoid this area? Did the reputation of the club keep them away? Her heart pounded, and fear threatened to smash her resolve. She could start the car and escape.

But she would never forgive herself if she didn't help her sister.

Taking time away from her financial analyst job in Denver hadn't endeared Dawn to her work-fourteen-hours-a-day boss. He'd grudgingly given her a week off when she explained her sister could be in grave danger. The boss from hell might use this trip as a reason to mark her down on her evaluation next month. If so, she'd start looking for another job, or another career.

"Shit." Cursing came easy to her now—she'd never been a potty mouth, but circumstances and stress made her do things she didn't think she would.

If she didn't watch out, she'd follow her sister Maureen's destructive path. She could still hear Maureen's chilling words when she'd called. *Dating a werewolf is a bitch.*

Well, her sister had given her life over to something unnatural, and now she paid the price.

Yet one fact plagued Dawn more than other concerns. If she left this vehicle, if she went into the fog-enshrouded night surrounding the club, she might not come back alive.

Plus, she didn't want to ask the help of one very, very dangerous man. A man she'd fallen for ten years ago and had never forgotten. Rumors about him abounded in New Orleans.

Was he a vampire?

Or a werewolf?

She didn't know if either applied to him, or neither.

No matter. She would find out tonight.

She'd located a parking spot as close to the club as she could. The streets were lined with cars, and she must traverse a block before the dubious safety of the club could embrace her. She smiled without mirth.

She glanced at her watch in the dim light from a streetlamp. *Close to midnight.* She unlocked her side of the BMW sedan, then stepped out of the car.

"Now or never," she said into the dank breath of New Orleans at night.

As she took the sidewalk quickly, her athletic shoes cushioned her steps. Her breath sounded loud in her ears, her heart pumping a steady beat of worry. Hair on the back of her neck prickled. She trembled and cold sweat broke out on her body. She hurried toward the entrance of the club. The low-key sign beckoned. She could hear the music, a thumping cadence more patently sexual than merely sensual. The rhythm lured her with its throbbing sound.

Please let Niall Machaire be at the club tonight. Please.

A horn blasted near her, and she jumped as a car swept by. She took a deep breath of thick air and continued onward until she reached the front door.

Den of Wolves.

An appropriate name for a place with a reputation like this. Reflective glass stared back like two onyx eyes. She reached for the glass doors, but they swung open before she could feel the metal handles beneath her nervous fingers.

She held her breath and stepped inside. A cacophony of wild shrieks and howls mixed with evil laughter. At first, she couldn't tell if the noises came from a Halloween soundtrack or from the occupants. Darkness stretched far in front of her, then broke where flickering purple and red candles lit various tables covered with plain red tablecloths. A few androgynous figures hovered near or sat at the tables. She didn't look too closely. A flash of red eyes here and there made her skin prickle with apprehension and her breath shorten.

Figures on the dance floor in the center writhed to a sinuous beat. Lyrics reached her ears.

Dark as night, your black soul,

Come taste the evening with me and go,

There's a wild thing inside me tonight,

Only you can free it,

Baby, you might…

Someone bumped her from behind. When she twisted around, Dawn saw a stumpy, slightly overweight woman with straight long black hair, tight red velvet bodice and flowing black velvet dress that reached her black pumps. Rimmed with black eye shadow, her dark brown eyes held contempt. Her mouth, outlined with heavy black lip liner and sanguine lipstick, curled with a sarcastic smile.

"Excuse me? Are you the door?" the woman asked in a high-pitched voice.

First impulse almost made Dawn sneer right back and tell the woman to shove it where the sun didn't shine. But she didn't want to draw extraordinary attention. After all, she already stood out in her plain green turtleneck, navy fleece jacket and blue jeans. Even her white athletic shoes would stand out in a place like this. She moved aside, and the woman swept by. An electrical sensation, almost like static, passed through her body. It stung the roots of her hair and Dawn gasped. This wasn't good. Not good at all.

"New here, *chere*?" The words rasped like old parchment, and she turned around to see who spoke.

Bald as a cue ball, and almost as white, the pink-eyed creature in front of her wore a floor-length red robe belted at the waist. Paper-white skin, smooth and blemish free, plus pink, glossy lips, completed the first impression. Man or woman, she couldn't say.

Dawn found her voice, raspy and choked with suppressed fear. "I'm looking for Niall Machaire."

The bald creature smiled and showed sharp white canines. Dread inched up Dawn's spine.

"He's here somewhere, sugar. You'll just have to wander until you find him." The creature gestured at the odd crowd, voice barely audible against the loud music. "That is, if he doesn't find you first."

Cue ball wandered away, and she shuddered. God, she couldn't remove the ice from her bones. The night had crawled up, bitten her, and hung on as tenaciously as a Gila monster.

She wandered the cavernous club and kept a straight face as relentless fear gnawed at her insides.

Damn it, buck up. You've never been a coward. Don't start now.

Suddenly, warmth heated her from the inside out. Someone watched her. She could feel it—the excitement rose up at the same time as caution. She glanced around and saw him.

Niall Machaire.

Ten years had passed since she'd seen him. Ten years since Dawn realized he wasn't exactly the man she thought he was. Niall had dated Maureen, but his kindness and good humor toward Dawn had endeared him to her young heart. Not only was he the most gorgeous man she'd ever seen, she'd sensed a core of extreme honor inside him. Over the month he'd been in her life off and on, Dawn had fallen head over heels in love with him.

Until he skipped town with Maureen for good.

And Dawn's heart had broken.

When Maureen left Colorado Springs, she vowed her life would never be the same. She wanted to make a difference. Take the world by storm. Instead, the world had taken her, stripped her, spat her out. Maureen long ago surrendered to hard living and shattered any chance she might have to exert that special something she believed she could accomplish.

A blue sheen bounced off the shiny black, long length of Niall's hair as it cascaded past his shoulders. Thick and wavy, his hair flowed around the most striking but starkly masculine face Dawn had ever seen. A Roman nose, carved jaw and firm lips graced his arresting face.

A dark angel, a fallen avenger, a man who had roamed this world longer than any mortal creature could. Her breath caught as his topaz blue eyes tangled with her gaze and held.

Dawn trembled as his gaze softened, went lambent and seductive. What caused that ruthless look to transform? Before she could blink, he stood. While others in this crazy place wore a variety of Goth-wannabe outfits, he sported a burgundy polo shirt and black jeans.

He strode across the dance floor rather than skirt the swirling gyrations. Time slowed, rippled. Dazzled and mesmerized, her will started to crumble. God, she couldn't do this.

Coward. The word whispered through her head. Self-recrimination pounded on her like a hammer. *Do it for your sister.*

Primal female attraction, stark and painfully fierce, tore through her the way it had years ago when she'd first seen him. Shame also intruded. She couldn't avoid it. Niall may have taken her sister away, but he'd snagged a piece of Dawn's sanity as well.

No. I can't. I —

She'd have to formulate another plan.

Fear rocketed through her, and she started away, dashing through the increasing crowd. She bumped into two people. Apologies tumbled from her lips. She'd made it halfway to her car when a dark form jumped from the darkness and wrapped steel-hard arms around her.

Dawn cried out, alarm blaring inside her as she struggled. Anger surged with hot intensity inside her. Self-defense training kicked in. Her right elbow went up at the same time her right foot aimed at the man's knee. The blow to his knee glanced off without effect. Her arm wouldn't budge. *No!* She'd missed her chance.

The man squeezed and her breath seized up. A wicked laugh hissed in her ears, rusted and filled with decay. She wrinkled her nose at the stench. He whirled her around.

Hard brick bruised her flesh as the attacker mashed her back against the wall and held her there with his body. She couldn't see too well in the dark alley. Shock held her immobile too long.

"You shouldn't have come here, sweet pea." The voice rippled like water, otherworldly in tone.

She jerked in the creature's grip as a stench more rancid than sulfur filled her nose. She choked, her breath cut off by the horrible smell. She gasped and struggled for breath.

Who — ? What — ?

"Let her go, Megla." The voice almost whispered in deep, brushed velvet.

Megla didn't obey. "She's mine."

"Bullshit. Let her go, or I'll rearrange your already ugly face," the voice said, harsh and certain. Salted with a distinct Scottish accent, the voice rumbled deep and husky.

The harsh pressure on her shoulders ceased, and Megla melted into the shadows and disappeared. While the sulfurous smell abated, her knees wobbled. Dizziness assaulted, and her stomach curdled with nausea. Stars visible in the night sky tilted and swayed. Overwhelmed, she groaned softly. Despair threatened. She'd failed her sister.

Tears filled her eyes.

Warm, strong hands gripped her shoulders, but her knees still threatened to buckle. God, she hated feeling helpless. Hated it.

"What in bloody hell are you doing out here?" the dark form asked. "Megla would've had you for lunch if I wasn't here to stop it."

"It?" Her voice quavered.

"Definitely an *it*." Amusement touched his voice.

Before she could answer, darkness gobbled her up.

Chapter Two

8∂

Dawn gasped, her heart leaping as she broke from a horrifying dream she couldn't recall. She jerked.

"No!"

Her eyes popped open to a room dimly lit by a bedside lamp. Nausea threatened, but not as overt as before. Her head felt clear. Her arms and legs ached as if she'd run hard and far. Disoriented, she took in her surroundings. A huge bed, easily larger than a California king, cradled her body in softness and luxury. Numerous pillows covered the head of the bed, including the fluffy one under her head. Cool sheets brushed against naked skin.

Naked. She lifted the sheet. Yep. Bare as a newborn. Who or what had undressed her? She glanced frantically about the room, trying to orient her scrambled world. Gauzy blue and green material acted as a canopy over the top of the bed. Wooden shutters blocked strong sunlight. A masculine, earthy scent teased her nose. It smelled wonderful, and she took another breath to ease it into her lungs. World traveler memorabilia graced the walls. Overall, the room comforted her in a way she didn't understand. Panic no longer nipped at her heels like wild dogs.

A movement in the bed changed that.

She gasped and looked to her right as the blue velvet comforter moved. A head emerged from under the sheets. Long, black, tousled hair, then the face she'd seen across the crowded Den of Wolves.

Niall Machaire.

She jolted with disbelief. *I'm in Niall Machaire's bed?*

Her mind ran in frenzied circles. She couldn't recall anything after the alley. Terror had wrecked her legendary control, her ability to hold back any outward sign of weakness. Megla could have done what it wanted until this man saved her. Gratitude mixed with uneasiness. A tremor ran through her frame.

With one flick of his wrist, he tossed the comforter and sheet off his body. Her mouth dropped open. While she'd admired Niall's gorgeous face, his body rivaled any fantasy she might have indulged on a lonely night. She propped up on her elbows to look. Broad shoulders led downward to ripped arms and chest. A dark sprinkling of hair fanned over his pectorals and a six-pack stomach. Nestled within thick hair at his groin, his cock thrust upright. Thick and long, his cock spelled demanding masculinity.

She blinked, stunned by the most exciting body she'd ever seen. Not that she'd seen many. She'd had two lovers, one in college many years ago, and one two years ago that ended in disappointed feelings and lousy sex.

Yet sex defined every inch of his sculpted body. Arousal curled low in her belly. Her breath caught as he moved. He rolled toward her with a groan, and his arms reached out and snatched her close. She uttered a soft squeak of surprise and clutched at his shoulders. His chest crushed against her breasts, the hair tickling her nipples into hard points. His legs tangled with hers, thigh muscles bunching. With a smooth move, his cock eased between her thighs and pressed along her clit and labia. She wriggled and gasped with mortification as her body heated and her brain rebelled against startling intimacy. His face buried against her neck, hot breath feathering along sensitive skin. She opened her mouth to wake him, to protest.

He awoke with a start and his powerful arms circled tighter around her ribs.

Halfheartedly, she pushed against his shoulders. "Let me go."

His eyes widened a second, as if surprised to find her wrapped in his arms.

Then his carved, beautifully masculine lips transformed into a wolfish grin. "Good morning."

"What have you done?" she asked.

One dark brow winged up. "Done? Brought you home with me. I carried you here after you fainted."

"I don't faint."

He grinned again, his gaze intense and probing. "You fell right into my arms. You were weak. Megla is a powerful mind bender. It would have subdued you, raped you, and left you in the alley. When I followed you, I knew you'd get into a wee bit of trouble."

"How long was I out?"

"Only a couple of hours."

He brushed one hand over the small of her back, and she quivered as sensual heat poured over her body. Everything about Niall screamed sexuality, his body raging with heat, power and testosterone. Even if she could ignore that, she couldn't disregard the thick, long cock pressing without remorse between her legs.

"Thank you for...protecting me," she managed to say.

"You're welcome." His voice rumbled, deep and silky on the air. "Damn foolish girl."

Indignant, she said, "I'm not a girl."

One big hand slid downward from her shoulders in a smooth, heated path. She quaked as he clasped one ass cheek and squeezed gently.

"Oh, yes. You're bloody well a woman." His lips touched her forehead. "A beautiful, hot woman." The rough, scintillating sensuality in his voice rippled over her skin like electricity. "How do you feel now? Are you all right?"

"I'm okay."

Okay. Well, that didn't exactly describe how she felt. Her skin prickled, awareness of him as a man causing her lower belly to flutter with steady arousal.

"Good." He nodded, though his serious expression belied his easygoing response. A few seconds later, he said, "You know the price for what you're seeking."

She looked into those smoldering eyes and saw lethal intent. "You don't even know why I came looking for you."

He chuckled, and the genuine warmth in his voice surprised her. His touch aroused, stimulated her wildest needs, but she realized with startling clarity one surprising fact. She wasn't afraid of him.

"You want me to help rescue your sister from her life with a werewolf," he said softly.

Amazement jolted her. "How — ?"

"Your mind is very open right now. I can read it."

Dawn's breath caught. "You can read minds?"

"Sometimes. Now, tell me why you think you needed to come out here and save her."

Confusion fueled frustration. "Four days ago she called me in a panic saying she'd made an awful mistake. She went to the Den of Wolves and met a — I can't believe I'm saying this — a werewolf named Valerian." Dawn shivered, equally frightened by her sister's insanity as by the sexy body pressed along hers. "She said she didn't want to be with him anymore, but she didn't know what to do. I told her to just leave him, but she said he's dangerous."

His eyes went sapphire, their depths cynical yet understanding. His touch turned soft along her back, comforting her. "You think she's crazy to run off with a werewolf, or that she's nuts for believing they exist?"

She wriggled, and his arms tightened. "I can't have this conversation with you this way. *We're naked*. And *why* did you strip me?"

A sardonic smile touched his lips. "You were wet through to your flaming red underwear. It started to rain the moment you passed out. I wanted to keep you here to make sure Megla hadn't done any permanent damage."

She didn't buy his humanitarian claim. "You crawled in bed with me."

"I was tired. It's been a long day." He rolled suddenly, and gently flipped her onto her back. One of his thighs pressed between hers, his hair-roughened muscle stroking against her pussy. "But you're beautiful naked." His gaze swept from her face to her breasts, then back up. "Fuckin' beautiful. Even more than you were ten years ago."

His low-pitched, husky Scottish accent seduced. Raw and masculine, his voice called to her basest instincts. Her nipples hardened. Slick moisture wet her folds. He smelled spicy, of sandalwood and heated man. Yet she hated him for what he'd done to her sister ten years ago. Most of all, she hated him for ravaging her equilibrium. For making her as hot and bothered now as he did ten years ago.

She forced a frown. "You seduced my sister. You made her fall in love and then dumped her in this city where she had no friends and family."

His eyes hardened, darkness replacing light. Still, his arms stayed planted on either side of her like a cage she couldn't break. "I didn't make her do anything. She didn't love me. She wanted an escape from her boring life."

Dawn felt an ache inside. "She could have escaped some other way."

"Could have. But she didn't. We all make our own way or allow circumstances to do it for us."

She knew he was right. Damn, but it was easier to blame him than admit Maureen hosed up her life on her own.

His eyes warmed. He brushed a stray hair away from her face. "And here you are again, rushing to her rescue at your own peril. When are you going to let go?"

"Let go?" She echoed him in confusion. "I'm not sure I know how." Her lips twisted in false humor. "I know I should stop rescuing her. Stop caring—"

"Not stop caring. Stop hurting yourself trying to fix something you can't heal."

"You make it sound so simple."

He snorted softly. She quivered as his right hand drifted along her shoulder to cup her rib cage. His big hand heated her skin, a touch at once gentle and intimidating.

"So small." His fingers trailed down her arm to her long fingers. "So damned fragile. You could be hurt easily in the night. You're not used to the warning signs and the rhythms here. New Orleans is a bright place and a dark place all at once. You can get too complacent."

As his fingers brushed over hers, she shivered. "That's why I've got to find Maureen. I need to help her before it's too late."

His cynical smile and hard eyes mocked her efforts. Niall's male beauty mesmerized at the same time it challenged. She sensed a lethal thread of danger around him, coiled and ready as a viper.

I should be horrified. Appalled. I'm buck naked in this bed with this gorgeous man as if I've been with him forever. It feels so right. Maybe I'm as insane as Maureen.

"Help her dodge old boyfriends?" he asked.

"Old boyfriends like you?"

He pulled her hands up until he pinned them to the bed above her head. "What I had with her was a mistake." His tone and face filled with solid regret. "I was at a bad place in my life when I met Maureen. The worst in decades. I'd nothing to live for, but no way to die."

She read a pain within his eyes that shook her to the core. Niall, ten years ago, had seemed invincible. Sexy and charismatic in a confident way, but not insincere.

"I don't understand," she said.

"If I'd been thinking straight about Maureen," he said, "I never would have tried to save her either. She can't be rescued, Dawn. She has to do it herself. How many times have you been to New Orleans and tried to get her out of messes she claimed were someone else's fault?"

Dawn's fingers clenched on his wide, rock-hard shoulders. "Twice."

"And you succeeded?"

"Yes." Pride didn't enter her tone, but neither did satisfaction. "And you think I should stop?"

"For your sanity." His soft burr, the rolling "r"s in his tone soothed and maddened. "Your self-respect. You're a damned competent, self-controlled, intelligent woman. Don't let Maureen's life choices destroy you."

He shifted and pressed his thigh harder against her pussy. She moaned softly as her body responded on a physical level she couldn't control. "Is that what you did? You left her when you realized you couldn't help her?"

"I left her one day after we came here. I realized she was pulling me down into darker depths. Her hell was a lot blacker than mine."

"You took what you wanted and then dumped her," she said with confidence and anger.

"No. She took what she wanted, and when I saw into her soul, I realized she didn't need me to love her. She wanted a diversion. A quick fuck. That's why I left her."

The idea this man—this creature, if you will—felt used by any woman astounded Dawn. The user felt used.

She quivered as he traced his fingers down until they reached her thigh. Arousal burgeoned inside her. His erection poked her hip. Her breath came tight, her craving more acute.

"What is the truth?" she asked. "What pushed you away from her and made you let Maureen go?"

"The club. I've owned the Den of Wolves for a long time. She told me I was evil. An abomination. She asked how I could harbor creatures of the night."

Surprise slapped her across the face. "You own the Den?"

"I do. She thought I was independently wealthy. I am, but the club is my life's blood. When she realized creatures like Megla, an energy vampire, frequent the place, she was scared."

Dawn waited for the crazy information to digest, but it stuck in her throat like a bone. "I've heard and seen too many weird things over my life to deny the supernatural. But you're nuts if you think I'm going to let you hold me in this bed against my will."

"Yet you want my help. You think if anyone can find Maureen, I can?"

"I figured you would know this Valerian character, or know someone who could help me find him."

He smiled, and the gentle grin made her heart speed up. He released her hands and they slid down to the solidness of his biceps.

He switched gears. "You were projecting your thoughts so loudly earlier tonight that half the telepathic creatures in the club could hear you." Niall drew his touch up to her neck, feeling the pulse point. "Since you first met me ten years ago, I felt the same powerful connection to you that you've felt to me."

Startled, she asked, "What connection?"

As his lips touched the joint between her shoulder and neck, she shivered. Spiraling desire coiled and leapt, heated and grew. Emotions battered her defenses. She shouldn't trust him, yet she did. She shouldn't believe his so-called mind reading, but she did.

"When I met you, I felt an attraction so strong, it almost brought me to my knees." His eyes shone with potent emotion— one she couldn't define. "It's never been like this with another woman." His gaze trailed down to her generous breasts. "Not in this life or any other."

Startled pleasure darted through her. She'd never realized that he'd been attracted to her all those years ago. "But you dated Maureen."

"You were fairly young and innocent. I didn't want to bring you into my many lives."

"Are you saying you're reincarnated?"

He shook his head, and his hair drifted over his shoulders. "Reincarnation is real enough, but not for me."

She gave him a shaky smile. "Why would everyone else have multiple lives, but not you? You're one big mystery rolled in an enigma."

"Because my chance to reincarnate was taken away long ago." Niall's eyes held an ocean of history, a shimmering kaleidoscope of dreams and wishes unfulfilled.

Curious, she asked, "Why do you live in New Orleans?"

"Bad memories demand it. In Scotland, at my family castle, I met my fate. My life ended and began when I met Elspeth. She didn't love me, but we were promised by our families. On our wedding night, I discovered her nature and it was too late to escape. She took my love and threw it back at me."

She realized suddenly that her hands had drifted to his chest. Springy hair tickled her fingers as she enjoyed the vitality of rock-hard muscle.

His gaze fired to life and he drew in a deep breath. "She was like you. Fire and ice. Damned pretty with the same jade green eyes and long hair curling down to cover her nipples." Niall slipped his fingers up to her left breast. He cupped the mound, and she gasped. Her nipple tightened and prickled. Dipping his head, he swiped his tongue with a long lick over her aroused flesh. Heat sparked low in her belly as her nipple crinkled tight. "But she didn't come in my arms. She didn't climax when I thrust inside her. At first, I thought it was because I was too eager and didn't arouse her enough. I found out the reason was a hell of a lot worse."

He swallowed hard. His palm slid down her torso and rested on her pussy. He twirled his finger, tangling it in her pubic hair. With slow deliberation, his fingers slipped between her partially open thighs. She gasped and moaned as he touched her creamy wet folds. God, it felt so good. Her breath quickened as he urged her thighs wider. One finger located her clit and brushed over it. She moaned softly as sweet pleasure sprang from the supersensitive tissues aching for release.

"She didn't respond to me the way you do. No sounds of pleasure." His voice rumbled in her ear as he started to kiss her throat.

"Oh God." She moaned the words, stricken by rising desire.

"But she took something from me when I thrust inside her that I can't get back."

He returned to her nipples. Dawn closed her eyes as he laved her right nipple, then sucked gently. She wriggled in his arms as heat burst through her body and she panted.

"What—" she gasped as he switched to sucking her other nipple. "What did she take?"

"My life. I can give pleasure to a woman. I can make her come and come until she's screaming for me to stop. But I can never climax."

Chapter Three

ᏕᏉ

Dawn's eyes popped open. "What? She took your life and you can't... I don't understand."

Without answering, Niall nibbled on her breast while plying her clit with long steady strokes of his middle finger. Sucking, licking, kissing, her brought her nipples to full peak. He kept them hard and aching. Repeatedly, he toyed with her slick little clit until she thought she'd go insane with the need to orgasm.

Arousal, stronger than anything she'd experienced, slammed her. How could this happen? Yes, she had ached for him ten years ago, but how could she long for this physical joining when she barely knew him? She pushed at his shoulders, but he didn't budge.

Grasping for rapidly diminishing control, she said with contempt, "You can't have an orgasm because your wife doesn't love you? You're still married?"

His eyes simmered with raging desire and gentle mirth. "No. She is long gone from my life. I'm cursed and that is why I can't climax."

"A curse?"

"Immortal life."

She nodded. "I heard rumors, but I didn't...I don't know if I believe it. Are you...are you a werewolf or a vampire?"

He laughed. "I sometimes wish I was either one, but I'm not. At least a werewolf or a vampire can find total physical love with a woman. I can't."

"Total physical love?" He looked down upon her for a long time, as if deciding how much he could tell her. She finally became tired of waiting and said, "Just tell me. You said you're cursed?"

Niall sighed. Turbulent emotions rolled through those soulful eyes. "Sex is the great equalizer in society, available to pauper and prince."

"So?"

"It should be enjoyed like a fine wine, or a fast gulp of best whiskey. Depends on what your appetite asks for." Her body shivered against his as he brushed the words into her ear with a whisper. "In your case, I think we should savor it like a cabernet sauvignon."

She struggled to keep her mind on the conversation, her body shifting against his involuntarily, wanting Niall with a fierceness that shook her. "You're trying to distract me. Tell me about your wife."

"After my bride had sex with me, she confessed. She couldn't climax because she had become a sex demon, designed to give pleasure and not take it."

Her mouth dropped open. "You can't be serious."

"Deadly serious. I came inside her one last time...and I mean that when I say one last time. I became immortal, but I can't climax. When my family found out that my wife was now immortal, and so was I, I left my wife, my home, and traveled the world."

Confusion warred with fascination inside Dawn. "You're trying to tell me you're an immortal sex demon?"

"I have been since 1450 on my wedding night."

She shook her head. "No. It's totally insane." She trembled against him, frightened by the implication. "Where do these sex demons come from?"

"No one knows for sure. There are several legends to explain it. You know the succubus and incubus tales?"

"Yes."

"We think that is the human explanation for the demon's origin. A sex demon is not inherently evil. We live in a half-world between dark and light. I opened the Den of Wolves because I could help other creatures with extraordinary abilities."

"Do you...do you have other powers?"

"Any wound I receive heals within seconds. I'm telepathic, and I'm physically much stronger than mortal men."

Her mind was dazzled by the information. Part of her wanted to escape, whereas the rest of her begged to stay and learn everything about him. She could try to run, but Dawn understood she'd never escape. Fear didn't rule her, though. His touch was gentle, his sexual aura wrapping around her in an intoxicating cloak.

"Maureen didn't believe me at first," he said. "She just became angry when I refused to fuck her. She begged me, but I wouldn't. I made her climax numerous times, but not because of intercourse. And I won't take you. Your mortal life is too precious, and if I thrust inside your pussy, you will become a sex demon and immortal." A flash of hope passed through his eyes. "There is one possibility. One thing..."

Her body hummed with high-wattage desire as he pressed against her. Emotional pain passed through his beautiful, passionate eyes, and she wanted so much to take it away. She craved to know him as she had ten years ago. A man both serious and filled with vibrant life.

"What is it?" she asked.

"There is one thing that could change my life and bring me eternal happiness. One possibility. Tonight there is an eclipse."

She nodded. "I heard about it."

"There is a legend." His mouth trailed along her chin, a gentle kiss pressed there. "The blood-red eclipse happens only once every eight hundred years. If a sex demon has found his true love and makes love with them, the sex demon is bonded for eternity with their mate. During sex, the mortal becomes immortal, and the sex demon can now climax. They will be together forever."

She looked up into his eyes, a new trepidation growing. "Does it work?"

"Legend says it has worked."

His mouth came down on hers briefly, a feather touch. He slipped one finger deep into her pussy, startling a whimper of pure ecstasy from her. Niall's finger pushed, then pulled back, establishing a gentle rhythm. "You need a hot, hard orgasm, and I'm going to give it to you."

She shivered under his touch. She wanted, needed, craved deep inside. She couldn't think, only vibrate on the edge of climax so tantalizing, so strong she knew she'd never wanted anything so desperately. He withdrew his fingers from her pussy, then gently clasped her clit. He tugged, working the hard button of arousal with tender attention. The tight ball of excitement in her womb exploded in a sweet, hot orgasm and a cry left her throat. He thrust two fingers into her pussy and she quivered as her tight channel clenched and released in rippling waves over his plundering fingers. Panting, moaning softly, she enjoyed the last beautiful pulsations of release.

"God, that was...I've never come so fast in my life," she said, stunned.

He grinned, his gaze glittering with scintillating desire. "It is my pleasure to give you pleasure."

His hands coasted over her skin with stunning gentleness. Her nipples puckered tighter as he massaged them between his fingers. She writhed in Niall's confident grip. He traced a finger over her chin and tilted her lips upward until his breath touched hers. Soft whimpers worked from Dawn as he tasted his way down her body, his tongue lashing against one nipple, then fluttering over it with tender touches.

"You don't trust me." He moved back and released her from his embrace.

He sat back on his heels, his thick cock still swollen into a huge erection. God, she wanted to touch him. She reached out on impulse and encircled his cock within her eager fingers. He gasped as she stroked steel encased in velvet-soft skin. His breath hissed inward as she took another leisurely brush over the head of his cock.

He grabbed her hand and held it still. "Stop. Remember, I can't climax."

She tried to imagine hanging on the balance and aching for the tremendous rush of orgasm and never achieving the final goal. For a foolish minute, she considered begging him to take her anyway. To thrust inside until he'd fucked her into oblivion, and her throat went raw from screaming in ecstasy.

Oh, yes. He could do it. She didn't doubt that he could send a woman into multiple orgasms.

Before she could speak, he rasped out his next words. "Your eyes are soft pools, and yet at the center they're hot with hunger." He gave a shaky laugh and ran his hand over his jaw. "Believe me, I wish I could fuck you until you can't come any longer. But we can't." His voice sounded hoarse with regret.

Hours later, he took her hand and urged her to leave the bed. "Let's watch the eclipse. It's almost time."

Modesty almost made her hold back. But how could she pretend false prudery?

She held his hand as he drew back a curtain and opened the wooden shutters. The huge full moon illuminated the city.

"Tell me more about the red eclipse. You weren't here for the last one?"

He slipped behind her and encircled her waist. He chuckled. "I'm not quite that old, remember?" Drawing her back against his powerful body, he murmured into her ear, "But I'm glad I'm here with you."

Dawn felt special as Niall held her. How could a man she'd known only a short time make her feel this way?

They stood for a long time, and while he remained powerfully aroused, his cock prodding her backside, she relaxed in his embrace. His arms around her didn't feel sexual so much as comforting. She sighed. She managed a smile. Her limited circle of friends would believe she'd lost her mind if they could see her now. Staying with this man—this demon, if you will—must have cracked her, they'd say.

"Happy?" he asked.

She grinned as the red haze came across the surface of the moon. "Right now I feel secure. I feel like nothing out there in the night can hurt me."

"Good." His accent thickened, his words rougher in tone and reminding her of his ancient origins. "I'd never let anyone or anything hurt you. Don't ever be afraid of me, no matter what happens."

Feminine power pushed through her in heady pleasure. Caution halted the feeling a few seconds later. "Is something strange going to happen?"

"Sometimes when I pleasure a woman, my eyes glow."

"Is that all? I think I could handle that."

He chuckled.

She would stay and experience Niall, discover the pleasure he promised. For once in her life, she'd have an adventure. An experience beyond most women's wildest dreams or nightmares.

"You're smiling," he said as he nibbled her shoulder with affectionate kisses.

"Isn't that what people do when they're feeling good?"

"Yes. But your smile says you have a secret."

Her grin widened. "Well, number one, my friends would never believe me. Two, I'm sure none of them would believe you. I mean, you're..." She wriggled her bottom against his cock. "Virile. I'm sure they don't know a man who can stay like this for as long as you have without..."

"Fucking?" He laughed softly.

"Umm. Yeah. That's a blunt way of putting it."

"I'm sorry. I tend to be direct when I've got a beautiful woman in my arms, and I want to make her scream with pleasure again and again."

They subsided into watching the red haze cross over the moon.

"A blood-red moon, the evil come near," he said. "Comes from a poem I remember hearing as a child."

She shifted, turning in his arms again so she could stare into the mercurial depths of his eyes. "Being immortal must be difficult. To see everything and everyone you love, friends and places, change beyond recognition. How do you do it?"

Niall's finely carved mouth, so beautiful and yet masculine, curved into a sardonic smile. "I've loved little over the years for that very reason. I ache to return to Scotland."

"Why don't you?"

"I hope to soon. I have the funds to buy back my ancestral home."

She skimmed her hands over the solid lines of his biceps. "That's wonderful. You could live in baronial splendor."

"The castle is livable but it needs a lot of work. There won't be anything baronial about it until I shell out the money to have it restored. There are big-ass taxes and upkeep to maintain after it's finished. Owning a castle can be bloody stressful. I've contacted solicitors in Inverness about the property. If all goes well, the castle will be mine in less than six months."

"How wonderful."

Excitement tingled through her. For a minute, she imagined standing in front of a huge castle and knowing within those walls her love resided.

Her love.

Niall.

Dawn shivered as sadness leaked through her. No. It couldn't happen. Loneliness she never remembered feeling before sliced like a knife. She'd always been independent, much like Maureen. She longed for connection, for a dream she never recognized until now.

His gaze intensified. "You're seeing my castle."

"Reading my mind?"

"You're broadcasting so loudly I can't help it. For a second you were sad. Why?"

She shook her head. "I don't know."

Lying was easier. Placing affection into the equation when she shouldn't only proved she'd let him slide under her skin too deeply.

She palmed his exquisite chest and sighed. She turned in his arms so she could watch the eclipse.

An eerie glow covered the city as moonlight disappeared under the dark circle of the earth. A red halo spilled out from behind the dark disk and bathed the land in its preternatural essence.

She watched in fascination. "It feels strange watching something I know won't happen again in my lifetime. But it might in yours."

He gestured toward the bathroom door. "Be that as it may, why don't you try and relax? You'll feel better after a bath. The tub is a whirlpool. It'll ease your muscles. After that, I'll give you a massage."

Savage desire rose inside her like a wellspring and demanded attention.

His gaze trailed thoroughly over her body. Heat rose into her face at his perusal. His attention devoured. Staked a claim. She'd never imagined a man's possessiveness, even in a look, could create longing in her heart.

She broke away from his stare and entered the bathroom. The luxurious bathroom, masculine and yet opulent in sumptuous emerald green and rich eggplant, held everything she needed. A huge shower big enough for at least six people sat next to a large whirlpool tub. Double sinks sat against one wall. Fluffy matching towels hung on towel racks.

She washed her hair in the shower and enjoyed fresh English milled soap. Afterwards she filled the tub and turned on the jets. She sank into the warm, frothing water and put her head back. As the water drew her into a dreamy state, she closed her eyes and relaxed. Dawn imagined how his hands would feel as he massaged her and shivered at the sensual promise. As her daydreams took form, she reached between her thighs and touched her clit. One wisp of her finger and her clit sang with excitement. God, yes. She needed him so much. She'd never had a one-night stand before, but she felt free, aching to discover what could happen when barriers departed and need overruled caution. Adventure never entered her life until now, and she was tired of rescuing her sister from her folly. For one night, she would forget responsibility and duty to her sister. This night was for her.

Chapter Four

ഔ

A gentle knock on the door brought Dawn out of a dreamlike state. She jerked upright, her heart pounding.

"Everything all right?" Niall's voice asked.

"I'm fine. Be out in a minute."

"It's okay. Take your time."

She left the bathroom a short time later, completely naked. She could have worn a towel, but he'd already seen every inch of her bare body, and she'd observed his. Playing modest at this point served no purpose, and she didn't play coy.

His gaze took her in, again cruising over her curves with such unabashed male hunger, excitement bubbled inside her.

She took a deep breath, crossed to the bed, and lay facedown. "I'd love the massage, if it's still available."

A soft chuckle left his throat. "Absolutely."

He went into the bathroom and when he came back, he placed several items on the bed stand. She drifted in a pleasant state. When his hands touched the back of her calves, she started.

"Easy, there. Relax."

She gave a tiny laugh. "I'm sorry. I thought I was."

"Not enough. We'll take care of that." His voice, husky and rich, flowed over her like the warm waters she'd experienced moments ago.

As he worked her muscles with gentle yet persistent strokes, the scent of rose and lavender teased her nose. He leaned down and added a kiss to her calves before he worked them with his hands. His tongue slid up the back of each thigh, his hands smoothed over the area he'd kissed. He nibbled, stroked with lips and hands. Her body quivered on a fine edge. Moist and hot, her pussy swelled and ached. God, she didn't know if she could take much more of this. Soft whimpers left her throat as he worked his way to her buttocks. He covered her ass with kisses, then swept his fingers over her ass time and again.

On the edge, she squirmed under this touch. "Niall."

"Mmm? What do you need?" His gentle question aroused her senses as exquisitely as his touch.

She didn't know what she needed, her passion so strong and new, putting coherency to it became impossible.

"Everything," she said in desperation.

Niall wanted to give her everything as much as he wanted to receive. Since she'd walked into his club, his mind and body betrayed him. Though she stood about five-six, her delicate, young-looking features reminded him of a pixie or waif. Her brown hair curled about her heart-shaped face and shoulders, corkscrew strands plumped by the humidity. She'd restrained it with a red ribbon, but sometime during Megla's attack the ribbon had fallen out. Her soft skin tortured his flesh in more ways than one. When he'd first seen her tonight, his body had come online, aroused within seconds. He'd yearned for her over the years, had almost gone in search of her more than once after Maureen departed his company. Yet the thought of bringing her into his dark world kept him away. If she was with him, he'd want to fuck her, and she would become immortal and suffer the plight of never having an orgasm again. Of outliving her family and friends.

Until she'd shown up at the Den of Wolves. He'd realized that he must protect her. In her zealousness to find her sister, she could be hurt or worse.

Fuckin' hell. He couldn't change the past or remove her sorrows, but he could give her this moment. He would satisfy her curiosity, help her find Maureen, then he'd send her away.

Curves and the sheer beauty of her peach-tinted skin made his cock ache until he wanted to howl. Throughout the centuries, he'd wanted many women, but none of them robbed him of breath, made his soul crave the way she did.

He groaned softly as his cock throbbed for a release that would never happen. He'd wring orgasm after orgasm from her flesh until she could do nothing else but sleep. He'd give her peace of mind if he could, for what little time they spent together.

Niall's hands trailed up her sides, over the slim curve of her rib cage, the flowing line of her back. Her skin gleamed with the oil as he worked it into her shoulders. He planted kisses along her shoulder blades, tongued her fragrant skin. He felt her surrender as he brushed aside her hair and massaged her neck. She sighed, the tiny whimpers leaving her throat a symphony to his ears.

He licked her ear and she squirmed and giggled. The girly sound appealed to him, and he smiled. "Get ready, love. Just feel."

He lingered over the sides of her breasts, then worked his hands down to her thighs. He urged her to part her legs and his hand slipped between and found the moist heat. She gasped as he thrust two fingers gently into her pussy. Slick cream eased his way, and he smiled. God, he loved it when a woman's pussy plumped with her arousal. He drew in a deep breath. Over the centuries, his immortal body had gained some attributes. His sense of smell, his taste buds, his hearing became more acute. He could smell her musky cream, sense the delicate quivers as her pussy trembled around his fingers. He worked her channel and spread her moisture over her clit. He felt her need grow to a razor-sharp edge. Deep in his soul, he felt a connection to her. She might fulfill centuries of loneliness.

Niall's strong, sensual touch, the sure thrust of his fingers in her pussy, brought Dawn exquisite enjoyment. Her internal muscles fluttered, quivered around his big fingers. He thrust them in and out repeatedly until she couldn't halt the moans leaving her throat. She wanted him to touch her clit, to bring her to the highest peak. Abandoning her inhibitions, she opened her thighs wider and tilted her ass upward, inviting more exploration.

He leaned over and whispered in her ear. "I can tell how much you want this. Would you like your sweet little ass filled, too?"

His suggestion sent a shock wave of excitement through her. She didn't hesitate. "Yes."

"Then we're going to fill your ass," he said, his breath hot in her ear.

He left the bed. She didn't look to see what he did—not knowing aroused her more. When he parted her ass cheeks and inserted his lubricated finger, she gasped at the unaccustomed pressure.

"All right?" he asked, his voice concerned.

"More than all right."

"Mmm. Good." Throaty with promise, his voice purred. "I'm going to work your ass like this until you're begging for relief."

Dawn's soft moans came more frequently as he slid two fingers into her tight hole and thrust slowly. Her pussy ached for orgasm, and each thrust of his fingers in her ass added to the storm swirling low in her belly and deep between her thighs.

She whimpered a plea. "Please. Niall."

"I've got a plug to ease you."

She'd never taken a butt plug inside her, and the idea thrilled her. Something wider than his fingers probed, then slid slow and deep inside. She shivered.

"Roll over," he said.

When she rolled over, she met his hot gaze. "It feels wonderful."

"Good. Now close your eyes."

She obeyed, and a few seconds later, he nudged her thighs apart. She sucked in a surprised, excited breath as he swiped his tongue in a long stroke over her pussy. He worked his tongue over one side of her labia and traced with delicate strokes. Oh yes, he knew how to touch a woman. After all, with centuries of experience, he would have a skill beyond mortal man.

Warmth pooled low in her belly, an urgency she grasped with all her being. She put her arms above her head and luxuriated in the moment. She inhaled deeply as he licked her with deep attention. He gripped her thighs gently and separated them more, and his eager tongue thrust inside her pussy. She writhed under the exquisite sensation, and his thumb smoothed over her clit. Heat increased with every torturous path his fingers and tongue drew over her slick flesh. She wriggled and thrashed as Niall continued to rub her clit and thrust his tongue inside. The butt plug added to her enjoyment and her senses pinpointed on the shimmering, boiling need surging higher and higher. Seconds later, he took her clit into her mouth and sucked gently. She came apart at the seams as heat burst inside her wet, aroused depths with breath-stealing force. Dawn gasped for air, shuddering and shaking.

"God, that was beautiful," he said softly.

More than anything, she wanted to give him an orgasm, to destroy his belief in the curse. God, a demon had just given her the biggest orgasm of her life. She should be frightened by him and questioning her sanity. Yet as he smiled at her, the warm, tender glow in those dangerous eyes drew fear away. She knew deep in her heart that he cared for her and would protect her without question. A heady rush of womanly power flowed inside her.

"You're still ripe, still needing another release." He smiled, cunning and determined.

"Sounds wonderful, but there's something I've got to do first."

She removed the butt plug and headed to the bathroom. When she returned a short time later, she urged him to lie back. His eyes narrowed. "What are you doing?"

"Wait and see."

His mouth tightened, and for a second she wondered if he was angry. Disregarding the possibility, she leaned over his body and started kissing him much the way he'd lavished kisses on her. She loved the hair on his strong, long legs, and they sent her libido rising.

"Sweet one, you shouldn't be doing this." His throaty voice rasped with desire. "It won't work."

"When was the last time a woman tried?"

He laughed softly, then moaned as she clasped his cock in her right hand. "At least a hundred years."

She grinned, feeling powerful. With steady movements designed to drive him insane, she licked and sucked his cock. Her tongue flicked over the tip and his hips jerked.

His fingers buried in her hair. "Damn it, this isn't—oh, shit. Oh God."

His breathy voice urged her forward. She did her utmost to give him what he thought he couldn't have. Every moan and twitch of his muscles made her work toward the ultimate explosion.

Inexorably, she licked up one side, down the other, pumping him with ruthless strokes. Her arousal surged in cadence with his—she could feel slick cream gathering deep in her pussy. She sucked, drawing his large cock as far into her mouth as she could.

"No," he said hoarsely. "Stop."

She halted, peering up at him with concern. "But—"

"No." His voice came sharp, his eyes tormented, his breathing coming fast. "It won't happen."

She frowned. "It surely won't if you keep thinking it won't."

118

With a growl, Niall drew Dawn up against him, then rolled her over onto her back. He glared into her eyes. He trembled, his chest rising and falling with fast breaths. "Are you trying to drive me insane?"

"Frankly, yes."

His handsome features stood out in contrast to the beautiful dark strands of hair tumbling about his shoulders. "Damn it, woman. Do you understand? If you keep taunting me, I don't know if I'll be able to stop. And you'll be immortal. Do you understand that? I can't do that to you."

"If you come in my mouth, will that change me to an immortal?"

"No. I have to thrust into here." He slipped a finger deep into her pussy. She gasped at the exquisite feeling. He kept his finger embedded. "I can even stick my cock up your sweet little ass. Just not your pussy."

His words, rough with desire, sent a raging need deep in her body. God, she wanted to try that. Wanted sex in every conceivable way. Wanted him thrusting into her, ass and pussy.

She slipped her hand into the long hair at the back of his neck. She drew his head down and kissed him deeply, thrusting her tongue into his mouth with an aggression she'd never wanted to show a man before. She felt his hesitation at first, then he responded. With a twist of his lips, he took control of the kiss. Niall's tongue plunged deep, driving in a rhythm. He anchored her head between his hands. His muscled body, hot and exciting, pressed along hers. One hard thigh pushed up against her pussy. His chest hair prickled against her nipples and she moaned into his mouth.

He grasped one nipple in his fingers and stroked. She moaned uncontrollably as arousal slammed through her. Love ached down deep, driving her toward insanity. As he tore his mouth from hers, his breathing came hard. His eyes glowed, the blue almost obliterated by golden light. Some fear battled with the excruciating need to take him into her body, to share an eternity with him.

Without warning, he lifted from her and with gentle hands urged her to turn over and come up on her hands and knees.

"Do you want me in your ass?" he asked.

"Yes. Please yes."

He retrieved the lubricant from the bed stand. She watched him cover his cock with lubricant, and her mouth literally watered. Hunger sent a rush of moisture flooding her pussy. Watching his big hand pumping his cock made her belly quiver, her heart pound. Her breathing quickened.

Niall's eyes, a glow hot and unearthly, added danger. An element of unknown. It thrilled her in ways she hadn't imagined.

He crawled onto the bed, and she felt one big palm on her ass cheek. "Spread your legs wide."

She did as he commanded. Two fingers slipped slow and deep into her ass. He thrust in and out to get her prepared. She squirmed, a whimper leaving her throat. After long moments, he removed his fingers.

"Don't be afraid." His cock head touched her tight hole. "Just relax and let me in."

She felt steady but gentle pressure on her anus and tightened up.

"Easy, Dawn. Come on, sweetheart. Open to me."

She took a deep breath, and when he pushed harder, the head of his cock popped through and entered. She felt only a slight pinch. He'd worked her ass with his fingers long enough to loosen her up.

"Oh God." His breath came ragged. "You feel so good."

"Show me. Show me how it's supposed to be."

He palmed her ass, then eased deeper. With a steady rhythm, he thrust his cock inside only a couple of inches. Dawn closed her eyes and took in the wonderful feeling of his body caressing hers. In and out, the beat continued. Her breathing quickened as soft moans left her throat. She wanted this, needed this as sweet craving built with fixed measure. Pleasure rose as his thick cock worked her tight channel with deepening movements.

"More?" he asked, his breath rasping in his throat.

Oh, yes. She wanted to know how much further they could go, how much more they could do. She knew he couldn't thrust all of his cock inside her—he was far too big for that.

"Yes."

He eased deeper, deeper yet. He groaned. Within seconds, he started pumping her ass again, his cock thrusting faster. He reached around and tweaked her clit, his fingers manipulating the aroused, tiny bud. Desire sang through her as she concentrated on nothing more than his fingers on her clit and his cock in her ass. Seconds later the pleasure burst almost without warning. A shout came from her throat as her clit tingled and her pussy exploded with climax. Her body writhed as she accepted the stunning beauty of his possession.

Niall pulled out of Dawn's body and she sank facedown onto the bed. A smile parted her lips. She quivered under the onslaught of growing emotion. When she approached Niall last night, she'd never expected this. Never expected to find growing love along with mind-altering physical joining.

She rolled over onto her back and waited for him as anticipation sang through her veins and heart.

Niall returned a few minutes later, his cock still hard and ready. The slightly cocky smile on his face charmed her.

"You look pleased," she said and stretched her arms over her head.

"I am."

She wanted more steel-hard cock, but this time in her pussy. She knew it would be even better than what she'd experienced with him moments ago.

If she allowed this, she would never be the same. But she would need to confess something first. Something that made her vulnerable to a ravaging pain if he rejected her.

"I want you, Niall. But do you love me enough to take the chance? To find out if we can spend eternity together?"

His expression hardened, eyes tormented and determined. As he closed his eyes, his face crumpled in pain. He took her in his arms, and cuddled her close. "God, you don't know what you're asking of me."

Power rose inside her. Confidence pushed her to force the issue. "What do you really want?"

His eyes popped open. "To live my immortality with you." In that moment, the fierce Highlander showed a vulnerability she never expected. "If the legend is wrong it won't matter how we feel about each other—"

She put one finger over his lips. "No. Don't think about it. Just feel." Tears prickled her eyes. She rubbed one hand over his chest in a soothing motion and dared look into his eyes.

His expression filled with intense hunger and undeniable love. His eyes turned moist, and his vulnerability made Dawn's heart fill with longing and desire to give him the ultimate relief.

"Damn us then. Damn us both," he said.

Chapter Five

ဆ

Niall's mouth covered Dawn's, his tongue plunging deep to taste her like a man starved for food and water.

He didn't wait this time to seduce her into lovemaking. Dawn shivered with growing need as Niall lowered his hips between her thighs. Her belly fluttered with deep excitement as he pressed the large head of his cock to her wet folds. Niall's eyes blazed with fervent passion. Darkening with desire, his gaze held her captive. She wanted and needed this joining of bodies, but beyond that, the connection of their souls.

"Tell me again this is what you want," he said softly.

"It's what I want. I can see in your eyes it's what you want, too."

He sighed, his chest moving against hers. "More than I thought possible. I want to feel you around my cock so badly I ache with it. I want you to move against me, beg me, give me everything you've got."

His words made her dizzy and breathless, ready for anything he might do.

"Don't be afraid. Feel me. Feel what I want to do to you," he said.

His raw words, unvarnished and fueled by heated need for sex, set her libido on fire. He kissed her ravenously, his control apparently broken. As he tasted her, she parted her legs wider and arched her hips.

With gentle persistence, he thrust into her inch by inch. He worked his hips back and forth in slow rhythm. She groaned against his lips and took a shuddering breath as he completed his penetration and possessed her wide and deep. He was so hard, so big, she couldn't believe she'd taken all of him. Seconds lengthened as he rested inside her. His kiss softened to tender appreciation, each small taste driving her desire that much higher.

Tiny shivers coasted down her spine. She quivered on the fine point of a blade, her body shivering with exquisite arousal. No man before Niall had filled her this way.

He stared into her eyes. "I love you."

His hoarse words, ragged with emotion, brought tears to her eyes. "I love you, too."

He started to move.

Heat blossomed within as the long, easy pumping of his hips generated exquisite friction. Deep satisfaction growled low in his throat. Control shattered as he kissed her, his tongue moving against hers in counterpoint to his thrusts. Her hands traced over the hard, flexing muscles in his back and down to his ass cheeks. Emboldened, she gripped his butt and urged him into faster motion. He tore his mouth from hers, his breathing coming harsher and faster. His eyes were closed, his teeth clenched as he drove for a climax he hadn't experienced in hundreds of years. He buried his face in her neck. Urgency rose higher as he quickened his strokes.

Scorching heat drove Niall to thrust harder and faster. God, she was so tight, so wet, so hot. Her slick passage embraced him fully, and the staggering pleasure it gave him made him want to howl. Heat shimmered in his belly and sparked raging flames. His heart thundered loud in his ears. As her head thrashed back and forth, his excitement grew. Naked emotion powered his drive to bring her satisfaction. Mingled with his craving to bring her to screaming orgasm was a selfish desire to know pleasure he'd not experienced in centuries. Torrid, driving, his passion gathered intensity until he felt nothing else, heard nothing but the urgency of their combined breathing and moans.

His cock jammed high inside Dawn, and she cried out as pleasure slammed her senses. As he jackhammered inside her, his grunts and moans of rising excitement stimulated her even more. His balls banged against her ass, his hips gyrating tirelessly to give her the most measure of soul-stealing pleasure. As her breathless rise to the top mounted, she closed her eyes and held on tight, learning a rhythm and tightening her pussy over the cock powering inside her.

His mouth and tongue made love to hers until her frantic cries were muffled under kiss after kiss. Blood-rich nerves deep in her pussy cried out for completion. Panting, quaking, she reached for the stars. With complete abandon, she caressed his ass, his back, his arms and shoulders, wanting to discover and caress every inch of him.

"Fuck me." His voice became commanding. "Come on, fuck me."

Orgasm broke her apart, and she cried out in ecstasy. Muscular spasms milked his cock as she groaned and shivered. With a last driving lunge, he stiffened and stilled inside her. He threw back his head and came with a roar of bone-rattling pleasure.

Racked by whole body shivers, he allowed the exquisite physical completion to mingle with the realization that the legend of the eclipse was true. He'd found his love, and the cataclysmic pleasure of coming within her hot depths.

Seconds after their orgasms started to subside, while he continued to rest inside her, a profound change sang through her body.

Her senses went painfully clear. She inhaled sharply. Prickles danced across her skin as cool air teased her. Objects around the room came into excruciating focus. Edges seemed intense, light brighter. She squinted and her eyes adjusted. Heat skipped across her nakedness, then a brush of cold. Sounds from outside the room teased her ears. The refrigerator clicking on, cars passing on the street, a dog's howl. A bombardment of sound ruled her world for an almost painful thirty seconds.

Niall's arms tightened around her. "Take it easy. This will pass."

She clung to him. "If I start screaming any second now, just call the little men in the white coats."

"You'll be fine. It fades quickly."

"I'm immortal now?"

"Yes."

She closed her eyes, the knowledge that in one blinding moment she'd achieved everlasting life shaking her to the core.

She opened her eyes, and he smiled down on her. "I'd almost forgotten what it felt like to climax, to feel a woman's tight body around mine."

She closed her eyes against his scrutiny. Dawn allowed the aftermath to take her, to relax in the special glow. His hands coasted with reverence over her back, her hair, as if he couldn't get enough of touching her. Comfort and satiation mixed with growing awareness that everything had changed.

* * * * *

A loud cracking noise vaulted Dawn and Niall straight out of sleep. Dawn cried out in surprise. Niall came off the bed, a fierce expression in eyes and face. Naked, he looked more powerful and invincible than he did clothed. She yanked the sheet up over her bareness.

Another crack and the door burst open.

Niall went into a fluid fighter stance. "Fuckin' A."

A huge man, taller and broader than Niall, strode into the room. Long tawny hair tossed around his head like a lion's mane. With his aquiline features and angry jade eyes, he looked like a berserker dressed in modern clothes. A black muscle shirt and black jeans curved over his well-honed body.

Stepping out from behind him was the one person Dawn didn't expect to see.

"Maureen." Dawn gasped and held the sheet tighter to her. "What are you doing here?"

"Rescuing you." Maureen's normally soft and silky tone went ragged. "Getting you away from this...this creep."

"Get out of my house, Valerian," Niall said.

The big blond man chuckled. "I don't think so." His voice held a breath of something Scandinavian. "Release this woman."

"Release her? What are you talking about?" Niall's harsh tone rasped across Dawn's ears.

"Let my sister go." Maureen sounded ready to kick some serious ass.

Shock kept Dawn immobile. That, and her sister's apparent transformation from slightly dumpy to all-out sex kitten gorgeous. Maureen's short-cropped black pixie hair went with her girlish features. Her belly-revealing yellow tube top and hip-hugger jeans made her appear twenty rather than thirty-five. She had the body to pull it off, though. She'd just never dressed like this before.

Niall kept one eye on the huge blond man he'd called Valerian. He reached for the jeans lying over the back of a chair and yanked them on without underwear. "Dawn isn't going anywhere with you. She is with me now."

Valerian smiled, but his gaze stayed cold.

Niall's stance, with feet apart and powerful arms at his sides, looked ready to rumble.

Horrified, Dawn clasped the sheet around her and left the bed. She stepped between the men. "This is ridiculous. What do you think you're doing?"

Niall grabbed Dawn's arm and maneuvered her behind him. "Stay behind me."

Valerian and Niall stared each other down, palpable tension stretched between the men like a rubber band. Valerian's hard-edged expression went ice-cold.

"Damn you, Valerian." Maureen sounded angry. "I wanted to convince her to come with us. Why did you have to charge in here with guns blazing? If somehow she wasn't turned immortal—"

"What the hell did you think you were doing barging in here?" Dawn asked.

Maureen's full lips trembled. "We talked to people around the French Quarter and they said you'd gone to the Den of Wolves. When we talked to people at the club, they said you'd been there. Niall left word at his club that he'd gone home for the evening. I figured if you'd come looking for me, this creep tried to take you against your will."

"That's not the way it was. He saved me from Megla."

"Ah, shit," Valerian said, his eyes glittering with irritation. "I know that bastard. He's a bad one."

Dawn's eyes filled with tears. "God, Maureen. Does everything have to be a huge drama with you? Look what happens when you go off half-cocked. People get hurt, feelings are destroyed. It's too late anyway. I'm immortal. And I'm with the man I love, just as you are."

Maureen looked stunned, then glanced at Valerian. "I do love Valerian. When I called back all I got was your answering machine, so I called Mom and Dad and they said you'd already left for New Orleans. I knew if you came looking for me at the Den of Wolves that something bad might happen."

A little of Dawn's anger with her sister dissolved. "Now this is a change. You trying to rescue me."

Maureen shook her head. "I think maybe I've stopped running."

A new humility penetrated Maureen's voice, and Dawn found the transformation amazing. She didn't know whether to give the change credence.

Maureen gave a half-smile. "I'm not the same person you've always known. I figure I owe you about a hundred years to make it up to you for dozens of times you came to my rescue."

Valerian had the decency to look contrite about breaking the door and barging in, even if he did keep a distrustful eye on Niall. "I'm sorry. I thought I was defending you, Dawn."

Maureen sniffed, and Dawn saw unexpected tears fill her sister's eyes. Maureen cried in earnest, tears flowing freely down her cheeks. "You're immortal because of me. Because you came to find me."

Niall grunted. "I tried to convince her not to look for you, believe me. I told her she had to let you go."

Maureen gave him a regret-filled look. "She won't have to rescue me anymore."

"Let's go," Valerian said. "Let them be for now. Your sister has a lot to adjust to in the coming days."

Without another word, Dawn watched her sister go. Now wasn't the time for long explanations or reconciliation. Dawn needed time to discover who she was from this point forward.

She turned toward Niall. He smiled, a genuine, loving expression that brought light into the shadowy corners of the room.

He cupped her shoulders and caressed the naked skin. "Now I have a wonderful reason to enjoy immortality, to have hope." His gaze turned hot and hungry. "Let's get cleaned up. The shower is big enough for both of us."

Once in the shower, Niall showed how he felt. He enjoyed his continued heightened senses, the fine edge of pleasure as he slicked soap over her delicate skin. He cherished the life pulsing through her veins and his. He caressed and kissed Dawn until his cock ached and throbbed to take her. After fingering her clit and dripping-wet folds, and sucking her nipples into hard tips, he lifted her against the shower wall.

"Live forever with me," he whispered against her lips.

With a solid thrust, he impaled her pussy and drove his cock straight into the hilt. She gasped and writhed, her eyes wide with pleasure.

He thrust hard. "Live with me forever."

"Yes."

Another spearing lunge. "Share my life in Scotland and here. Anywhere we want to go."

Another jabbing thrust, and she let out a soft moan, her breathing accelerating. "In your castle?"

"Yes." He jammed deep, then started a hard, ruthless pounding. He groaned. "God, yes. Yes!"

Dawn absorbed every hammer of his hips as he fucked her hard and without pause. She loved it, arched against him as his hands cupped her ass and kept her prisoner for his unremitting possession. As hard flesh stroked her deep inside, rubbing her into a screaming orgasm, she cried out.

And she came.

And came.

The orgasm crashed through her relentlessly, longer than anything she'd imagined. He fucked her through the climax and prolonged the throbbing, heat-filled moments until with one last thrust, he came with a deep, loud shout. His hips ground into hers, his body shaking as he took his pleasure. As they rested in each other's arms, the water pounded down upon them.

She shuddered with wonderful fulfillment. "I've never felt anything like that before. I thought I was never going to stop coming."

His breathing came harsh and hard. "That's a bad thing?"

She laughed softly. "No. But I think I have a lot to learn about this immortality thing."

He chuckled and they left the shower. After they toweled dry, they returned to the bedroom.

She stopped in front of the window. "Look."

He came up behind her and slipped his arms around her waist. "What is it?"

"The eclipse is over."

He kissed her ear. "Any regrets?"

She laughed and turned toward him. "No. Do you have any regrets?"

He smiled, and she saw a deepening warmth and emotion that might be love in his eyes. "Are you kidding? Not only am I still immortal, but I can have a bloody orgasm."

She matched his amused expression with one of her own. "Now and forever."

"Forever."

The End

Also by Denise A. Agnew

ଛ

By Honor Bound *(anthology)*
Deep is the Night: Dark Fire
Deep is the Night: Haunted Souls
Deep is the Night: Night Watch
Ellora's Cavemen: Tales From the Temple IV *(anthology)*
Meant to Be *(Cerridwen Press)*
Men to Die For *(anthology)*
Special Investigations Agency: Impetuous
Special Investigations Agency: Jungle Fever
Special Investigations Agency: Over the Line
Special Investigations Agency: Primordial
Special Investigations Agency: Shadows and Ruins
Special Investigations Agency: Special Agent Santa
The Dare
Winter Warriors *(anthology)*

Genesis

B.J. McCall

ഇ

Chapter One

ॐ

"Kysis Station, this is *Currus*. *Currus* hailing the Kysis Station. Do you read?"

Dr. Tria Anara listened as the communication unit translated the words of the male speaker. Contact. Others in the galaxy had survived.

"This is the *Currus* of the Sarruian Expeditionary Force hailing Kysis Station. Repeat. *Currus* hailing Kysis Station. Do you read?"

Tria clasped her hands together and thanked the Mother. Salvation had arrived.

"Station Kysis hailing *Currus*."

"Kysis, I am Captain Dax Rann of the Sarruian Expeditionary Force. We are responding to your signal. Are you in distress?"

This male voice was deeper, richer, more mature and confident. Instead of masking the voice, the translator enhanced the tonal quality.

"Negative. This is Dr. Tria Anara of science station Kysis. You are the first contact since the invasion."

"Status of station?"

The strength in the Sarruian captain's voice filled Tria with hope. After the Purge had passed through the Zyrai system decimating the population, Tria had feared all intelligent life in the galaxy had perished.

"Secure. Functional."

"How many on station?"

"Five. Females."

Seconds ticked by before the captain responded.

"Four hours to your position. Permission to land?"

Tria thanked the Mother. "Standby for landing beacon and coordinates."

When the ship had entered orbit about the mother planet, Zyrai, Tria started an analysis scan. Ever cautious, she'd suppressed her excitement and allowed the *Scan-net* to evaluate the vessel before making contact. Her excitement had grown as *Scan-net* spit out information giving her specifics about the Sarruian ship. The scan had picked up five compatible life forms, all male, and although the *Currus* was armed, Sarru had never shown aggression against Zyrai.

The Sarruians had made peaceful contact over a century ago and were perfect male specimens to begin the genesis mission.

Tria uncloaked the station's docking portal. "Landing beacon initiated."

After signing off, Tria left the communication center. She hurried through the lush gardens, her feet flying along the pathway leading to the bathing pool. Edible and medicinal plants, and a variety of flowers graced the vast science laboratory and station conceived and built by her grandfather. Seven years had passed since the Purge had invaded the Zyrai system and destroyed all sentient life forms. Only Tria and her young charges had survived on Kysis.

Before her, four beautiful young women representing the future of Zyrai bathed beneath one of many recycling waterfalls. "Dr. Tria, join us."

"Thank you, ladies, but something important has come up. Naci, will you accompany me to the communication center?"

Naci rose from the pool and stepped beneath the drying station. Cyna, Phedra and Sala continued to bathe. Using her hands, Phedra soaped Sala's firm breasts. Her movements were tender and sensual. Laughing, Sala stepped beneath the fall's gentle spray. When Phedra cupped Sala's breast and leaned down to suckle, Tria knew she'd made the right decision in hailing the passing ship. The five Sarru males were well suited to her purpose. She wanted to shout her news and dance, but given Naci's stature as the only remaining member of Zyrai royalty, Tria held her tongue.

Tria waited while Naci turned beneath the gentle currents of warm air. Within minutes the blowers ceased.

"I'm ready, Dr. Tria."

Although Tria continued to dress in the jumpsuits bearing the Kysis station insignia, she couldn't recall the last time any of the girls had worn clothing. They were as comfortable with their nakedness as they were with their sensual experimentation.

Walking side by side, Naci and Tria headed for the communication center. Glancing over, Tria thought about how much Naci and the others had changed in the last seven years.

The four were children when Naci's father had brought his daughter and three exceptionally gifted girls to spend the better part of a year in science camp. When word of the impending invasion came, the Zyrai Council headed by Naci's father had summoned every available adult to the capital city. Tria's parents along with the group of scientists working at the station answered the summons. Tria and the four children remained.

Her father's final message still haunted Tria's dreams. *No defense against Purge. We surrendered, but the slaughter continues. Cloak station. Save yourself. Protect Princess Naci. Stop all transmissions. Cloak station.*

She'd followed her father's instructions. Located on an insignificant lifeless moon, the cloaked station remained safely concealed from the Purge's cruel wrath. On Zyrai, every man, woman, and child were gone in a matter of days.

The Mother had provided compatible males. Tria's prayers had been answered. Genesis.

"Dr. Tria, why are you smiling?"

"The day we have prayed for has come."

Although she remained in step, Naci touched Tria's shoulder.

"A contact?"

"Yes, a Sarruian ship called the *Currus* has answered our signal."

"They have traveled far. Will they help us?"

"I think we can convince them. I've uncloaked the station. Our beacon will guide them into the landing portal."

The cloaking device her father's scientific team had invented and were testing on Kysis had saved her life and the lives of the four girls. Now it served to protect them against an outside world that was alien and hostile. With the station cloaked, a scan would reveal nothing but an uninhabited moon.

Naci followed Tria into the communication center and closed the door.

"After all these years, others exist. Will they like us?"

Tria detected some trepidation in Naci's voice.

"Yes, they will like you."

Although Tria had prayed for this moment, she understood the introduction of men would change their peaceful existence on Kysis, but the Sarruian males were the key to a new generation.

"The *Currus* will dock within hours and our time is short. I must know your thoughts, Naci. All of you know the importance of our mission, but until now it's been theory. *Scan-net* evaluated the voyagers as healthy, compatible, male life forms. These males can provide genesis.

"We can choose to extract their seed and send them on their way or we can use the *cinsi* flower for the purpose it was developed and institute the ancient ways. Are you prepared to mate?"

"It is our duty to repopulate Zyrai. It is the reason we were spared by the Mother."

"The life source the Mother has provided is a gift."

Before the Purge, Tria's father and grandfather had cultivated the *cinsi* flower as a sexual stimulant to revive a dying Zyrai. She and her cousins were the products of the first testing phase. Naci and the girls were the second phase.

After years of education, Tria would find out if her charges were willing to embrace the ancient ways and rebuild Zyrai.

"My parents supported the ancient ways, but so many did not."

"Centuries ago, Zyraian culture turned its back on traditional methods of mating and embraced celibacy. Powerful drugs were used to suppress the male sex drive in favor of a peaceful euphoric state. Cultivation and use of the *cinsi* flower was illegal and the plant was destroyed if discovered. Eventually the females joined the movement, but this peace brought about a dramatic decline in population."

Although Tria had lectured her students over the years, she wanted to remind Naci of the necessity and purpose of the genesis project. "You and the girls have never been given those drugs. The *cinsi* had revitalized the primal needs long dormant in Zyraian females. I've observed you at play. All of you delight in the sensual pleasures of your bodies."

"We can give one another pleasure, but no offspring. These Sarru males, will they wish to mate?"

"According to our records, the Sarru demonstrate strong mating instincts. Their society has advanced despite this."

"I have studied the historical recordings." Naci clasped her hands together. "Bless the Mother. They're so big and they have hair on their heads."

"They are men with the necessary equipment to accomplish our mission."

"In the recordings they all wear clothes. I wish I could see one naked, before they land."

"They are similar in form and body to the Zyrai, but taller. Sarruian males have short hair on parts of their bodies."

"You've seen one naked?"

Tria worried the girls might reject the Sarru. "Not in the flesh, but I studied the Sarru and educated myself in their sexual practices. I can't wait to feel the hair on their heads."

Naci touched her smooth head, running her fingers to the topknot. Grasping her hair, she slid her fingers down its blonde length.

"Do you think their hair will feel like ours?"

"I imagine it does. I read that the Sarru have hair surrounding the genitals. Some males have hair on their chest. Many centuries ago, our males were similar to the Sarru."

"But we were barbarians then. Men fought wars instead of advancing society."

"We sought peace and harmony. We advanced, but as we did the majority chose a life of meditation and study, denying all things primal. As a society, we stopped having children. Instead our scientists redirected their efforts on extending life instead of creating it. If we do not complete the genesis mission, Zyrai dies with us."

"We have followed your guidance since we were children. You have taught us to love our bodies and enhance our senses. We will follow you now."

"Mating with men is nothing like the sensual play all of you enjoy with one another. They will penetrate you and seed your wombs."

"You have educated us in the mating rituals. We have practiced with our tongues and fingers. We are well prepared."

Tria recalled the rich voice of Captain Rann. Soon Naci would learn the difference between a thick cock and a slender finger. "Males can provide amazing pleasure. I want each of you to explore this option."

"The Sarru will find pleasure with us?"

"The four of you represent a perfect example of Zyrai heritage and beauty. The Sarru will be eager to mate."

Tria did not exaggerate. Naci was gifted with perfect features, blue eyes, golden skin and pale hair. Although the color of their hair, eyes and skin tone varied each of the girls were representative of the Zyrai people. Despite her golden hair and green eyes, Tria knew her looks were ordinary when compared with her young, healthy charges. All were blessed with sharp minds, women's curves and bodies ripe for childbearing. Each would contribute their inherited features to a new generation. With the arrival of the Sarru, the time had come to introduce them to sensual delights of the mating ritual.

Rejection of natural procreation had dwindled the peaceful Zyrai population. Against the cruel invaders, they were defenseless.

Naci touched her belly. "It is my duty, my responsibility to rebuild the house of Ayrd. A new generation requires offspring. Those pictures you've showed us of naked men, they excite me."

The pictures on record were of Zyrai males. Besides having shriveled reproductive equipment, the Zyrai men were completely hairless.

"Cyna, Phedra and Sala, do they understand?"

"Cyna speaks of little else. She's fascinated by the mechanics of mating and the male phallus." Naci laughed. "Sala worries she will not find as much pleasure with a man as with Phedra. I think the male size frightens her."

"Perhaps attraction will override her fears. What of Phedra?"

"She knows her duty."

Five healthy males. "Then we will proceed."

Naci's lips curved into a half-smile. "Is mating truly pleasant?"

"It is. After the *Currus* has docked, I'll secure the port. When they leave their ship I'll open the garden. The *cinsi* perfume will begin to take effect immediately."

Naci's brow furrowed. "Are you sure they'll have no memory of their experience on Kysis?"

The decision to remove the donors' memories after completing semen extraction and the mating process was made to protect the future of Zyrai and rebuild the house of Ayrd with Naci's offspring in the traditional position of power. Alien males might be tempted to claim Zyrai for themselves or their government. Now that the Purge had wiped out the Zyrai council, would the Sarru accept Naci's royal status? It might be years before they were visited again.

"I have prepared canisters of tenre. My father discovered the gas erased short-term memory. The mating should exhaust the Sarru. While they sleep the tenre gas must be released. Under the influence of the tenre and the *cinsi* they should be mobile, but open to suggestion and completely cooperative. We'll escort them to the garden, help them to dress and suggest they return to their ship to rest. When the effects of the gas wear off, the station will be cloaked and they will be safely in their ship on a lifeless moon with no memory of us or what happened here."

"But what will we do if the *cinsi* has no effect on the Sarru?"

"*Cinsi* should have a powerful effect upon them, but if ineffective I've armed the cleansing chamber with tenre. I'm confident the *cinsi* will work. Their brains will be drugged and their bodies will be stimulated, allowing us time to accomplish our mission."

A grin curled Naci's lips. "You mean the phallus will be erect?"

"Remember, they must ejaculate inside you several times so you must crush the *cinsi* petals and rub it on your body, especially your breasts, and let them suckle. Absorption through the tongue will accelerate the effect. This opportunity may not come again for years. You cannot mate with every species traveling through our system. The Mother has blessed us with compatible males. They will provide healthy offspring."

"I will embrace the ancient ways and pray to the Mother."

Tria reached out and placed her hands on Naci's delicate shoulders. "I cannot describe the pleasure or the fulfillment a man will give you. But I can assure you will enjoy the Mother's blessing. Gather the others, we must prepare for our visitors."

A hand splayed over her flat belly, Naci left the communication center.

Tria thoughts returned to the Sarru. Determined to remain the teacher, Tria had never indulged in the sensual play the girls enjoyed. Instead, she practiced self-stimulation in the privacy of her quarters and prayed for the day compatible males might visit Zyrai system. The Sarruian captain's voice had awaked a smoldering need. Opening the seam of her jumpsuit, Tria pushed the garment off her shoulders.

Touching her bare breasts triggered an exhilarating response. Fire raced through her body, heating skin, muscles and bone. Her nipples peaked in anticipation of a hot mouth suckling and licking her, of a thick cock driving into her again and again. Slipping a finger inside her pussy, Tria imaged the captain's cock penetrating her, fucking her. Pummeling her sex with her fingers, she climaxed.

Bowing her head, she prayed to the Mother for her gift.

The familiar pulse of sexual need thrummed through Tria's middle. Self-manipulation could not entirely satisfy that need. The Mother knew she'd suffered these many years. Her memories of mating had faded, but Tria had enjoyed the process. Only fifteen years Naci's senior, Tria prayed the Mother would bless her and the Sarruian captain would fulfill her needs.

Chapter Two

Captain Dax Rann checked the viewing monitors and hailed the science station. He'd followed the landing beacon, but except for boulders and craters the moon's terrain was desolate. Receiving no response, Dax turned to Loc, his first officer.

"Nothing, Captain. If there's an inhabited station on this rock, I can't find it. Did we make a mistake?"

Dax shook his head. "The beacon came from here."

The instrument panel went blank. Dax checked the instruments. The panel flashed to life, numbers and symbols scrolled wildly for a few seconds then all appeared normal. "Scan for weapons, life forms."

"Weapons negative. Life forms negative." Loc's fingers flew over the controls. "Captain, we're sealed inside some type of dome. We're trapped."

"Trapped with five females on a remote Zyrai moon. That's a situation we never anticipated."

"Females." The three voices had spoken in unison. The crew gathered around the com-unit.

Medical Officer Jai Kresi spoke up. "It's been a long run. Months since our last leave."

Dax needed little reminder of how long it had been since he'd touched a woman. Just the thought of seeing anything female made his balls hum.

"What do Zyraian females look like, Captain?" asked Specialist Anicc.

"The Zyrai are similar to us, except smaller in stature. Full trade and diplomatic relations were established long ago."

"Remember your mission training manuals? Zyrai males are hairless," offered Jai.

Anicc's eyes widened. "Hairless? Are the women hairless?"

Specialist Brace leaned toward Anicc. "As long as they have pussies, what do you care?"

"The women have topknots," Dax said. He studied the Zyrai culture before embarking upon this mission. "The rest of their bodies are perfectly devoid of hair."

An image of bare pussy flashed in Dax's mind. A subtle contraction rolled through his loins.

"I'm up for a bit of exploration, Captain," injected Brace. He nudged Anicc in the ribs. The two were the experts with the heavy equipment resting in the belly of the ship and could construct a livable shelter within hours. After searching for survivors, Dax had turned his attention to the selection of a landing location. The unexpected signal from the small Zyrian moon had diverted his focus.

"I'll volunteer," offered Anicc.

Dax grinned. "Our mission is to locate survivors and set up an outpost. We've finally made contact. It's our duty to assess the situation. This station may provide an excellent location. Just because these survivors are females, don't underestimate them. They've managed to survive the Purge. Remember your history. The Dairon wars taught us women are formidable foes."

"Weapons?" Brace asked.

Again, Loc checked the instruments. "None detected."

"Breathing apparatus required?"

"None required. The atmosphere within the port dome is compatible," Loc reported.

After making the required entry into the ship's log, Dax met his four crewmen at the hatch. "Let's go."

Followed by his crew, Dax stepped into a large docking port lit by long tubes of bright light. At the far end of the port was an enclosed garden filled with large pink flowers. The lack of communication since landing bothered Dax. He reminded his crew to remain alert. As they approached the garden filled with pink flowers, an interlocking panel slid open. Someone or something had detected their arrival.

Once they entered the garden, the panel slid closed and sealed the area with an audible hiss. Perfume, unique and pleasing, filled Dax's nostrils. The crew moved forward toward the flowers.

"By the Father!"

Dax understood Brace's exclamation. The flowers were rosy pink with five long petals. Two succulent pink petals encircled the deep, rose-colored slit at the center. A small hooded bud protruded from between the lush pink petals. His nostrils quivering, Dax suppressed a grin.

When Brace reached out to touch the blossoms, the ship's medic grasped his wrist.

"These flowers could be poisonous."

Using a pair of long-bladed scissors, Jai snipped off pieces of the outer and inner petals and removed the delicate pink bud. He dropped the items into his portable analyzer. Within seconds the instrument gave a negative readout. "Clear."

Dax slid his finger along one of the petals. Fleshy and damp, the center petals were smooth and moist. He pushed his fingertip between the petals into the damp, rosy slit.

"Tell me, Jai, what do these plants look like to you?"

"A woman's pussy."

"My thoughts exactly." Dax glanced around. He and Jai weren't the only ones fascinated with the flowers. Brace, Anicc and Loc plucked blossoms.

Anicc stuck his finger between the petals. "It's wet."

Brace touched his tongue to the pink fleshy petals. "Soft." He plunged his tongue into the center. Lowering the flower, he licked his lips. "It's sweet."

Not to be outdone, Loc and Anicc stuck their tongue into the center of the flowers. After licking the nectar, the men reached for another blossom and another.

Brace licked his lips. "Ohhh. You should taste these, Captain."

Jai plucked two blossoms and handed one to Dax.

When Dax raised the flower to his mouth, his crew grinned like schoolboys. He dipped his tongue dipped into the moist center. The moment the sweet nectar touched his flesh, his cock stretched.

Embarrassed by his physical reaction in the presence of his crew, Dax withdrew his tongue.

"I glad the inhabitants of this moon are female," Jai said. "I'm hard as stone."

The men nodded in agreement. Dax turned to Jai. "Is that an official medical observation?"

"It is, Captain. We should gather plants and cultivate them."

"We'd make a fortune selling these," said Loc.

"I was thinking more of a scientific discovery than a commercial venture," said Jai.

"I just want to get laid," said Brace.

"We are visitors, rescuers if necessary," Dax reminded his crew.

At the far end of the flower garden a portal opened and a female in a jumpsuit walked toward them.

A lone, attractive female and handful of horny males wasn't the best mix. After ordering his crew to stay put, Dax approached the woman. Her honey-colored hair fell from her topknot to her waist. Bald except for her topknot, she was a beautiful woman.

Her features were delicate, her eyes were green and her lips a soft pink. If she was an example of the average Zyrai female, this mission may have unanticipated perks. The provocative smile she bestowed upon him sent a message straight to his cock. Dax stopped a few feet short of her and introduced himself.

The woman approached him and placed a small device in his left ear. "Welcome to Kysis. I am Dr. Tria Anara. The translator will allow us to communicate."

As she spoke, her words were translated. He repeated his introduction.

"Captain Rann, you and your crew are welcome. The station's ecosystem is a delicate balance. Introduction of bacteria or viruses could prove destructive." Dr. Anara directed his attention to the portal connecting the flower garden to the station. "You must remove your clothing and pass through the cleansing unit."

Jai stepped next to him. Dax held up his hand to prevent the rest of the crew from moving closer.

"We pose no threat to you or your crew, Captain."

The *Currus* had orbited Zyrai, scanning for life forms, but had discovered only animals. No people on an entire planet, but five females survived on a lifeless moon. Dax's curiosity was piqued. "Only five of you inhabit the station?"

"I have four female students."

Dax's excitement plummeted. "Children?"

"My students are young women, not children." Dr. Anara inhaled. Her breasts lifted, straining the thin material of her jumpsuit. Dax forced his gaze back to her face. "We are not in need of food or medicine, merely companionship."

Five women on an isolated moon seeking companionship? By the Father!

"We've had no contact with Zyrai or the outside world since the invasion."

"Sarru joined forces with the Rhijt and defeated the Purge. As for Zyrai, we've no response to our signals or probes. Other than you, we've found no survivors. I'm sorry."

Dax detected a subtle tremble of her lips and sadness shadowed her eyes. "We suspected as much. Please refrain from communicating your news to my students."

"Our council had hoped for survivors." Dax removed a disc from his breast pocket. "A message from Sarru."

The doctor accepted the disc. "A representative of the Zyrai royal family is present to accept your government's message. As survivors of Zyrai, we wish to honor our Sarru visitors for destroying the invaders. Join us for a few hours of leisure."

"Thank you, Dr. Anara."

After issuing each crewmember a translator, the doctor introduced herself.

"You must leave your devices and clothing here in the garden. The cleansing process is short. You'll see a series of lights. When the chamber is filled with blue light the process has ended. Nothing will harm you."

If his ship's scanner had picked up weapons on Kysis, Dax would refuse the attractive doctor's offer, but the longer he remained in her presence the more secure and unthreatened he felt. Dax ordered his men to remove their instruments, weapons and clothing.

Dr. Anara stepped inside the portal. "You first, Captain. Your crew should step in behind you."

Naked, Dax followed Dr. Anara inside the long narrow chamber. The doctor directed him to place his feet upon oblong plates that were about eighteen inches apart and to grip a bar running along the sides of the chamber.

Once his crew was positioned, the doctor sealed the portal.

"How did the five of you survive?"

As Dr. Anara removed her slipper-like shoes, her gaze settled on his partially erect cock. When it jerked in response, Dax waited for her reaction. She smiled.

"The Purge bypassed Kysis."

"I'm amazed you were undiscovered."

She slipped her fingers between the seal of her jumpsuit. "During the invasion, we shut down everything emitting a signal."

"Still, the Purge's scanners—"

Dax's words froze in his throat as she stripped out of the jumpsuit. Her skin was golden and her breasts firm. Need surged and his blood heated. Anticipating the feel of her lush nipples tightening to taut beads in his mouth, he licked his lips. By the Father, his cock ached.

The doctor faced him and placed her feet on oblong discs and wrapped her hands around the bar. His gaze dropped her bare pussy. A conspicuous bud of inviting pink flesh protruded. He wanted to slip his tongue deep inside her, taste her as he had the flower and lick her nectar.

Concentrate. Forcing his mind to focus on the mission, he dragged his gaze back to the doctor's face. Why did he feel so lightheaded? *Concentrate.* "What is the name of the pink flowers in the garden?"

"*Cinsi.*" A wanton smile curled her lush lips and her eyes blazed with a woman's hunger. Aching to ease that hunger, Dax's cock stretched.

"Did you like their perfume?"

A greenish glow filled the chamber. Beneath his feet the oblong plate grew warm. The bar hummed and heated. He tried to shift his fingers and failed.

"Yes, they tasted sweet."

The light changed to yellow.

"You tasted the nectar? All of you?"

"Yes." Despite his efforts, his gaze dropped to her pussy. His brain felt fuzzy as if he'd drunk too much wine. Dax blinked several times and tried to clear his thoughts, but the only thing his brain acknowledged was the growing ache in his cock and the tightening of his balls.

The doctor checked out his cock. It was pointing at her.

Dax ached to touch her and feel the softness of her skin beneath his hands. The thought of her breasts pressed tight to his chest brought forth another intense rush of desire. Never had he felt so horny. He tried to move his feet, but they were sealed to the floor.

"Do not move," she ordered without lifting her gaze.

A reddish glow filled the chamber. The red faded and the chamber went dark, then blue lights began to flash.

"Would you like to know the reason you are here, Captain?"

Her voice had changed to a sultry invitation. "Call me Dax. And yes, I'd like to know."

When she released the bar and moved closer, Dax tried to open his hands. Again, he failed.

"We need to repopulate Zyrai. I am hoping your crew will accept a few hours of pleasure as payment for performing the service."

"You want us to f—to copulate?"

"We need male seed."

"Breeding stock?"

She reached out and grasped his cock. Moving her hand along his length, the doctor's touch was clinical as if testing his length and width. When she stroked him, his cock jerked. If she kept tugging on him, he'd come in her hand. Releasing his cock, the inquisitive doctor examined his sac. A sweet, urgent ache burned in his balls.

"Your semen in exchange for pleasure."

Dax didn't care why he was here. Need surged, piercing his groin. By the Father, he hurt.

Clutching his balls, she brushed her breasts against his chest. Hornier than he'd ever been in his life, Dax swallowed hard.

"I need your consent, Captain."

"You have it," he managed through gritted teeth.

When she released his balls, he gasped. His cock was so hard it hurt and his balls so tight they ached.

She opened a small compartment built into the side of the chamber and extracted a large *cinsi* flower. A long, flexible tube replaced the stem.

"Your discomfort will soon ease, Captain."

The doctor slid the flower onto his cock. The warm, moist petals wrapped around him, tugging gently on his swollen flesh. A petal slipped down to his balls, caressing him with the finesse of a woman's tongue.

"I must see to the needs of your crew."

Leaving him to the mercy of the *cinsi* wrapped around his cock, the doctor ducked beneath his arm. The flower suckled him gently at first then the tempo increased. Behind him, Jai moaned.

One lush tug followed another. Better than the mechanical pleasure devices provided for the crew and used regularly on lengthy expeditions. Dax surrendered to the pleasure. His climax shot from his balls. Euphoric, he groaned as he ejaculated into the warm moist petals. After months of nothing but the occasional sucking off by a pleasure device, the intensity of the release left him weak-kneed.

Would he have anything left for the beautiful doctor? Or was the pleasure exchange limited to cock-sucking flowers?

Like dominos falling, each member of his crew groaned in pleasure. The flashing blue lights ceased and a soft golden glow filled the chamber. Finally, the doctor reappeared.

"You will rest and the process will begin again."

Again? The chamber lights lowered. Dax tried to move.

"Do not be impatient, Captain."

A soothing liquid covered the tip of his cock. Despite his recent climax, his balls began to hum with desire. The petals pumped his flesh until his cock was rock-hard. Hot and moist, like a woman's mouth, the flower suckled him. As he climaxed, Dax heard the lusty moans of his crew.

The lights glowed brighter and the doctor smiled at him as she removed the flower. After replacing the apparatus into the compartment, she turned to him.

"How do you feel?"

"Drunk. Horny." Despite two climaxes, he remained unfulfilled. Flesh-to-flesh couldn't be replaced by a pleasure device or a cock-sucking flower. The best mechanical device couldn't replace a real woman.

Dax wanted this woman.

Her scent filled his nostrils and his blood ran hot at the thought of sinking his cock into her soft, wet pussy.

"You can move now."

He released the bar and flexed his arms and stretched his fingers.

The doctor stepped close to him. "It's been a long time since I've mated," she whispered as she touched a triangular disk. Behind her, four interlocking metal sections retracted, opening the sealed hatch. The doctor stepped through the portal into a massive chamber filled with trees, plants and flowers. To one side, standing before an inscribed obelisk, stood four naked, nubile beauties.

Paradise exists or I've died and gone to the forever beyond.

The doctor joined the young women. "Welcome to Kysis."

Swaying slightly, Dax moved forward into the station. His crew stumbled after him and Jai mumbled something about feeling intoxicated. When his crew spotted the naked girls, they gaped.

"We prayed to the Mother and she has answered by bringing you here. We need your help to repopulate Zyrai. Are you willing?"

His crew answered quickly in the affirmative.

"Captain, my students have never known the touch of a man or experienced the mating ritual. I ask that you instruct your crew to initiate them gently."

"You heard Dr. Anara. Be gentle."

Her eyes blazed with desire. "Please, you must call me Tria."

Tria introduced her students one by one until the only one left was a young woman with full, ripe breasts. "This is Princess Naci. The child she bears will be of royal blood."

Although each of the women was beautiful in face and form, Dax preferred Tria. He craved the feel of her soft hands stroking his cock and caressing his balls. Everything about her, her voice, her grace, her fine body and her scent was an erotic caress.

When Naci stepped toward Jai, Dax realized that the doctor was allowing the girls to pick their mates. When a beauty with long black hair looked his way, Dax took action. He stepped forward and pulled Tria aside.

Snaking an arm around her waist, he pulled her tight against him. As skin touched skin, every cell in his body reacted. Need heated his blood. "You are my choice, Tria."

"But I must see to my students."

"Look, they have already made their choices."

The young people stepped toward one another. Brace picked the black-haired beauty. The pale-skinned vision called Phedra reached for Loc. Anicc stepped up to Sala and placed a fingertip beneath the blonde's chin. He whispered something to her. She raised her head and smiled.

Taking the lead, Naci and Jai started down a garden path. Arm in arm, the other couples followed leaving Dax and Tria alone.

"Tria."

When she looked at him, Dax trailed his fingers along her back to the sweet slope of her hips. Beneath his hands her skin was silky and warm, and so soft his heart thumped hard in his chest.

"My men are experienced, but hardly barbarians. Anicc will be gentle with the shy one."

Cupping her ass, he cradled her belly against his swelling cock. She gasped softly and Dax knew he had to taste her. Hot and moist, her mouth opened beneath his. He stroked her with his tongue, deepening the kiss, testing her response. At the easy roll of his hips against hers, his body tightened and ached. Hers went soft, utterly yielding.

Need rose. Blood rushed to his cock. Guiding the doctor a short step backwards, Dax lifted her and braced her back against the obelisk.

"Do you require a gentle introduction?"

In answer, Tria shook her head and wrapped her arms around his neck and her legs around his hips.

"Guide me."

Grasping his cock, she placed the thick crown to her center. Her scent filled his nostrils and a deep throb of need pounded in his groin.

Nostrils quivering, he pushed inside her. "Your scent—"

His words died in his throat as her hot, wet pussy accepted him. With each thrust, he buried his cock deeper into her soft, moist flesh.

Slick and ready, she welcomed him. Her throaty moans and clutching walls told him she wanted more. Believing he could fuck forever, he rammed his cock deeper, faster. Nothing existed except her heat, her softness.

Soft, strangled gasps of pleasure told him she wanted more.

His heart pounded against his ribs, threatening to explode in his chest. Relentless and beyond reason, like an animal in rutting season, Dax thought of nothing but the pleasure. The feel of her tight, wet pussy drove him with mindless urgency. Like an animal driven by instinct and the primal need to procreate, Dax answered an ancient call.

Heat poured from his body, slicking his skin with perspiration. Each thrust sweeter than the last. Her pussy grabbed at him, squeezing, milking, taking him to the edge. He climaxed, exploding into her tight heat.

By the Father!

Dax's knees threatened to give out. He'd taken her fast and hard, without gentleness.

"Tria. Did I hurt you?"

"I've waited years for you, for this."

Never wanting this moment to end, Dax found immense comfort in her softness.

He remained buried inside her until his cock was limp and his breathing returned to normal. Yet the urge to fuck her had not waned. "Do you have a room, quarters that are private?"

Sliding her thighs slowly down his, she lowered her legs. Taking him by the hand, the doctor led him down a path opposite from the one his crew had taken. She stopped before a bungalow. Nearby a waterfall spilled noisily into a large pool.

"The waterfall, the water." He looked up at the dome. "The light, the artificial sky." He inhaled. "The clean air? How?"

"My grandfather and his group of scientists created a system of light, air and water processes. The system circulates and cleans the air. The plants aid the cleansing process and produce moisture. Within the hour, a gentle rain will fall."

"Rain. I haven't seen rain in months. This place is amazing. I've never seen anything like it."

"The Kysis station was built by my grandfather for scientific research. He cultivated the *cinsi* flower to stimulate our people and rebuild the Zyrai population."

"On Sarru we're trying to control population growth."

She opened the bungalow and invited him inside. "Since we have no males, we've chosen you and your crew to assist us."

He glanced about the room. After months in his ship's tight quarters, her bungalow was open and airy. The chairs were plush and the bed, strewn with *cinsi* blossoms, was large enough for two. A vase filled with *cinsi* sat upon the table.

His mind latched on to the reason for Tria taking him to her bed. "We're breeding stock."

She plucked a blossom from the container. "You're saviors. If all of Sarru was reduced to the five of you, what would you do?"

He moved closer. "Search the cosmos for compatible females."

"Lick the nectar, it will make your cock strong and eager."

Dax plucked the flower from her hand and lapped the flower's nectar. "The flower is as sweet and wet as a woman's pussy."

Taking his hand, she guided it to her breast. He cupped the firm flesh and slid his thumb over her plump, rosy nipple. It responded immediately, puckering beneath the pad of his thumb. The nectar triggered his physical urges. Dax wanted, needed to fuck, but knowing he was nothing more than a source of semen remained unsettling.

"I have read that Sarruian males like to lick pussy? Is that true?"

Surprised by her question, Dax lifted his gaze. "The Zyrai do not?"

"Our men lost their desire to mate. We have forgotten the ancient ways."

She moved closer. The touch of her soft, warm body sent a deep throb of need coursing through his middle. He slid his hand down over her hip, across her flat belly to her bare pussy. Dipping a finger into her moist flesh, he teased her clit with his thumb until she moaned. Soft, sweet moans of pleasure.

"Then I must teach them to you."

Dropping to his knees, Dax licked her. Her pussy was as sweet as the *cinsi*.

His cock stretched and ached. The urge to fuck her, to come deep inside her, overwhelmed him.

When he started to rise, she fisted her hands in his hair and held him fast. Lifting her leg, Dax tucked his shoulder beneath her thigh and cupped her ass in his hands. He thrust his tongue deep into her wet heat and moved his lips over her soft, hot flesh.

Hot and lush, she yielded to the stroke of his tongue and caress of his lips. He latched on to her clit and suckled.

Beneath his hands, her hips rocked. Willing and eager to learn, the doctor pushed her pussy against his mouth and moaned softly. When she whispered his name hot cream touched his tongue.

Dax lifted his head and inhaled deeply. The sweet, delicate scent of her made his balls ache.

"Did you enjoy your lesson?"

Tria slid her leg from his shoulder. "Bless the Mother, I did."

Dax stood. His head felt light, his balls full and tight and his cock strained to the point of pain.

The doctor plucked a flower from the vase and crushed the delicate blossom in her hands until they were slick with moisture. Grasping his cock, she stroked him, working the *cinsi* nectar into his eager flesh.

"By the Father that feels good."

Following her lead, Dax sat down on a padded footrest and grasped her by the hips. She straddled his lap, spreading her thighs over his, exposing her sweet pussy.

"Fuck me," he whispered. "Fuck me hard, please."

The *cinsi* had worked its magic.

His brilliant blue eyes were glazed. Never had anyone else looked at her with such need and intensity.

The broad tip of his cock pushed into her throbbing flesh. Tria gasped as he drove deep. His thrusts filled her again and again, the heat and friction activating the *cinsi*, making them both mindless with need.

The captain's big body surged against hers. Loving the feel of his hard cock, Tria rode him hard and fast. She wanted his seed, but her mind and body ached for the pleasure he wrought. Her breasts felt heavy, her nipples sensitive and her pussy tingled. Hot and tight, her skin felt as if she might explode. Pounding her pussy onto his hard cock, Tria reached for the sweet oblivion of pleasure.

The scent of *cinsi* surrounded them, the fragrance stronger as her skin heated. Eager to mate, she'd bathed in perfumed water and rubbed the nectar into her skin before greeting the Sarruian men. Grabbing and releasing, her needy flesh met each thrust of the captain's hard cock.

Reaching up, he grasped her by the hair and pulled her head back. Tria arched her back and pressed her breasts firmly to his heaving chest.

"I'm coming." His voice was harsh and raspy. A smile tugged the corners of his mouth and his eyes blazed hot. "By the Father! It feels so good, it hurts."

Her pussy quivered, grasping his cock as she climaxed.

He released her hair and his chest heaved as he caught his breath. Breathless herself, Tria slumped against him. For several minutes, they clung to one another.

"What is that sound?" he asked.

She rose from his lap. "It's raining."

He pushed himself to his feet and walked outside to stand in the rain. Eyes closed, he lifted his face. The soft rain drenched his hair and ran in rivulets down his chest and back. A masterpiece of bone, muscle and sinew, his physical beauty, the power of his body appealed to Tria far more than she'd had expected or hoped for.

Opening his eyes, Dax turned, lifted his arm toward her and smiled. "Join me, Tria."

The rain would reduce the effect of the *cinsi*, but his happiness, his joyful appreciation of the rain she'd accept as uneventful, overrode the scientist. She stepped out of the doorway and into his arms.

He cupped her face in his hands. "This place is amazing. You are either a dream or a gift."

His lips covered hers, teasing and tasting her. Heart pounding, Tria shuddered. With each touch, he gave her a new sensation and introduced her to a new world of sensuality. She wanted to experience more of the ancient ways.

When the rain stopped, they returned to the bungalow and stretched out on her bed. Tria considered releasing the tenre gas, but after so many years without intimacy she wanted more time with Dax.

She caressed his cheek. "Rest. I'll be here when you awaken."

Soon his eyes drifted closed and his breathing became steady. Although she had a healthy amount of his semen in reserve, Tria wanted Dax to impregnate her the ancient way. While he dozed, she indulged her scientific and sensual curiosity.

Dax was a healthy specimen. Instead of passive features, his face was rugged and his nose slightly imperfect. She slid her fingertips over his jaw, fascinated by the stubble of his facial hair.

"By the Mother."

She ran her fingers through his hair. Deep brown in color, the short strands covered his head like a thick, soft pelt.

His muscled body fascinated her. Slowly, she gave him an examination, touching and caressing him from head to toe. His chest was broad and smooth, his arms bulged with strength and his legs were strong. She recalled how he'd lifted her as if she'd weighted nothing. Tria slid her open hand down Dax's chest to the flat plane of his belly. She brushed the tight curls of dark hair nestled about his cock and the soft down on his balls. Picking up his limp cock, Tria caressed the broad crown with her thumb. To her delight, his cock jerked in response.

"How do you expect me to rest with those soft hands of yours playing with my cock?"

Caught, she released him.

His eyes opened. "I like your touch."

"Your body is so different. Our males had no hair on their bodies and muscular strength was discouraged. Robots were given the manual chores and men were judged by their intellect."

Grasping her hair, he rubbed the strands between his fingers. "You are different, but I want you more than I've wanted any female."

Tria understood his words were influenced by the *cinsi*, but the compliments she'd received from Zyrai males had been restricted to her abilities as a scientist. Repopulating Zyrai was her mission, but as a woman she ached for companionship. She wanted those tender moments she'd witnessed between her mother and father. Those special tender moments they shared as a man and a woman.

She shouldn't think about companionship. Although Dax had given her an official message from the Sarruian government, Tria couldn't place the future of the Zyrai in his hands. She'd protected her charges and the station for far too long.

"I should check on the girls. Especially Naci."

"My men will treat them well. Jai is my medical officer. He won't hurt Naci."

"If you were in my position and your charges were having their first mating encounter, what would you do?"

He released her hair. "I'd check."

Tria rose. "Rest. When I return, I'd like to mate again."

Despite her request, he stood. "I take responsibility for my crew."

The last thing Tria wanted was exposing more of the station to the inquisitive captain. Although the *cinsi* had the anticipated effect, he'd demonstrated a curiosity about the operation and functional aspects of the station. She'd have to keep her motherly instincts in check and Dax distracted until she released the tenre gas.

"I have read that Sarruian females suckle a man's cock. It is pleasurable?"

"To the male, definitely. As for a Zyrai female, you'll have to judge for yourself."

Plucking a *cinsi* from the vase, she kneeled before him and slid the flower over the head of his cock. "Do you feel the moisture?"

Low and throaty, he groaned. "It's cool, soothing."

She removed the flower and massaged his cock, working the nectar into his skin. The expansion of his flesh from a flexible, warm appendage to a hard, throbbing instrument was a lesson in pleasure. Just the feel of him in her hand excited Tria. She licked the crown.

"Again," he said. "Take me into your mouth."

Tria dipped the tip of her tongue into the center of a fresh flower then formed her lips and mouth about his cock. The sensation of flesh against flesh sent a wave of need through her middle. She tested the width and length of him.

"Take it deeper, love me with your lips, caress me with your tongue."

Following his instructions, Tria slid her lips along his hot flesh. Drawing him deeper, she tugged gently as first. His moans of pleasure encouraged her. Finding her sensual rhythm, Tria pulled greedily on his flesh. She cupped his balls and gently caressed his sac.

"By the Father! That's it."

Tria loved touching him, feeling him, caressing him. His muscular body a playground of sensation of taste and touch, his reactions made her blood heat and her body hum.

He grasped her hair and pulled her head back. Releasing his cock, she looked up at him.

"I'd like to teach you another lesson."

Wrapping her hair about his hand, he positioned her on her knees and kneeled behind her. Splaying his free hand across her belly, he held her firmly as the broad head of his cock nudged her wet pussy.

Tria wriggled her hips, urging him deeper. His slow rhythmic thrusts teased and tantalized. Wetting his fingertips, he rubbed her clit. The heat, the pleasure intensified as he stroked her flesh. Aching for more, she arched her back and shifted her knees. He slapped her on the ass, a sweet connection of flesh. She wanted more.

Again, he slapped her ass.

The captive position touched a primal response the *cinsi* had stimulated. The ancient needs awakened within her were pure pleasure.

Tria gave in, begged for more. "Fuck me."

His breathing became more labored as he responded to her demand and increased the tempo. With the next gentle slap, she climaxed.

"By the Father!"

Dax's anguished words told Tria he'd joined her in the mating pleasure. His body shuddered.

He slumped against her back and rolled to the one side. Momentarily exhausted, Tria stretched out next to him. Lying upon his back, Dax looked at her and smiled.

"Have I told you how beautiful you are?"

His softly spoken compliment touched Tria. When he took her hand and lifted it to his lips, she considered asking Dax to remain on Kysis but she couldn't risk the mission for her own selfish needs. Instead, she would pray for a male child and ask the Mother to keep him safe.

"Rest. I will require your strength."

A smile curled his lips and his eyes drifted closed. After a short time Tria rose and dressed. She retrieved several small canisters of tenre gas and a respirator from her closet.

Looking upon Dax's handsome face, Tria resisted the urge to kiss him goodbye. She managed a softly whispered, "Thank you."

After placing the respirator over her mouth and nose, Tria opened two canisters and placed them on either side of the bed. She left her quarters to ensure her charges had successfully released the tenre. Once the Sarruian crew had been led back to their ship, she'd assist them in erasing their ship's records. Then she'd cloak the station. The Sarruians would awaken on a lifeless moon with no memory of their short and hopefully fruitful visit. By the time the Sarru returned, if they returned, the new generation would be born.

Chapter Three

∞

Forcing one foot in front of the other, Dax entered the medic's small office. Needing to speak with Jai in private, he closed the door. Six weeks had passed since awakening on that lifeless moon. Then the dreams had begun. Strange dreams. Erotic dreams. The dreams had to stop before he doubted his own sanity and was forced to abandon the mission and return to Sarru.

Every planet and moon in the Zyrai system required exploration and except for the visit to the Kysis moon, the mission continued without incident or contact. Cities and towns were devoid of all life, yet it was that odd little moon he couldn't forget. Why?

"Can't sleep again, Captain?"

Dax raked his fingers through his hair. Jai was leaning back in his seat in a rumpled pair of pants with his bare feet propped upon his desk. Although Dax found no fault with his medic's abilities, Jai's approach to the job was relaxed. Given his easygoing personality, the crew never suspected the medic had scored at the extreme top on his intelligence evaluation. Dax often wondered why he'd chosen the military, but he never asked. Each man had his own reasons for choosing exploratory missions. For some it was the mission itself, for others it was the pay incentives. Dax had always sought the unknown.

"I need something stronger."

Jai pulled his feet off the desk and swiveled around in his chair. His blue eyes focused on Dax. "If I give you anything stronger, Captain, you'd be unconscious."

Dax leaned against the door and folded his arms across his chest. "There has to be something you can do."

"We could try a brain mesh."

"I don't want you or that computer of yours inside my brain."

"I don't get into your brain. I attach sensors along your hairline. When your dreams come, they are recorded. Do you have a better solution for finding out why your dreams are so disturbing you can't or won't sleep?"

How could he admit the dreams were so erotic that he awoke in a sweat with his cock so hard he ached? No matter how many times he jerked off or used the suction reliever, the dreams returned and so did the manic hard-ons.

Dax scrubbed his face with his hand. Why did he dream of only one woman? A green-eyed female he couldn't recall by name or place, yet knew intimately. The taste of her lips, the firmness and the size of her breasts and the tight wetness of her pussy were familiar. He'd fucked her many times, but he just couldn't recall where or when.

"Have you considered contacting Doctor Nivt?"

Doctor. Green eyes. Soft voice. Gentle hands. He tried to recall a face. The memory slid away. Maybe he should speak with Dr. Nivt, but opening himself up to a military psychiatrist on a distant space station could have the *Currus* ordered back to port and he'd be placed on medical observation. Amazing wet dreams were the last thing he wanted on his official record.

"That's not an option."

"At least tell me what you're dreaming about. Perhaps I can help?"

When Dax hesitated, Jai again offered the brain mesh as the best solution.

Talking about his wet dreams, especially to an officer ten years his junior made Dax uncomfortable. As the ship's medic the young man performed a full examination every three months as required by headquarters, but letting him view the dreams in detail wasn't acceptable.

"I dream about a place, a woman. Over and over, every night the same type of dream."

"I have dreams about a beautiful girl with long hair and this flower that looks like—I can't believe I'm gonna say this—"

Dax's body tensed. "A woman's pussy?"

As Jai described the flower, Dax's heart thumped in his chest. He'd thought he was going crazy, but if Jai was having a similar dream... By the Father, nothing made sense. He grabbed a water container from the medic's cabinet and drank half the contents.

"Do you remember that flower wrapped around your cock, extracting your semen?"

"It really happened." Jai pushed his chair away from his workstation. "That part of the dream had me baffled. Dreaming about a beautiful woman, that's natural, but a flower sucking you off is weird."

"Have Loc, Anicc or Brace complained about sleeplessness? Have they mentioned dreams?"

"No one but you. But perhaps they're having dreams and are reluctant to mention them."

What if the woman was real and not some erotic image he'd conjured up in his brain? Surely he and Jai couldn't imagine the same flower.

"There were no survivors on Zyrai, yet we're having a similar dream."

"Are we dreaming about the same woman?"

No! She's mine! Dax sloshed water on his arm. He stared at the droplets on his skin. A memory came and slid away. "Describe her."

The relief Dax felt as Jai told of his dream female was as peculiar as the odd fit of jealousy. "That's not the woman I dream of."

"Captain, remember how we all felt dazed and confused after the Zyrai moon search? No one could recall any details.

I've tried meditation, but nothing has helped. If we hadn't found ourselves parked on that barren rock, I'd think we'd never been there."

"The ship's computer shows no record of our landing or our flight path. Loc ran a complete system check. We've experienced solar particle storms, traversed a major section of the galaxy, slid through wormholes and never experienced a recording failure. Loc couldn't explain the glitch. He speculated we had passed through a force field."

"Could the Zyrai have activated a field to ward off the Purge?"

"A force field that wipes out the ship's recording system for twenty-four hours and gives erotic dreams about beautiful Zyrai females?" Dax shook his head. "I don't buy it."

"Zyrai females. No Zyrai survived the Purge, but we both dream of beautiful Zyrai woman."

"Something happened on that moon." He paced a few steps. "What if there were survivors? Female survivors."

"Naci."

"Naci?"

"My female. Her name is Naci."

"Tell me, Jai," Dax began. Asking the question made him uncomfortable. "Do you feel possessive, jealous about the woman in your dreams?"

Jai just looked at Dax for a couple of heartbeats, then nodded. "Now that you mention it, yes. But it's more than jealousy. It's protective. I fear for her. She's alone. She needs me."

Protective. Yes, Jai had touched on something Dax hadn't realized before. He wanted Tria, but she needed him. She needed his semen.

The doctor needed his semen and the crew's semen.

Tria!

Since when did the women in his erotic dreams have names? Usually they were vague images and they were Sarruian.

"She wanted our semen."

"For what purpose?"

"Repopulation. We were donors." Dax brushed the water droplets off his skin. As if a door opened, images came. Rainfall. Wet skin. Laughter. "Do you remember rain?"

"No, but I do remember fresh air and an abundance of plant life."

"Speak with the others. Find out if they're having dreams." He turned to leave. "I'll be on the bridge."

"Are we returning to Kysis?"

Feeling better than he had in days, Dax glanced at Jai. "I can't doubt my sanity for the rest of my life. I have to see her again."

* * * * *

"*Currus* hailing Kysis."

"No response, Captain. I've scanned this moon with each orbit. The sensors haven't picked up any life forms. I've checked the charts. The moon was desolate before the Purge."

Three orbits. No response. *Answer, Tria! Answer!* "Continue transmission."

Dax's training told him to trust his instruments, believe in the physical facts presented, but his instincts told him Tria was real, she existed and this moon was more than a lifeless, pitted rock circling Zyrai.

"We're landing on the next orbit. I'll assume transmission."

Dax took a deep breath and prayed his crew wouldn't think him a total fool. Loc, Anicc and Brace were experiencing highly erotic dreams, but not one recalled specific details when Jai questioned them.

"Tria, this is Dax. We're not leaving until you respond."

He repeated his message several times. When Loc gave him a couple of curious glances, Dax lost his patience.

"We're landing, Tria, with or without your assistance. I'm not leaving until I find you. If necessary, I'll begin firing laser bursts until you answer. Final transmission."

Loc's eyes widened. "Captain, you can't be serious!"

"It's called a bluff."

"Permission to speak."

"Granted."

"Sir, the moon is lifeless. We've no means to replenish our weapon stores."

"Your official observation is on record."

Loc's lack of confidence shouldn't surprise him. If Tria didn't call his bluff, he'd question his mental capacity to remain in command.

She wasn't a figment of his imagination. *Was she?*

No. Jai had described the flower. Dax had to trust his heart. Tria was real and she needed him. As the *Currus* approached the area where they'd landed before, the sound of her voice set a shock through his body.

"*Kysis hailing* Currus. *Hold your fire. Landing beacon initiated.*"

Loc's eyes widened. "Captain? Someone is answering."

"Tria, meet me in the garden. Alone."

Chapter Four

&

Heart hammering, Tria waited for Dax as he entered the garden. Dressed in a dark blue jumpsuit bearing a military patch on his right breast, his stride exuded confidence. This time, he wasn't armed. Although his gaze remained on her, the set expression on his face did not bode well. When the *Currus* had returned, joy had filled Tria's heart. The tenre gas should have erased the captain's memory, yet the Surru captain had remembered her. When she heard his voice, she'd agonized over whether to respond. At his threat to release laser bursts, her worst fears were realized. Although most of the station was underground, the direct impact of a burst above the station or near the entrance would have serious consequences.

Did the Sarru intend to rule Zyrai and to take command of Kysis? And if they did, how could she stop them?

"Captain."

Instead of speaking he reached out and placed his palm gently against her cheek. With his thumb he traced a slow trail over her lips. Her breath caught as he cupped the back of her head and drew her close. So close, the heat of his body penetrated the cloth of her jumpsuit.

His lips crushed down on hers, possessive and demanding. Then he pulled back his head and spoke. Unable to understand, Tria placed a translator in his ear.

"Was I, were we just specimens? Experiments?"

"You were chosen to father a new generation. Zyrai must survive."

His fingers slid around her throat. "You wanted me to forget." The strength of his hand, his ability to comfort or do harm was more than apparent as his hold tightened.

"Kysis has no weapons, no means of defense. I was protecting my students, the future of Zyrai."

"Without us Zyrai has no future."

"Children are the future."

Abruptly, he released her. "Do you think five women with children can stop the Purge or the Rhjit?"

"The Purge was defeated. You said the Rhjit were your allies."

His eyes blazed. "What if the Purge returns? We did not destroy their homeland. As for the Rhjit, they will claim whatever they have the ability to take and defend. The invasion did not change that. Did you forget why the Zyrai broke from their isolationist path a century ago?"

The Rhjit threat had sent the Zyrai government running to Sarru for protection. Faced with the might of the Sarruian military, Rhjit turned its attention to other worlds. "I remember."

"The Purge may not return, but the Rhjit surely will."

"Unless the Sarru have established a presence. That is why you are here."

"My orders are to search for survivors, make contact with the Zyrai government if any exists, and to establish a warning post on Zyrai. Within months a fleet of ships will arrive. We intend to build a permanent base of operations for the Sarru Expeditionary Force."

"You will remain on Zyrai?"

"I'm committed to building the base. Did you play the disc?"

"Yes."

"Zyrai and Sarru still have a protection treaty." Dax bowed. "As authorized by the Sarruian government, I formally recognize Princess Naci as the leader of Zyrai. I suggest we work together and prepare the princess for her official presentation to the Sarruian Council."

"The Sarru will not claim Zyrai?"

"If the Sarruian government wanted to overtake Zyrai we would have and could have long ago." Placing his fingertips beneath her chin, he tilted her face toward his. "There is only one thing I want to claim."

"And what is that, Captain?"

His gaze slid to her mouth and his voice dropped to a whisper. "The woman who haunts my dreams and makes my cock so hard I awaken in the night wanting her more than I ever wanted anything or anyone."

"Erotic dreams are a side effect of the *cinsi*, but otherwise it's harmless."

"Harmless! When a man dreams of cock-sucking flowers he starts questioning his sanity. When he can't get a woman out of his mind despite her best scientific efforts, he has to accept the inevitable."

The strength of his arm around her waist and the hot brush of his lips to hers set Tria's heart thumping hard and fast against her chest wall. "The inevitable?"

"The time comes in every man's life when one woman reaches deep inside him. There are some things science can't explain."

Tria wrapped her arms about his neck. "Sometimes the woman has to forget she's a scientist and accept the inevitable.

Also by B.J. McCall

❧

Deep Heat

Ellora's Cavemen: Legendary Tails I (*anthology*)

Icy Hot

Short, Tight & Sexy

Slumber Party, Inc.

Things That Go Bump in the Night V (*anthology*)

About the Author

❧

Born a coal miner's daughter, B.J. McCall now lives in California. Thanks to an older sister who was also a librarian, reading became B.J.'s favorite pastime. Reading a romance novel is B.J.'s perfect way to spend a rainy afternoon or a day at the beach.

Her love of romance and science fiction came together in the *Aktarian Chronicles*. The creation of her futuristic world challenges B.J.'s imagination. Princess Tayra's dress in *Icy Hot*, the first story in the chronicles, is a perfect example of her imagination at work. The chronicles are a work-in-progress.

The phrase "do what you love" applies to B.J. She loves to write and each story is special. She hopes her readers will enjoy each and every one of them.

B.J. McCall welcomes comments from readers. You can find her website and email address on her author bio page at www.ellorascave.com.

Blind Date

Elisa Adams

လ

Chapter One

ଛ

"A penny for your thoughts, Ruthie. A quarter if they're dirty."

Ruthie shot a teasing glare across the couch at Mike. "*Please.* If my thoughts were dirty, I wouldn't share them with you, of all people."

He shook his head and let out a dramatic sigh. His blond hair, a little shaggy on top, drooped over his forehead. "Why not? We share everything else."

She snorted and gave his shoulder a swat. He was only kidding, and they both knew it. He was her best friend. Her confidant. The down-to-earth guy she could confess her worries and fears to and know he'd always be willing to offer an objective opinion. Whether she asked for one or not.

"Not everything. Some things aren't meant to be shared with *friends*."

"Friends? Is that all I am to you? A shoulder to cry on?"

Pure sex and sin flashed across his gaze and it made something flutter low in her stomach. Something that had been fluttering an awful lot in the past few months. But she knew better than to take him seriously. He was playing around with her, trying to get her temper going. No way was she taking the bait.

"Nah, you're pretty good for taking out my aggravation on, too."

She'd had a crush on him once—when they'd first met in their senior year of college. But she wasn't a kid anymore and that crush was long gone. Mostly. It was hard not to be a little bit attracted to him, but her attraction was more of an appreciation of the male form in its absolute perfection rather than a desire to want him in her life as more than a friend. Women drooled over him all the time. Damned near swooned at his feet, despite the fact that swooning had gone out of style eons ago. The last thing Mike needed was to find out that his best friend, of all people, harbored a teeny, tiny little infatuation. Not even an infatuation. It was more like an involuntary twinge. Just because her body reacted didn't mean her mind had any interest in him—or that he had any interest in her.

Of course, a girl could dream, right?

And dream she did. About his long, muscled body honed from ten years working as a personal trainer. About his thick blond hair that just about screamed for her to sink her fingers into it. About his warm brown eyes and strong jaw and the goatee she'd always found so sexy.

She took a big gulp from her can of soda to wet her suddenly dry throat. Maybe she wasn't as over her crush as she'd thought.

Mike cupped her chin in his big palm and swiped his thumb across the corner of her mouth. His touch lingered for a beat too long, his gaze locked with hers, and something passed between them that she couldn't explain. She wanted to pull out of the amazing, discomforting touch, but she couldn't make her muscles move even an inch away from him. Her nipples pebbled against the soft material of the tank top.

His finger trailed down her chin as he pulled away.

She gulped. "What was that for?"

"You had diet cola dripping down your face. Didn't want it to land on that little shirt of yours." His gaze dipped to the white tank top she'd wisely—or not so wisely—chosen to wear for their usual Friday night rented movie and pizza non-date on Mike's couch. His eyes darkened and he licked his lips before returning his gaze to hers. "It might stain."

"Thanks." The word came out as little more than a strangled whisper and she cursed herself up and down for being such an idiot. If she had any sense, she'd get out now before he figured out what she was thinking and kicked her out on her ass. He'd never given any hint that his interest in her went beyond friendship. At least there hadn't been any *serious* hinting going around. The words, the little actions, were just part of his easygoing personality. What was happening right at this second was nothing but a fluke. But if he ever did hint that he wanted more, she was ready and willing.

A charged moment of silence stretched between them before Mike shook his head and glanced back toward the TV screen, his face a little flushed. "Good movie, huh? You picked a great one this week."

Definitely not interested. Not in her. *Damn.*

"Yeah, it's great. Just *perfect*." With a frustrated sigh, she slumped back against the couch cushions. He was her friend. She shouldn't be thinking about him in any other way.

Too bad her body wasn't giving her much choice.

* * * * *

Mike tried to keep his focus on the movie Ruthie had selected, but it couldn't seem to hold his interest. The movie, a thriller that had gotten great reviews, would normally have kept him glued to the screen from the opening to closing credits. But not tonight. Tonight something else had snagged his attention. His best friend.

He'd always been attracted to Ruthie, with her wild, curly brown hair, tanned skin, and bright blue eyes. She had a cute, curvy body that was soft in every place he was hard, and just thinking about all those curves made him even harder. He'd never done anything about it, though. They'd both been dating other people when they met and had formed a friendship he didn't want to risk by pursuing more now that they were both single.

She wouldn't stay single for long. Ruthie Ryan never did. She was cute, but that wasn't what drew men to her. Her personality, the spark of life that not many women had, made her damned near irresistible. He knew firsthand. He'd been trying to resist her for as long as he'd known her and with each year it got more difficult.

She finished her pizza, wiped her lush mouth with a paper napkin, and snuggled against his side much as she'd done every Friday night for the past two years, since they'd started their ritual. But tonight it felt different. No, not just tonight. It had been two months since the first time he realized he'd lost the fight and his feelings for her had moved out of the realm of friendship into something more. Something deeper and stronger.

She felt it too. He saw it in her eyes every time she looked at him. Teasing hadn't prodded her to admit it and up until now he hadn't been able to work up the nerve to tell her the jokes weren't jokes at all. He'd been content to ignore his feelings for her. At first. But now *someone* had to make the first move or he ran the risk of losing his mind. It was time to try another tactic. One that would leave no doubt in her mind about his intentions.

He stroked his fingers through her silky, dark curls. "So how's that guy you've been dating? What's his name again?"

"Bradley?" She glanced up at him and wrinkled her nose. "Ack. What a clingy little mama's boy he was. I dumped him last week."

Mike had known that. He knew more about her than he let on. He'd always been observant, and in recent weeks he'd turned his observations skills on Ruthie. He'd spent the better part of the past two months collecting little bits of information about Ruthie. His best friend. The one woman who knew him better than anyone else. He knew her, too. Better than anyone. And he was about to prove it.

She'd never go out with him, though. Not if he asked outright. Something held her back from admitting her true feelings for him, threatened what she perceived as a safe relationship. Her defense mechanism would kick in and she'd pretend any suggestions he made were just part of the easy banter they'd always shared. So a week ago he'd come up with a foolproof plan to get the woman where she belonged. At his side, and in his bed. It would involve a little deception, but nothing she wouldn't forgive. He hoped.

"I swear, you go through men as fast as I change my underwear."

She scooted away from him and pinched his side, laughing. "Just because I date a lot doesn't mean I'm *going through* all of them."

She meant she didn't sleep with all of them. He'd known that, too. The fact brought a smile to his face.

"Besides," she continued. "I haven't had a *good* date in so long I think my social skills are going to fade away into nothingness. I might as well face it now. I'm destined to life as a spinster with a houseful of cats and homemade quilts."

"What would you say if I told you I know someone who would be perfect for you?"

One dark eyebrow shot up, her gaze flashing challenge. "I'd think you were lying."

"I'm not. Honest." He raised his hands in front of him, palms up, in a gesture of mock surrender. "I know this guy you'd just love. You have a lot in common and you'd get along great. I mentioned you to him and he's definitely interested."

"Are you trying to set me up on a blind date, Mike?"

He chuckled at the suspicion in her eyes. Such a trusting woman, his Ruthie. "Would that be so horrible?"

"That depends. What's wrong with him? Let me guess, he's five-foot-two with a comb-over and soda-bottle glasses, is an obsessive fan of fantasy role playing games and lives with his parents."

Mike burst out laughing. "Not hardly. He's a normal guy, early thirties, with a great job and his own place. He just happens to be a little shy about asking women out so I offered to help him. He's free tomorrow night. What do you think? You up for a little adventure?"

"Is he good-looking?"

He fought the urge to roll his eyes. He'd known it would be this difficult. It wasn't in Ruthie's nature to make anything easy. "I'm not really a good judge of that, since men do nothing for me, sweetie."

"Okay. Understood. But he's not hideous, is he?"

"No."

"Okay, then." Ruthie let out a dramatic sigh and flipped her hair over her shoulder. "I'll go out with him. But it's not because I'm desperate. Because I'm *so* not. Well, not much. And if this doesn't go well, it's your head on a platter."

"Have I ever let you down before? I have a feeling it'll be great." He gave a lock of her hair a little tug, trying to keep the smug smile off his face. "Perfect, even."

Her *date* would be the last person she was expecting, but hopefully the only one she really wanted.

Chapter Two

ဆ

Ruthie walked into the restaurant with hesitant steps, almost afraid to find out what the night would bring. She had yet to even speak to her date, who still remained nameless and faceless thanks to Mike's secrecy. Mike had called her that morning with instructions to meet the man at Tello's, the new Italian place downtown, at seven o'clock and give her name to the hostess. He hadn't been willing to tell her any more than that, no matter how much she'd begged.

All day long she'd been waiting with nervous anticipation to find out what sort of adventure the evening would bring. Would he be handsome? Tall? Would he have dark hair or light? What did he do for a living? Would he turn her on the way Mike could, with just a single glance?

She shook her head, shoving all thoughts of Mike Allen to the back of her mind. Comparing her blind date to her best friend wouldn't be the best way to start the evening.

"May I help you?" The hostess, a small, fair-haired young woman, asked from her post behind a small podium.

"I'm supposed to be meeting someone here. I'm Ruth Ryan."

The hostess—Lisa, according to her name tag—glanced down at her list. "Okay, I have you right here. Follow me and I'll show you to your table."

Ruthie followed Lisa through the dimly lit dining room, taking in the romantic sights of the candles on each white linen-topped table, the iron sconces on the beige walls and the tiny white lights strung along the edges of the ceiling. She wrapped her arms around herself and shivered. Though she'd never admit it to anyone under penalty of death, she was a closet romantic. All her life she'd been waiting for the man who could sweep her off her feet. She had yet to find him, and, at thirty-two, had nearly given up hope. Her blind date couldn't have picked a better place to make a first impression. And what an impression it was. She only hoped he lived up to her expectations.

As they wove amongst the tables on their way to the back of the room, Ruthie glanced around, searching for men sitting alone. There were only a few, and any of them could be her date. Her heart sped up and her palms broke out in a sweat. Which one was it? The tall, thin man in the dark suit? No, Lisa led her past his table. The distinguished-looking older man with graying hair? No, they passed by him, too. She was starting to get worried, her prospects looking slimmer by the second, when Lisa opened a set of French doors and stepped out onto a private terrace lit only by candles in tall, wrought iron stands and the late spring moonlight.

A small, round table sat in the center of the terrace, draped in a white tablecloth that sparkled in the pale blue light. A bowl of water holding floating candles and rose petals sat in the center of the table. More rose petals lay scattered on the table around it, as well as the tiles under her feet.

"This is my table?" she asked Lisa, sure there must be some mistake. Men didn't usually go all out like this for a first date, especially a date they'd never seen or even spoken to.

"This is it. Why don't you have a seat? Your date will be along shortly." With that Lisa stepped back into the restaurant and closed the doors behind her, leaving Ruthie all alone in what could possibly be the most romantic setting she'd ever seen.

Holy crap. The guy really *did* know all about making a good first impression.

She walked the few feet over to the edge of the terrace and leaned on the rail surrounding it. It was so peaceful out here in the warm spring air, surrounded by the muffled sounds of traffic and voices from the busy downtown streets on the other side of the restaurant. She was only steps away from all that activity, and yet this place had a sense of peaceful isolation. He couldn't have picked a more perfect place. No one had ever taken her out to a restaurant like this, let alone sprung for a private table. She usually got the Saturday night special at the local pizza joint, or beers at one of the many downtown bars. Never this. It overwhelmed her, and she had yet to even meet the man who'd planned it all.

The sound of the terrace doors opening and closing made a lump form in her throat. She turned slowly, wanting the moment she first set eyes on him to be forever imprinted in her mind. This would be a perfect night, no matter what he looked like. No matter what his interests were. He'd already made it magical for her and she had yet to learn his name.

Her first hint of a problem came when she laid eyes on the man standing by the closed doors. Her heart dropped to her knees. It wasn't the blind date she'd been promised. It was Mike.

And why was he wearing a suit?

* * * * *

Mike stood by the doors, unmoving, his gaze on Ruthie to watch her every reaction. He shoved his hands into the pockets of his pants to keep from grabbing her and pulling her close. She looked so beautiful tonight. Red had always been her color—especially when it involved a short little dress with a billowy skirt, tiny straps, and a plunging neckline. She'd swept her hair up into some sort of a knot at the back of her head, with a few curls trailing down here and there. So sexy. His fingers itched to pull the pins from her hair and let the mass of curls tumble down her shoulders. He swallowed hard. She'd gone all out for this guy.

She'd gone all out for him.

But she didn't know it yet. Confusion etched her pixie-like features. "What's going on? Did he change his mind?"

Mike shook his head.

"Is he going to be late?"

"No. He's right on time." *Standing in front of you, waiting for you to notice him as more than just a buddy.*

"So where is he?" She craned her neck to look over his shoulder, squinting as if that would help her see through the dark drapes on the other side of the terrace doors. It took her gaze a little while to return to his, but when it did he caught the understanding that filled her eyes. Her throat worked as she swallowed, and she let out a tiny, quiet sigh. "Oh, Mike. What did you do?"

He expected complaints, expected berating and scolding for the ruse he'd pulled on her. But he should have known to expect the unexpected. Ruthie was a lot of things, but no one described her as predictable. And her reaction was definitely unexpected. She didn't yell or moan or sock him in the arm. She didn't storm out amid a string of curses and threats.

She smiled.

* * * * *

Ruthie's hand flew to her lips. She didn't know what to say. He'd done all this for her. She tucked an errant curl behind her ear and a single word slipped from her mouth. "Why?"

"Because you deserve it."

His answer couldn't have been more perfect. Tears welled in her eyes. Silly tears—she had no right crying over this. Over something so sweet it took her breath away. He was her best friend. Of course he'd known what would make her happy. But this…she'd never voiced this particular fantasy to anyone. Not even to Mike.

"How did you know?"

"I pieced some little bits of information together. The way you sigh at romantic movies. The look in your eyes whenever we pass a flower shop. Those romance books you read—the ones you keep hidden and think no one knows about."

A watery laugh bubbled up in her throat. *I think I love you.*

She *loved* him. It had only taken her until just this moment, on the heels of his confession, to see it, but now that she had she couldn't deny it. "This must have cost you a fortune."

He shrugged and offered her a small smile in answer. "This has nothing to do with money. It has everything to do with you, and the way I feel about you. You deserve a lot better than what you've had and I want to give it all to you."

Her knees went weak. "Um, thanks. But why didn't you just ask me out?"

"I have. On several occasions."

"I never thought you were serious."

"I wasn't always. But lately things have been changing." He took her hand and led her to the table, pulling out a chair and gesturing for her to sit. "I have to warn you, though. Tonight isn't just about your romance fantasy."

"It's not?"

"No. It's about your other fantasy. The one you told me about that night we had a few too many beers."

She thought back to the night in question, to what she might have confessed to him, and when it came to her, her stomach dropped to her knees. Her other fantasy. The secret one she'd confessed...

Oh crap.

Chapter Three

∽

Mike watched the play of emotions across Ruthie's face—surprise, pleasure, and a healthy dose of fear—and he couldn't hold back the smile. Just the thought of acting out her other fantasy, one a hell of a lot different than a candlelight dinner, had his cock hardening against his fly. If she kept looking at him like she wanted to eat him alive, yet run in the other direction at the same time, this would all be over before it even began.

He'd sworn to himself that he wouldn't touch her until they'd made it through at least half the meal, but standing over her, looking down into her big blue eyes, he couldn't resist a little tease. He leaned down, placed his hands on the armrests of her chair, and kissed her.

As soon as their lips touched, he knew he was in trouble. Flames burst to life at the spot where his lips met hers, flames licking down his body and heating his blood. His tongue traced the seam of her lips before dipping into the hot cavern of her mouth. The soft, feminine taste of her exploded on his tongue, nearly making him forget his vow to keep his hands to himself. Why hadn't he gotten up the nerve to tell her he was serious sooner? It could have saved him a lot of lonely, horny nights.

There wouldn't be any more of them after tonight. Not if he had his way.

He broke the kiss and Ruthie's hand came up to cup his cheek. "What are we doing?"

"What we should have done a long time ago." He straightened to his full height, smoothed the front of his shirt down, and settled into the chair across from her. He wanted to be closer, but couldn't risk it. Not before they'd made it through at least the appetizer.

* * * * *

Ruthie pushed her salad around on the chilled glass plate, taking a bite of the crisp lettuce here and there but mostly leaving it alone. Not long after he'd sat down, a waiter had come out onto the terrace to take their orders. He'd disappeared without a word as soon as they handed him their menus, leaving her alone with Mike and the silence that had settled over them. He'd come back briefly to deposit their salads on the table, but he didn't linger. Mike might have paid the restaurant extra to see they weren't disturbed.

As soon as the waiter had left, Mike had dug into his salad with the fervor of a man who hadn't eaten in weeks, but her stomach tossed and turned too much to let her enjoy the fresh greens. Did Mike really expect her to eat after the little stunt he'd pulled? She should be angry with him for lying to her, but she couldn't quite manage to dredge up the emotion through the layers of anxiousness. She never dreamed he'd be the one to make the first move. And what a move this was. She lifted a bite of romaine lettuce to her mouth and chewed thoughtfully, her gaze lifting to Mike for what seemed like the hundredth time this evening.

He sat back in his chair, his plate empty, staring at her with a mix of lust and amusement in his eyes. She frowned at the amusement, but it was the lust that really had her worried. He'd told her they would act out her secret fantasy. The one she'd never dared to tell anyone about. At least not when she'd been sober. But she'd confessed the whole sordid thing to Mike after downing a couple of beers. Or six.

She was never, ever drinking again. Not one single drop.

She set her fork on her plate and moved it away from her. "I can't take another bite of this. How can you eat right now?"

Mike laughed, but it sounded a little strained. "Am I making you nervous?"

"Well, duh. A little warning would have been nice. You could have told me you were my date. Why make up the story about some guy who's shy meeting women?"

"I didn't make it up. What I told you is all true."

She raised an eyebrow. "*You?* Shy meeting women? Not hardly."

"Sometimes I am. When it comes to certain women."

She could see in his eyes how much that little confession had cost him. Mike wasn't a guy who could easily admit his weaknesses, even to her. It endeared him to her even more. "But you've never been shy with me. We see each other all the time, and we've never had a problem talking."

"The problem, sweetheart, is that lately talking is the last thing I want to be doing with you." He propped his elbows on the table and leaned forward. "I could think of so many more interesting, pleasurable things I'd rather be doing."

Just like that, her panties went damp and her nipples pebbled against the lace cups of her bra. She licked her lips and let out a small, nervous laugh. "Really?"

He nodded. "Uh-huh."

She swiped a stray curl away from her face, her fingers shaking so much it took three tries to get it behind her ear. The need to lighten what had suddenly become a tense moment kicked in and she forced a bright, teasing smile. "Oh, yeah? Prove it."

She expected him to take her words for the joke they were, but he didn't. The heat that flared in his eyes told her he'd taken them as a challenge. She gulped. She was *so* dead now.

Mike pushed out of his chair, holding out his hand to her. She took it and stood on wobbly legs. The heels had been a definite mistake tonight. If she'd known what she was in for, she would have left them at home.

"Come with me." He threaded his fingers together with hers and started off down a stone path leading to a small garden a few dozen feet away from the terrace. The path cut through groupings of sweetly scented flowers and stopped at a small, dark fish pond surrounded by stone benches. In the light of the moon she could just about make out orange and white koi below the surface of the water.

"This place is unbelievable. I never realized how beautiful it is back here." Ruthie glanced around at the buildings surrounding the makeshift courtyard. Most of the windows were darkened, but lights burned in various businesses. Through the panes of glass she saw a few shoppers milling around in the eclectic shops and galleries that attracted the tourists around this time of year. The stores would be closing soon, nothing but the restaurants and bars stayed open much past eight, but now they were open and Mike had promised her a fantasy she wasn't sure she even wanted.

She pulled out of his grasp and clasped her hands together, squeezing to stop the shaking she couldn't seem to control. She turned away and pretended to study a small flowering tree with thin branches that reminded her of a waterfall. It was delicate and striking, and she was so nervous she felt like she was going to throw up all over its slender trunk.

It seemed like an eternity before Mike moved up behind her and put his hands on her hips. Her body swayed, leaning back against him before her mind even had a chance to react. His fingers squeezed her hips, his breath hot against her neck, and a sigh escaped from her lips. It felt so right to have him holding her. He was so warm, so strong, and so close.

He leaned in and placed a kiss on the sensitive patch of skin just under her earlobe. Ruthie shivered. Somehow he even knew where to kiss her to make her melt. Her hands came up to cover his and she loved the feel of his rough, strong hands under hers. She'd touched his hands before, but never like this. Never in this context. Now, in the space of a single evening, everything between them had changed.

Mike pulled at her hips, drawing her closer to him so that his erection rested against her lower back. She whimpered. She couldn't stop the way her hips wriggled, settling him more firmly against her. The feel of him, of that hard flesh so close, made her mouth turn dry.

He nipped at her earlobe. "You smell great."

She opened her mouth to thank him but stopped when he stepped back and she felt his fingers at the zipper on the back of her dress. How had they gone from a single kiss to...this so fast? It wasn't that she didn't want him touching her, undressing her. She did. She'd just prefer somewhere a little less public.

"What are you doing?"

He didn't answer. Instead she heard the rasp of her zipper as he slid it down, his lips trailing down her spine along the skin he'd exposed. Her knees buckled and threatened to give out. He stopped when he reached her strapless bra, and the next thing she knew his fingers were working to unhook the clasp.

No, no, *no*. Whatever she might have told him about her so-called fantasy was a lie. It had to be. She'd been drunk. Didn't he know better than to take her seriously? Public sex might sound fun in theory, but she'd never put it on her Things to Do Before I Die list. She straightened up and spun around, gripping the top of her dress to keep it from falling down and exposing her to Mike—and whoever else might be watching. The date was one thing. This was taking things a little too far.

At least her mind thought so. Her body protested the loss of contact.

"What's the matter?" he asked, his tone laced with challenge.

"We're in public."

"Yeah, I kinda noticed." He reached for her arm and pulled her back until she stood half a foot from him. "What's the problem with that? I thought that was what you wanted."

"Having a fantasy and actually following through with it are two very different things."

"They don't have to be."

"Mike." His name came out as a soft whisper, not the protest she'd intended. The look in his eyes — half dare, half something much more tender, made all the fight drain out of her. Damn it, the fantasy *did* turn her on. And he knew it, too, the jerk.

He bent his head and kissed her. His lips played over hers in a teasing touch at first, brushing and stroking, daring her to kiss him back. One of his hands rested on her waist while the other still gripped the arm she refused to drop from her chest. A curl of arousal spiraled low in her belly and she swayed toward him. She was in so much trouble and couldn't think of a single way to get out of it.

When he broke the kiss, he smiled down at her, his tone reassuring, coaxing. "It's just you and me here. No one else."

She glanced around and swallowed hard. "There are people in the shops, and the restaurant. They could see us if they looked outside."

"Not very likely. It's dark."

Not that dark. They shouldn't be doing this. Not here.

His fingers circled around her wrist and gave it a gentle tug. She dropped her arms to her sides and her dress dropped with them, revealing the black lace of her bra. Mike's gaze heated and a muscle ticced in his jaw.

A little thrill shot through her. This was what he wanted. And, if she had to admit the truth, she wanted it too. Had for so long she ached inside. Yes, she'd entertained this particular fantasy. If she could trust anyone with her fantasies, it was Mike.

Mike reached out and crooked his finger around the bra material that rested between her breasts. He gave it a little yank and the undergarment slid away from her body. With a wink he folded it and slipped it into the pocket of his suit coat.

"Can I have that back please?" She shivered, unsure of where to put her arms, so she just let them dangle uselessly at her sides. Her body had become a ball of nerves, over-sensitized, reacting to the slightest touch of the gentle breeze across her skin. Her pussy felt heavy, waiting to be filled, her clit tingling and her inner muscles quivering. For a long time Mike just looked at her, his gaze filled with heat and want and a thousand other emotions she couldn't read. An eternity passed and she was ready to throw herself at his feet and beg him to put her out of her misery.

Then he leaned down, cupped her breast in his palm, and took the distended nipple between his lips.

As soon as his warm, wet mouth closed over the peaked flesh, a trickle of moisture wet her panties. She arched into him, bringing her hands to his shoulders to steady herself. His tongue circled over the little bud of flesh, his lips suckling and his teeth lightly scraping. Every touch, every small contact, sent a riot of sparks through her core. Just when she thought she couldn't take another second, he moved from one breast to the other and offered the same treatment to her other nipple. His goatee brushed her skin in an erotic caress of soft hair against sensitive flesh. By the time he pulled back she was panting and barely in control of her body.

Mike didn't look like he was in much better shape. He stood in front of her, his shoulders squared, his hands clenched into fists. His breath rushed in and out of his parted lips and his eyes had taken on a hard, lust-filled glaze.

Oh boy. She'd seen him many ways, but she'd never seen him like this, hot and hard and all hers. She'd never wanted him more.

"Aren't you warm in that jacket?" she asked him. If she had to stand out here in the middle of the garden half-naked, he should too.

"Hot. Too hot." In the next second the dark gray jacket hit the ground, followed by his tie. He undid the top three buttons of his shirt, exposing the white undershirt beneath. But he didn't go any further than that.

"What about the shirt? Don't you want to cool off even more?"

He shook his head. "Sit down."

She sat on the stone bench behind her, her mind working overtime, wondering what he had in mind. Her heart beat hard against the wall of her chest and a line of sweat broke out across her forehead. "Mike?"

He dropped to his knees, placed his hands on his legs and kissed her again, his lips more insistent this time. An urgency filled the kiss, one that matched the urgency flowing through her veins. She wrapped her arms around his neck, a little excitement swelling inside her at the thought that someone might be watching. She no longer cared if anyone was, maybe even hoped they had an unseen voyeur. Right now she just wanted Mike, and she wanted nothing between them.

His hands came to her skirt and he edged it up until he could reach under it. "Lift up a little."

When she did as he requested, he slid her panties down her legs. Once she settled back onto the bench, he pulled them off and stuffed them into the pocket of his pants.

"I'll get those back later, too, right?" she asked.

He nodded and smiled. "Much later."

His gaze traveled down her body, heating every inch of exposed skin it touched. Her back arched a little, pushing her breasts toward his face. Sitting in front of him, naked from the waist up, completely bare under the soft material of her dress, even more moisture trickled from her pussy to wet her outer lips. Her muscles quivered and her breathing hitched.

"What next?"

Mike laughed, glanced up at her and shook his head. "We've been through this before. Just relax and enjoy. This night is for you."

He settled his hands on her thighs, his fingers caressing her skin as he trailed his big, warm palms up until his thumbs brushed the thatch of curls over her mound. She gasped, her hips bucked and she nearly fell backward off the bench.

"What about dinner?" Her sensible side chimed in, making one last attempt at control of the situation. "The waiter will bring the food out any minute. We really should get back to the table."

"We won't be disturbed."

"Mike, I don't think—"

He smiled up at her, his thumb dipping between her legs to stroke the length of her slit. She whimpered.

"Don't think what?"

What had she been saying again? Rational thought seemed to have floated out of her mind, leaving only an aching, burning need. A need for Mike, and whatever he had planned for her. "Never mind. By all means, keep going."

Her words dragged a laugh out of him, but the humor didn't last long. His expression darkened, filled with intent. He leaned down and brought his mouth to her pussy, and then she was lost.

His fingers spread her lips apart while he dipped his tongue inside her. Short, fast thrusts that had her panting and biting the inside of her cheek to keep from crying out. About five more seconds of this and she'd come. There was nothing gentle about the way he ate at her, his thumb swirling over her clit while he fucked her with his tongue, pushing her to the very edge of sanity. She threaded her hands in his hair and let her head drop back. Her eyes closed and her lips parted. She reveled in the feel of his warm, wet tongue against her pussy, laving and sucking and driving her body to places she hadn't been in too long to remember.

He groaned softly and pulled her clit gently between his teeth. That was all it took to push her over the edge into a heart-stopping, breath-stealing orgasm. Even the deluxe vibrator she'd splurged on last year had nothing on this. Her grip tightened in his hair and she knew she was probably hurting him, but that was secondary to the pleasure rocketing through her body and making her hips buck against his mouth. He didn't stop until he'd wrung every last spasm out of her body and she didn't think she had anything left to give. And then he straightened up and opened his arms. She collapsed against him, her head dropping to his shoulder and her lips brushing over his neck. He hissed out a breath and his arms tightened around her.

Once she was able to think again, which seemed to be an inordinate amount of time later, Mike smoothed her skirt down and helped her up. "I think our dinner is ready."

She glanced over to the table, which had been set with two plates of food, and her face flamed. A chill ran down her spine. "You said we wouldn't be disturbed."

"No one bothered me. Did they bother you?" He winked.

She pulled her dress back up and zipped it, the whole time plotting her revenge.

Chapter Four

∽

Mike signed the credit card slip and passed the leather folder back to the waiter. Ruthie had been right. The meal *had* cost him a fortune. But it had been worth every second. To watch her come apart like that, out in the open where anyone could be watching, where the waiter had walked in on them at one point... It wasn't just her fantasy they'd been playing out. It was his, too.

He glanced to where she sat next to him. As soon as they'd walked back to the table after the incredible moment in the garden, he'd moved his chair around the side of the table and set it next to hers. Being close to her wasn't enough. She'd been well satisfied but his cock still ached for release. He'd get that release as soon as he got her home.

All through the meal he'd wanted to pull her onto his lap, but he'd resisted the urge. Tonight he wanted to keep her on her toes, to surprise her when she least expected it, and so far he'd accomplished that objective. He hadn't kept his hands off her during the meal, not hardly, but he'd kept his touches small and fleeting. A brush of his finger down the line of her jaw, a soft kiss on the spot where her neck met her shoulder. She'd seemed to melt into every touch, which only made his cock throb even more. He needed to take her home and sink into her, stay there for the whole night. A little play in public was one thing, but there were some things he wouldn't chance, especially in a restaurant owned by a client. He needed to at least make an attempt at behaving himself, not matter what his body screamed for him to do.

"Are you ready to go?" he asked Ruthie.

"Sure."

A look of disappointment flashed across her eyes, but he ignored it. As much as he wanted to push her up against a wall and bury himself inside that tight, wet cunt, he couldn't do it. Not until they had a little bit more privacy.

He walked over to the garden and grabbed his jacket and tie before coming back to the table, taking her hand in his, and leading her out of the restaurant onto the now-quiet street. He glanced around as they walked toward his car. Every darkened alleyway between the brick buildings made him think about Ruthie, and sex, and sex in places he shouldn't be thinking about sex in. It took everything he had to keep walking, to resist dragging her into some small, dark space and acting out a few of his more lurid fantasies.

"That was one heck of a first date." Ruthie laughed and squeezed his fingers. "But it seems that I'm the one who had all the fun. What about you?"

If she so much as thought about touching him, he'd come in his pants. He'd waited too long for her. Couldn't wait much longer, but he'd have to wait just a little while more. "I'm fine. Or I will be once I get you somewhere with a bed. Why don't you come back to my apartment for the night?"

Her eyes widened, but she managed a bright, sexy smile. "Sounds like a plan."

He understood what she felt. All the emotions in her eyes echoed somewhere inside him. Fear of the unknown, and of ruining the friendship. Lust—and something that ran a lot deeper than that. He loved her. Had for a while. Probably since not long after they met, but he'd refused to classify it until a few months ago. She felt it too. Now all he had to do was get her to admit it. Tonight wasn't just something he did to talk her into his bed. It was real, an expression of how he felt about her. She had to know it. He'd give her the world.

The date had been a huge risk on his part, but in the end it would all be worth it. She'd be his. "Where's your car? I'll walk you to it and you can follow me home."

A blush crept up her cheeks and she looked away.

"Ruthie?"

"I didn't bring my car. I took a cab."

"Why would you do that?"

A second after he asked the question the answer hit him like a hammer between the eyes. A painful knot twisted in his gut and he clenched his free hand into a fist. She'd been hoping her date would go well that evening and she wouldn't be going home. She'd wanted to go somewhere with her *date* instead. Knowing he was her date didn't appease him. Ruthie hadn't known that when she'd left her house.

Her laughter broke through the jealousy clouding his mind. "Relax, Romeo. My car wouldn't start this afternoon when I wanted to run out to the grocery store. I have to call and make an appointment at the shop first thing Monday morning."

All the fight left him in a single, sharp breath. She was baiting him. He'd been afraid of things changing too much, of losing the easygoing friendship, but she apparently wasn't going to let it happen. A smile curled his lips. "Okay, we'll take my car then."

It would be difficult to sit that close to her in an enclosed space, but at least driving would give him an excuse to keep his hands to himself. Once they got back to his apartment, though he couldn't be held responsible for his actions.

* * * * *

Mike opened the door to his building and Ruthie followed him inside, her whole body thrumming with a nervous, sensual energy she couldn't contain. What had happened at the restaurant was just a warm-up for what would happen as soon as they made it to his bedroom. The tension in the air had become a palpable thing stretching between them, reminding her that they weren't finished yet. They'd barely gotten started. She couldn't wait to have him inside her—but he'd been right to stop things at the restaurant before they'd gone any further. The rest of what would happen between them belonged in a bedroom.

She grabbed his hand and started walking toward the door leading to the stairs.

"What's wrong with the elevator?" he asked.

"No closed spaces until we get upstairs. Now I know what a dirty mind you have and I'm not taking any more chances."

His hint of a smile made her narrow her eyes. "What are you up to, Mike?"

He shook his head, the picture of innocence when the man was anything but. "Absolutely nothing."

As if she'd believe him after the little blind date stunt he'd pulled. If she wasn't so damned happy, she might have been able to be angry with him for lying to her.

She walked ahead of him up the stairs, the clack of her heels against tile echoing through the empty stairwell. She practically raced up the stairs and reached the platform that led to the second-floor apartments in record time.

"Hey, Ruthie?"

She glanced over her shoulder at Mike. "Yeah?"

"Have I ever told you what an amazing ass you have?"

She spun on him, her hands on her hips, ready to lay into him for his crude words, but Mike had plans of his own. The second she turned around he pulled her into his arms and crushed his mouth down on hers. His hands were all over her, reminding her of how bare she was under the thin fabric of her dress. He cupped her breasts, his fingers brushing over her peaked nipples. Hot, sensual flames licked up her middle and an ache settled in her pussy. It seemed she wasn't the only one who liked the idea of a little risky public fun.

He backed her into the wall and raised one of her legs over his hip, rocking his cloth-covered erection against her. She moaned into his mouth, the feel of his pants rubbing her bare pussy almost too much to take.

She broke the kiss and let her head drop back against the wall. Her gaze met his and locked. The heat, the intent in his eyes made her even wetter. She'd known Mike as a friend, a confidant, but never like this. She'd been missing out on something good for far too long.

She ran her hands down the backs of his shoulders, met his hips thrust for thrust. The stirrings of orgasm started low in her belly and didn't take long to reach the boiling point. Another few of his expert thrusts and she'd come. She angled her hips, arching toward him to deepen the contact, but he pulled back. Her leg dropped from his hip.

"What's wrong?"

"It's not enough. I can't take this anymore." He dug through the pocket of his pants until he pulled out a small square packet. A condom. She gulped. He couldn't possibly be thinking...not here. Not where anyone could just walk in on them and catch them in the act. Kissing was one thing, but this...

"Open this." He handed the condom to her and with shaking fingers unzipped his pants and freed his cock from the confines of his boxers.

Her fingers just as shaky as his, she had trouble tearing the corner of the package. She barely had the condom open before he took it from her and rolled it over himself. And then he lifted her, wrapped her legs around his hips, and drove his cock into her waiting pussy.

It was all Ruthie could do to keep from screaming as he slammed into her, over and over, pushing her back against the wall with every sharp thrust. His back heaved under her hands with each breath he took. His hands came to her hips and he tilted them. It was enough. More than enough. Within three furious thrusts she came, biting her lip to keep from crying out as the orgasm washed over her. A scream caught in her throat and she thrashed her head from side to side, the world around her shifting and turning.

Mike pounded into her, his strokes hard and fast, dragging out every last sensation racing through her. Her pussy muscles gripped him tight, trying to draw him deeper with every thrust of his hips. It was perfect. Rough and hot, raw in a way she'd never experienced, but with someone she could trust. Someone she loved.

He leaned in and nipped the skin of her neck, not hard enough to break the skin but with enough force to send another round of tremors through her center. With his teeth still on her, he found his own release, his body stiffening as he emptied himself inside her. It seemed like hours that they stood there, suspended in time. Nothing in the world existed but the two of them and the magic they made together.

She let out a soft laugh. "Holy crap."

Mike pulled his softening cock from the cushion of her pussy and set her down on her feet, pressing his forehead against hers. "Did I hurt you?"

"No, but even if you had I wouldn't have minded. That was amazing."

He laughed, his chest still heaving from his ragged breaths. His hands stroked her hips, her sides, her face. "Yeah, it was pretty intense. Awesome."

A door slamming from one of the three floors above them followed by heavy footsteps on the tiled stairs broke her out of her sensual spell. "Damn. Mike, someone's coming."

He glanced at her, confusion clouding his eyes for a few seconds before those warm eyes widened and he let out a sigh. "Shit. Okay, we'd better head to my place now. I, uh, have to get cleaned up anyway. And then maybe we can find something to do to occupy our time."

A rush of heat flooded her body at just the thought.

Chapter Five

ଚୈ

Mike stepped out of the shower, quickly toweled off, and threw on a pair of cotton boxers. He ran a comb through his wet hair before making his way down the hall to the kitchen to get a pot of coffee started. It was still early, a little after six a.m., but he hadn't been able to sleep. He'd woken Ruthie up twice during the night and couldn't bear to do it again. She needed her rest. Just because he couldn't sleep didn't give him the right to deprive her.

All the while he'd concocted his little scheme to turn his friendship with Ruthie into something more, he'd never thought about the morning after. Now guilt hit him hard. He'd tricked her into everything they'd done. She might have wanted him last night, but he knew Ruthie. She'd never forgive him once the truth sank in. She'd hate him, and the thought made his whole body numb.

He filled the coffee machine with water, spooned grounds into the basket and pressed the on button. Within minutes fresh, hot coffee had started to drip into the carafe. He leaned his hands on the counter and hung his head. What the hell would she say to him when she woke up? How long would she yell at him before she stomped out of his life? He'd seen how she was when she ended a relationship. Seen her when she got angry in general, and it wasn't a pretty sight. He didn't relish the thought of being on the receiving end of that kind of anger.

He heard soft footsteps on the kitchen floor, but he didn't turn around. Couldn't bear to face her after the way he'd taken her like some crazed animal in the stairwell. That had been wrong and he deserved her wrath, no matter how harsh her words.

"Mike?" Her voice sounded as uncertain as he felt.

His heart hitched, his arms aching to hold her and stroke her hair and promise everything would be okay. But he held back. She wouldn't want his touch now.

"Yeah?"

"Why'd you get up so early?"

"Couldn't sleep."

She came up behind him, pressed her front to his back and wrapped her arms around him. She kissed him lightly between the shoulder blades before she rested her cheek against that spot. "You're having second thoughts."

"No." He'd passed second thoughts an hour ago. Now he was working on tenth thoughts.

With her so close, his body soaking up her heat, his cock chose that moment to spring to life. Good thing he was facing away from her. His mind was a jumbled mess of thoughts he'd never be able to sort out. She deserved better than him, though it would kill him to see her out with anyone else. "No second thoughts."

"Don't lie to me. That's one of the things I love about you. You're always upfront with me, no matter what. Don't let what happened last night change that."

"Maybe last night shouldn't have happened."

She stiffened behind him. "You don't mean that."

"I could have hurt you. I would never, ever want to hurt you. I'm not a gentle guy, Ruthie. I shouldn't have done what I did."

"You're so stupid sometimes, you know that?" She backed up with a sigh and gave his arm a playful punch. "This doesn't change anything between us. If you hadn't wanted it to happen, you wouldn't have set up that date."

He shook his head. "I didn't say *I* didn't want it to happen. What I'm saying is that I didn't give you much choice."

"Okay, so you tricked me into going out with you. I'd be upset about that, if it had been someone else. But it's *you*. What you did was amazing. No one has ever done anything even close to that romantic for me before. I love you even more for it."

He spun around, his eyes widening. "You love me?"

Ruthie nodded slowly, her teeth snagging her lower lip. She clasped her hands in front of her before releasing them and raising them, palms up. "Maybe it was a mistake to say that, but it's the truth. I think I've loved you for a long time. I just didn't let myself admit it until last night."

The breath left his lungs in a whoosh. *She loved him.* His lips curled into a smile and his rioting nerves quieted down. That sure made things a hell of a lot easier. "Do you know why I set that whole thing up last night?"

She gave him a crooked, teasing grin. "Because you wanted to get into my pants?"

"No. Because I love you, too. It's taken me two months to confess that to you."

"Well, I have to say I was very impressed with your confession." She walked over to him and wrapped her arms around his neck, pulling his head down until his lips nearly touched hers. "And with everything that happened last night. You mean a lot to me."

She meant a lot to him, too. If she didn't know it yet, she would. He'd prove it to her every day. "So where do we go from here?"

She leaned back and looked up at him, mischief dancing in her eyes. "As far as the future goes, I think that's something we can figure out as we go. We have ten years of friendship on our side, and that's got to count for something. But for now, I think we should just go back to bed. We can sort out all the details later."

He couldn't agree more. Ten years of friendship counted for *everything*. He lifted her in his arms and started walking toward the bedroom. For as long as she put up with him, he would see that she got whatever she wanted. All she had to do was ask.

Also by Elisa Adams

തു

Dark Promises: Demonic Obsession

Dark Promises: Flesh and Blood

Dark Promises: Midnight

Dark Promises: Shift of Fate

Dark Promises: Tarnished

Dirty Pictures

Dream Stalker

Eden's Curse

In Darkness

In Moonlight (*anthology*)

Just Another Night

About the Author

തു

Born in Gloucester, Massachusetts, Elisa Adams has lived most of her life on the east coast. Formerly a nursing assistant and phlebotomist, writing has been a longtime hobby. Now a full-time writer, she lives on the New Hampshire border with her husband and three children.

Elisa welcomes comments from readers. You can find her website and email address on her author bio page at www.ellorascave.com.

Sir Stephen's Fortune

Sahara Kelly

ഌ

Chapter One

ଞ

"Hell and devil *confound* it."

Stephen O'Mannion swore luridly as his horse pulled up lame. He was hot, dusty and thirsty, and this was the second horse in as many weeks that had proved unworthy of its purchase price—little though that had been.

For the umpteenth time, Stephen yearned for one of his own Irish thoroughbreds, a sturdy mount between his thighs, a creature that would respond to the slightest command either by voice or a light touch on the reins.

And for the umpteenth time a cloud of darkness settled on his shoulders as he remembered—it was now all gone.

Lost to the vicious whim of a parent who'd surrendered to the awful truth about his much-needed firstborn son.

Shrugging, Stephen slid from the saddle and examined the weary horse's hoof. The shoe had cracked and there were several pebbles deeply embedded—it would be a cruel sin to ride this animal further. Stephen O'Mannion was many things, but he was not a cruel man. Not to horses, anyway.

Human beings? Well, after these last few months, that was another matter that might well prove fodder for debate.

The road he was on led nowhere in particular, which was fine with him, since he had nowhere in particular in mind to travel. But an inn would have come in quite handy at this moment, along with a blacksmith.

Looking around him, Stephen noticed a wraith of smoke in the distance, which—he presumed—indicated life of some sort. Given the scarcity of any better options, he gathered the reins and started walking.

And thinking.

"You're no son of mine. Get out of this house and never come back."

Would that phrase haunt him for the rest of his days? Lionel O'Mannion's roar of rage still echoed in his ears, even though Stephen had been gone now for over half a year.

He paced onwards trying to block out the sound of his father's screams, to no avail. His mother had been dead less than a day when the storm broke—when Lionel O'Mannion finally released the anger that had been brewing within him for Stephen's entire life.

It was not unknown for a gentleman to accept a child as his own, even though he had not fathered it. Such things were necessary for the continuation of the lineage—an heir being tantamount to a treasure in the aristocratic way of things. And Lionel had accepted Stephen as his heir since there were no others forthcoming from his third marriage, to Stephen's mother.

But the birth, some twelve years later, of a son of Lionel's loins had been cause for a mighty celebration—and the beginning of Stephen's downfall.

His brother Michael had been the recipient of all the affection Stephen had never received. The youngster had been reared, tutored, educated and instructed as the son and heir. Ruefully Stephen admitted that the writing had been on the wall even then and he didn't need his finely tuned intuition to detect it.

Michael hadn't been at fault, even though his attitude had progressed from confused to withdrawn and finally condescending. As he grew up he'd sensed the undercurrents that swirled within O'Mannion Towers, alert to each and every nuance betwixt members of the family.

Had it not been for his mother, Stephen's life would have been a misery. But she had interceded between him and his father, buffering the currents of distaste, protecting him from the worst of his father's volatile temper and his brother's vicious taunts.

Now Stephen could understand the emotions. Could easily see how Lionel would not view him as his son and heir but as an interloper fathered by another. This awareness did not ease the pain he felt, but as a man he could at least understand.

Even armed with that knowledge, he'd been unprepared for his instant dismissal. Preparing for his mother's funeral, his father had stormed into the room waving a small book that Stephen recognized as his mother's diary.

"A filthy gypsy. That's who sired you, boy. A filthy *gypsy*. And to think today I have to pretend to grieve for the death of that—that—*whore*, your mother."

Stephen was caught unawares, shocked at the vitriol in his father's voice. He knew he'd said something in response, but couldn't remember what.

"She admits it. *Relishes* it, the doxy. It's all here..." Lionel had thrown the small diary at Stephen, hitting him on the shoulder. "I knew it was a mistake from the start. You've been nothing but trouble your whole life."

"Father, that's unfair..."

"*Father*?" Lionel's veins had stood out on his forehead as his temper approached apoplectic. "I'm no father to you. You're no son of mine. *Get out of this house and never come back.*"

And there they were again, those heated and angry words that haunted Stephen. He had ridden away from his mother's grave, vowing never to return.

He was a *bastard*. A homeless, landless bastard with nothing to recommend him to anybody. As if in sympathy, droplets of rain began to dapple his shoulders and he sighed. A fitting conclusion to a perfectly rotten day.

He rounded a bend in the lane and stopped short. Here was the source of the smoke...a small country fair, tucked into a fallow field miles from anywhere. The hardiness of the local residents showed quite clearly in the small crowd which must have walked or ridden for quite some distance to get here and enjoy a day away from their labors.

Music and laughter assailed his ears and the most delectable smells of good hearty fare crept around his nostrils and made his stomach rumble.

Trying to remember if he'd eaten anything that day, Stephen led his horse toward the fair. There must be a blacksmith around someplace who wouldn't mind taking a look at the injured hoof.

In spite of the rain, children ran around the few stalls, giggling at their own games while their parents tried their hand at throwing a ball at a target or discussed the finer points of one or two large sows and their litters. It was the quintessential gathering of simple country folk and Stephen found himself smiling as he walked through the raindrops to join the throng.

Tethering his mount to a convenient post, he looked around—just as the skies opened and produced a heavy downpour. Stephen cursed and darted in to a small colorful tent beside him.

"Sorry. It's the bloody rain…"

"Welcome. Yer here just in time…"

He blinked. "In time for what?"

The old woman shadowed in the darkness moved a little, letting the necklaces and bracelets that festooned her body jingle like the harness of a horse. She was seated on the far side of a low table and between them lay some cards and a tapestry tablecloth that looked like it had seen better days.

Stephen squinted at her, trying to discern her features as he waited for an answer. Something disturbed him, unsettling him and making him itch. It was that annoying intuition of his once again. He ignored it and hoped her response would be forthcoming. Soon.

None did. She simply acknowledged his arrival with a wave of her hand. "Sit down, lad."

"Look…" Unwilling to raise her hopes, Stephen opted for the truth. "Ma'am, I have barely a shilling to my name. I cannot cross your palm with silver, nor afford the luxury of you telling my fortune." He sighed. "Actually, I'd just as soon *not* know what that might be."

She ignored his protests. "Sit down. Honest words are better'n gold. They'll do."

Somewhat stunned at this bit of folkloric wisdom, Stephen sat.

"Gi' me yer hand."

She held her own hand across the table, palm upwards, waiting for him to obey. As the rain thrummed against the roof of the tent, he laid his right hand in hers, also allowing his palm to face up.

She glanced at it then pushed it away. "T'other one."

"What's wrong with this one?" Stephen stared at his hand.

"Nothin'. It's yer *present*. I can tell you what's goin' on right now from that. Nothin' you doesn't know already."

"Really?" Stephen quirked a disbelieving eyebrow and did his best to keep the sarcasm from his voice. She was only doing her job and trying to make a few pence, after all.

She sighed. "Yer in trouble, family trouble and that's the worst kind." She tipped her head to one side, reminding Stephen of an elderly sparrow. "You don' know where yer headed. Or if you'll get anywhere in one piece. Yer heart has pain in it—a lot of pain—and none of it's yer fault. Sometimes we gotta carry burdens on our shoulders that're put there by others. I need to see if yer gonna lay 'em down any time soon."

Stunned, Stephen obeyed, silently stretching his other hand towards her. He hadn't expected such accuracy from a simple gypsy fortuneteller.

She gripped him hard, pulling and turning his hand this way and that, running rough fingertips down creases, grating a nail against lines. "T'isn't enough. I can't *see*."

Gloomily Stephen stared at her. "I don't have any future, do I?"

"Don't be daft. We've all got a future, one way or 'nother." She rummaged in a large fabric bag and produced an object wrapped in silk. "Now, let's see what we've got here, shall we?"

Oh yes, do let's. He stifled his sarcastic answer, reminding himself that it was wet outside and dry in here and *this* wasn't costing him anything. His attention was caught fair and square, however, when the silk was withdrawn to reveal the most perfect crystal orb he'd ever seen.

Stephen loved glass. He'd visited Murano in Italy on his Grand Tour and fallen in serious lust with the process that created such masterpieces from such simple ingredients. He'd even been permitted to try "blowing" a piece himself, with quite terrible results. But his passion had been caught, and he'd retained an appreciation for the glassworker's skill.

And this crystal ball was quite a magnificent piece. He reached out a finger and brushed the smooth surface wonderingly. "So lovely…"

"Yep. Come down to me through me mam and her mam before her."

The solid sphere was flawless yet hinted at a slight bluish tinge, the sort of color that one wasn't quite sure existed or not. It rested on a simple wooden base and must have been about as tall as Stephen's handspan.

It radiated light quite vividly, drawing the soft rays from the small lamp and amplifying them into a pure glow. *Like moonlight captured in a still pond.*

"Yep. 'Tis indeed like moonlight." The woman smiled at him, sending a decided chill down his spine as she eerily echoed his thoughts. "Now. I need yer to look deep into the heart of the crystal."

Stephen needed no second bidding. His eyes had been drawn to the center of the globe as soon as she'd placed it on the table. He was already staring into it.

"And look wi' yer *heart*, lad, not yer eyes."

Stephen was drifting. The soft shadows of the tent, the bright glow of the crystal ball—he was seduced by the magic of the moment.

A rough breeze flapped the canvas of the tent around them, but it was lost on him. The crystal ball was clouding beneath his gaze, gentle swirls of some sparkling viscous substance beginning to roil within.

Waves danced and parted only to merge and blend once more until they finally cleared and he found himself staring, not into a crystal ball, but through a broken window—*at a naked woman.*

Chapter Two

ജ

Stephen's breath caught in his throat. "*I see —*"

"What?"

"I see — a woman."

The room in which she stood was blurred, dark and shadowed. But what light there was shone directly onto her body — and what a body it was. Skin like alabaster glowed softly, hair the color of fine whiskey poured down her spine in a tumble of curls, and between her legs a soft mound of the same-colored curls drew his eyes.

"Where is she?"

Stephen vaguely registered the questions as his gaze remained solidly on the vision before him. "In a room. A dark room. Her bedroom perhaps — I can't tell."

He swallowed as the woman moved to stand in front of a tall mirror. She stared at her reflection, as did Stephen. He was looking over her shoulder now, seeing what she saw, admiring what she admired.

And when she raised a hand to cradle one full breast, he gasped.

"*What*? What is happening?" The fortuneteller's voice distracted him and he tried to pull back, but found his wrists anchored to the table by two gnarled hands. They were stronger than he'd have imagined and for a second or two he could have sworn that heat poured from the calloused palms into his arms and up through his body.

The burning energy settled in his groin and his cock stirred as he once again returned to the vision in the crystal ball.

"Tell me what you see, lad. *Tell me*." The fingers tightened around his wrists.

Helpless to resist the command, Stephen obeyed. "She is — touching herself. Looking at herself in a mirror."

The dream woman tossed her head back and closed her eyes as one hand fondled the peach-red nipple beading at the tip of her breast. It was a sensual and erotic gesture of pleasure that brought a slight groan to Stephen's lips.

"Go on."

"I *can't*." He licked his lips. "I can't describe this — *please* don't ask me to."

The fingers loosened slightly. "Very well."

He drowned in the image, watching the fingers of her hand as she teased the nipple to erect hardness, pinching it and rolling it between her thumb and forefinger while her palm supported the heavy weight with ease.

Her lips parted on a sigh he could hear in his mind and his cock hardened as she moved to treat the other breast with the same loving attention. It was agonizing for Stephen to watch, the tension in his crotch rising with each breath that lifted her breasts from her chest.

He stared fixedly at her, biting his lip as her other hand began a leisurely slide down over the silken curve of her belly to her pussy. She tightened her fingers and pulled on the little curls, every muscle in her body quivering at the small pain she inflicted.

Stephen quivered too. He'd had his fair share of women in a variety of ways, and enjoyed every one. But never had he been privileged to watch such an erotically intimate moment.

Her fingers spread wide, parting the outer folds of her pussy lips, revealing a hint of the lush pink and swollen folds between them. Tiny sparkles of moisture reflected brilliantly in the mirror and she found them with her fingertips, spreading them languorously over her pussy and her thighs.

And all the while Stephen watched.

Need snaked around his throat, choking him. He wanted to be the one spreading that honey. He wanted his fingers to be teasing her nipples, his mouth delving through her tight curls to find that pearly bud and make her sigh with pleasure.

She rubbed herself, parting her thighs, changing her stance slightly to allow her hand freedom to reach where she could find the most delight. Her hips swayed a little, in concert with her movements.

Stephen's breath kept pace. Who was she? Why could he see this? Why could he not look away? Would his cock survive this experience or explode before she reached fulfillment?

"Don't look away, lad." The hands kept him anchored to the table and his desire kept him looking into the crystal ball. He couldn't have *stopped* looking now if the tent had collapsed around them.

The woman had raised her head again and opened her eyes, her lowered lids clearly showing him that she was watching her hand as eagerly as he was.

She stopped for a moment and Stephen nearly cried out for her to continue. But she simply reached into the shadows and picked up a small object—a short wooden spindle of some sort with a gently rounded snout.

With deliberate movements she lifted it to her lips and licked it, letting her mouth slide over it, slicking it with her own saliva until it was moist and shining. It took no imagination at all for Stephen's cock to respond.

Would she lick him like that? Would she like his cock between her red lips instead of some inanimate tool? He ached but could not withdraw from this painfully exquisite torture.

She took the little spindle and lovingly drew it over her pussy, adding even more moisture to its surface. Strands of her honey clung lovingly to it and Stephen held his breath as she finally lifted it away from her body and looked at it. She gave a small nod and then leaned forward, resting one hand on the frame of the mirror.

What she did next took his breath away and he coughed out a strangled sound as she delicately parted her buttocks and slid the wet spindle between them into the tight little rosebud of her arse.

Standing erect once more, her face shone with color, the flush spreading over her skin as her arousal burgeoned within her. And her hand slid back to her pussy.

Stephen was on fire. Desire, lust, heat—he scarcely knew where he was or what day it was. All his senses were attuned to the woman in the crystal ball and he swore he could smell the juices from her cunt. Had she been there at that moment he'd have freed himself and taken her on the spot, plunging as deeply as he could, thrusting himself into her any place she wanted.

With increasingly rapid movements she was bringing herself to climax now, her mouth open, her eyes vague and unfocused as her hand found the places that aroused her.

Stephen saw her stroke her clit, bury two fingers inside her cunt and then return to stroke her clit once more. No detail was obscured, no shiver or shudder unnoticed. His fingers twitched as she became more frenzied and he shifted on his chair, his cock a solid length of agony restrained within his breeches.

She was coming, reaching that peak of pleasure, stimulated by her own hand and a tool within her arse. Her head dropped forward, hiding her face for a moment with the curls that fell loosely over her shoulder and Stephen almost sobbed—he wanted to see her face as she orgasmed.

He wanted to be there, to share it, to take his pleasure with her, to drive her higher than just a simple climax—to show her things she'd never dreamed of.

As his eyes remained glued to her image, the woman came.

He could almost hear her cry as her face contorted into a grimace of fulfillment and her body shook with the force of it. He wanted to cry out with her, to hold her close, to feel the shudders that racked her, to lick the sweat that dewed her breasts and glowed on her face.

He moaned, a guttural sound that would have easily emerged from his throat had he been experiencing his own orgasm along with hers. His fingers scrabbled absently on the surface of the table and then suddenly—

She was gone. The silk fabric had obscured everything, the crystal ball, the stand and the woman within.

"Rain's stopped. Best you be on yer way now."

He blinked and gaped, still shaken by the force of the lust that had billowed through him. "What?" His hands were free and with difficulty he moved his arms, finding them strangely limp and unresponsive for a moment or two.

"Rain's stopped." The fortune teller gathered her things, whisking the crystal ball back into the recesses of a large bag and folding the cloth that had covered the table. "'Tis late. I must be home before dark." She glanced up at him. "You'll be needin' help for that horse of yers, I'm thinkin'."

"*How…*" Had he told her about his lame horse? Stephen ran a hand through his hair and tried to summon his wits from his cock where they were still thrumming about, screaming at him to let them go in an explosion of his own.

"You walk a couple miles down yon lane you'll find a barn. Cousin o'mine takes care of the farm. He'll help you out. Mebbe you can get yerself a meal at the main house. Not promisin' or anythin', mind you…"

"The main house? What main house?" Stephen wanted to sob. His ears were still ringing from the moan he'd released, his body ached because his balls hadn't released anything at all, and he was totally confused.

The old woman smiled, an odd contorted little smile, but a smile nonetheless. "Relax, lad. It'll all work out. Yer here now. Best follow yer fortune."

And she was gone, leaving Stephen staring into nothing at all and wondering what the hell hit him.

* * * * *

Ileana Baxter shivered as the cool air chilled skin that had been overheated just moments before. It wasn't just the temperature either.

She'd seen...something — *someone*...behind her, a reflection of a face in the mirror. Watching her as she came, watching her pleasure herself — watching her as she fell from grace and took what little delight she could in her own body.

Even now his features were imprinted on her brain. Dark hair, a lush moustache, eyes that burned into her. Harsh planes that hinted of strength and perhaps anger — she didn't know, couldn't be sure from the brief glimpse she'd had of him.

And of course there was nobody there at all. She sighed, removed her toy and slipped back into her nightgown.

Bi kashtesko merel i yag. Without wood the fire would die.

The Romany phrase slid into her mind. She'd provided the wood to keep the fire of her body alive.

But it would seem that her *mind* was beginning to die, since it was creating images to accompany her occasional lapses in behavior.

It was early yet, too early to be dressed for bed. But what else was there?

Ileana sighed. Alone and lonely, she wished for the twentieth time that Ben was with her, to cheer her and make her laugh as he always did.

But she'd willingly sent him on his way to his cousin's, knowing he'd have adventures and stories to tell upon his return that would last them through the coming winter. How her heart ached for the sound of his voice and how empty the house was without him.

A door slammed somewhere below and Ileana listened for a moment or two. It would be Callie returning from the fair. Perhaps she'd have some news — local gossip — something to alleviate the cloud that was settling into Ileana's soul.

Was this all there would be for her? Eking out a meager existence on a tiny stipend and in a house that was all but falling down around her ears?

"It's your own fault, you whore. Be thankful I am allowing you this much."

She blocked out the words. No point in revisiting the past. Although God knew the future wasn't much to look at either.

Footsteps rang on the bare staircase and a tap on the door preceded Callie's entrance. The old woman erupted into the room in a flurry.

"Get dressed, girl. Lazin' around in yer nightrail at this time of day? What are you *thinkin'*? We might be havin'…visitors or somethin'."

Ileana laughed wryly. "Callie, we've had no visitors in the past year. Few even know we exist in this out-of-the-way place. Why on earth would you think we'll have visitors today?"

Callie dropped her eyes.

"*Callie*. What did you do?"

There was no answer, just a shuffling of feet underneath the muddy hem of Callie's serviceable gown.

Nervous now, Ileana put her hands on her hips. "Did you do something *foolish*?"

"I did *not*." The old woman's head snapped up. "I did nothin' at all. *You* did it with yer woman's body and woman's needs."

"*Me?*" Ileana blushed, the color heating her cheeks.

"He has the sight, lass. *He has the sight*. He's the one." Callie turned quickly. "Get yerself dressed. He's comin'."

Chapter Three

℘

The knocker on the door was hanging half off and gave an unimpressive thud when Stephen lifted and dropped it. He'd found the barn as the old woman had promised, and given his mount into the hands of somebody who looked like they knew what they were doing.

At least he hoped so. But he had no other options, so when bid to "Go over t'house. They'll feed yer…" by the dour farmhand, he'd done precisely that.

"T'house" itself was less than impressive. Several windows were cracked, others boarded up completely. Only a small portion looked habitable and there were few lights showing in the dusk that had fallen during Stephen's long walk.

He was tired, filthy, hungry and still aching a little from his unrelieved arousal. There was no way he'd bring himself ease with his own hand in some forest glade. He had to draw the line somewhere.

He might be almost penniless *and* homeless, but he still clung to something of his former life. A code of behavior perhaps. Whatever it was, it had prevented him from doing a damn thing to take the edge off his lust, which added to his less-than-happy state of mind.

Once again he rapped on the peeling door, cursing as the knocker gave up any pretense of usefulness and came off in his hand. With an oath he flung it away into some nearby straggly bushes.

And finally the door opened.

"Good evening."

Stephen blinked and his jaw dropped. It was *her*.

Or possibly her. Or maybe not.

He blinked again. *This* woman was elegantly garbed, although her gown was old-fashioned. Her hair was coiled neatly and severely at the back of her head and her face was expressionless. No soft smiles of desire or heavy-lidded eyes.

She was simply staring at him with mild curiosity. "May I help you?"

Stephen gathered his wits and closed his mouth with a snap. "Yes. I mean — sorry. I was told — er — your man said — "

Very good, you brainless idiot. She'll slam the door in your face within two seconds if you keep this up.

He tried again. "Forgive my disturbing you, ma'am. My horse is being tended to by one of your people and it was suggested I might obtain a meal while I wait." Dredging up a smile from somewhere, Stephen patted himself on the back as he actually produced an intelligible phrase.

She stepped back into the dimly lit hall. "Of course. Please enter." She waved him inside, glancing over her shoulder as he closed the door behind him. "Please excuse our informality. We live quietly here. I have no servants to speak of, just a couple of faithful retainers."

"I understand." And looking around him, Stephen did. The house had once been magnificent, he guessed, but now — it was not in very good shape at all and showed quite clearly the ravages of time and neglect.

However, the small salon she led him to was warm and well lit and he sighed with pleasure at the sight of a small decanter half full of what he guessed might be brandy.

"This is quite charming. My thanks." He bowed. "I should introduce myself. I am S—Stephen O'Mannion." His tongue stumbled as he deliberately left off the title he'd fought to retain. It wasn't the one he'd expected, but it was all he'd been allowed. For some reason he didn't feel the need to share it.

"Welcome, Sir Stephen."

She'd caught it without a blink. Stephen reminded himself never to underestimate a woman.

"I am Ileana Baxter." She dipped a slight curtsey. "Please do me the honor of sharing my meal?"

"Thank you…ma'am." She'd given no hint of a husband or suggested any form of address that would enlighten him. Damn her.

"It would appear you have been on a long journey. Would it be presumptuous of me to suggest a bath? I know how insufficient inns can be when one travels. If you would care to…" She waved her hand.

"You are most kind, ma'am. I would indeed appreciate the opportunity to make myself presentable."

"In that case…" She tugged on an aged bellpull, which— miraculously—stayed attached to the wall and produced a knock on the door. "Enter."

An elderly man peered into the room. "You rang?"

Stephen noticed a lightning-quick smile cross her face then vanish as she reassumed her politely social demeanor. "Yes, Rodney. Would you show our guest to the spare bedchamber and prepare him a bath? And care for his clothes too, I think…"

"You are most gracious." Stephen accepted the offer gladly, only to narrow his eyes as the servant spoke once more.

"'Tis all ready."

He frowned. "I don't understand…"

She curtseyed in dismissal. "Dinner will be served in a little over an hour. Shall we meet here at that time?"

Uneasily, Stephen nodded and followed the man from the room to find that indeed a steaming bath was awaiting him in a sparse upstairs chamber. This was, to coin a phrase, *bloody* strange.

But then again, nothing about this day had been normal, in any accepted sense of the word. He simply stripped and availed himself of the pleasure that awaited him.

A blissfully hot *bath*.

* * * * *

Ileana's hands were shaking as she entered her own room to change. Callie was already there laying out her gown and cackling with glee.

"He's a right one, isn't he, lovey?" She smoothed the folds of silk lying on the bed. "I'm thinking he'll ride yer body hard, and warm the cockles of yer heart with his...cock." She cackled again at her own joke.

"*Callie.*" Ileana opened her eyes wide. "I'm shocked. *Shocked*, I say."

A wise gaze met hers. "Don't be, lovey. You need what he's got betwitxt his thighs. Always have needed it. T'isn't yer fault, lass. Some needs it, some don't. Yer one that needs it right enough."

Ileana raised her palms to her flushed cheeks. "I'm a whore, Callie. A wanton whore to be even thinking such things."

Callie pulled Ileana's hands away from her face sharply. "Enough o'that kind of talk. Yer *no* whore. Yer a healthy woman. He's a healthy man. 'Tis natural enough ye'd find an attraction there. 'Tis even more natural to act on it."

Ileana allowed Callie to unlace the gown she'd donned only an hour or so before. "If he *knew*, Callie..."

"He's got the sight, love. He'll know."

"Are you sure?" Ileana's thoughts gave rise to a shiver that was purely sensual. He was, as Callie had said, a *right* one. "I can't *ask* him. That would be outside the pale."

"You won't need to. He's ready. Ripe an' ready."

"Callie..." Her voice was muffled by her dress but she had to speak. "I think I saw him once before."

Callie paused as she tugged the skirts from Ileana's head. "When?"

"Earlier—this afternoon. Just a reflection. In—er—in my mirror. Behind me." *As I screamed out my pleasure.*

Callie grinned. "Told you he'd got the *sight*, lass. Mebbe he saw you too. Mebbe he's *meant* to be here this evenin'."

"Do you think so?" Ileana felt a little dart of hope rise within her. "But if he *leaves*…"

"He won't." Callie sounded so certain. "He's seen *you*, lovey. The real you. He looked with his heart, not his eyes. He's the one. I know it." She grinned suddenly. "But just to be on the safe side, let's go take a quick look…"

"*Callie.* You *wouldn't.*"

But she would and she did and before Ileana knew it, she too was hurrying along a small corridor, wrapped in a dressing gown, to do the unthinkable—spy on their guest in his *bath*. After all, justified Ileana to herself, he'd seen her, hadn't he?

It was only fair that she have a chance to feast her eyes in her turn.

And when they found the tiny peephole into the spare guest chamber and pressed their eyes to it, Ileana couldn't regret her action.

What a feast he was!

* * * * *

Stephen O'Mannion hummed to himself as he luxuriated in the large copper tub. The water had been hot enough to turn his arse red and he'd sunk chest-deep into it with a sigh of delight.

The soap was new and smelled slightly of herbs, not unpleasant or overly flowery. There were towels warming by the fire—and for the first time in ages, all was right in Stephen's world.

Or almost right.

If he'd had the lush beauty of his hostess naked in the tub with him, *then* everything would have been bloody *perfect*. He soaped and rinsed his hair, noting the dust that now coated the surface of the water. God, he must have looked a fright. His last bath had been outside under a cold pump and done nothing much to clean him, just refresh him.

This was a proper cleansing, one that went soul deep. And refreshed more than just his skin.

A tingle at the nape of his neck caught his attention. *I'm being watched.* Stephen had long accepted his "gift" or his curse, depending on whom he listened to. He could sense things, feel things, anticipate things long before anybody else did. It was something he'd tried to suppress in the past as a shameful skill to be concealed.

Now he knew it had been inherited from his real father. The Romany blood that ran in his veins had produced a special awareness—something else his pedestrian parent had held against him.

He shrugged. Let them look. In fact—a brazen thought tickled his fancy and he stood, nude, letting the water roll down his body into the water. For a moment he opened his mind, trying to locate the source of his observer. *To the right. Behind that paneling.*

Under the pretense of reaching for a towel, Stephen turned towards that part of the room. His cock stirred and lengthened, spurred on no doubt by rather lascivious images of what he'd like to be doing to one Ileana Baxter.

He could have sworn he heard a gasp and schooled his features into blank unconcern as he toweled off his chest.

Slowly. Might as well make it worth the while for whoever was getting an eyeful.

He rubbed his hair hard and then tossed it back behind him, moving the towel down to his belly and beginning the job of drying his lower half.

Stepping out of the water, he turned right around, treating the wall to a nice view of his buttocks and then moving closer to the fire—and the right side of the room. He leaned over and stoked the logs, letting the warmth evaporate the moisture on his legs.

And then he began to toy with his watchers. And himself.

The towel slid over one muscled thigh and back down, just brushing his cock and his balls. As expected, he hardened. He stifled a chuckle at the sense of breathless silence emanating from behind the paneling. She—they—whoever it was, waited for what he might do next.

Hmm. Stephen O'Mannion promised he'd do penance for this, but could not resist the imp of mischief that whispered naughty things in his ear. He reached between his legs and cradled his cock, enjoying the touch of his own hand around the solid and sensitive length.

He stroked, gently, just bringing himself to a full erection, no more.

And then—blatantly—he turned his arse to the fire and stretched out his arms, thus heating his buttocks and baring all that he had to the allegedly empty room. This time he could not hide his smile as two very audible breaths sounded quite near him.

He stood, enjoying the exhibitionism of the moment and hoping that one of his onlookers was Ileana. He wanted her, desired her in the most elemental of ways, longed to fuck her senseless and drain himself dry at the same time. If physical attractiveness was what she wanted, he modestly hoped he could offer *that* at least.

If a good fuck was what she wanted—well, he was more than ready to oblige her in that department, too. His cock agreed, a tiny drop of lust seeping from the small slit, reminding him that unless he wanted to come right then and there, he'd better redirect his thoughts into avenues less stimulating.

There'd be time enough for fucking after dinner. Or at least he hoped so. With a sigh he began to dress, wondering if she was sighing too as he slipped his breeches back on and waited for his shirt to be returned to him.

Strangely enough, his thoughts of her were eager and curious, not simply lust-filled, although *that* was there in more than sufficient measure. He realized that Ileana radiated sensuality from every pore.

Not a blatant invitation to bed, unlike many women he'd known. Hers was a subtly attractive appeal, something hinting of fire beneath her proper exterior. She was no hungry whore looking for coins, nor a bored aristocrat looking to add him to her conquests.

She was, thought Stephen, the most beautiful woman he'd seen in quite some time—and she had a heat burning inside her he longed to ignite. It called to him on some fundamental level he had yet to fully comprehend.

His sixth sense kicked him solidly. *She will light fires within you too.*

A cleaned shirt having been returned by a silent Rodney, Stephen shrugged himself into his jacket and prepared to leave the room. His self-possession had received a blow with that message from somewhere deep in his head. He didn't know if he wanted any fires lit by anybody.

And yet—something gnawed at his brain. A foreign phrase he'd heard his mother whisper occasionally.

"Now, Stephen. Do it now." She would urge him to finish whatever it was he was doing. "*May angle sar te merel kadi yag.*"

He'd asked her what it meant. She'd looked sad for a moment then smiled. "*Before this fire burns out…*"

He shook his head at himself and his absurdity.

When fires were lit, somebody got burned. He'd been burned too many times to take such a prospect lightly. So it was with an uncertain and unusual amount of apprehension that he allowed Rodney to lead him to dinner—and Ileana.

Chapter Four

଼ଡ଼

"Would you care for brandy?" Ileana waved her hand at the tray on the sideboard.

"Thank you. That would be nice. May I pour you some?"

The conversation had been trivial, desultory even, making Ileana more than a little frustrated. Stephen was an easy companion, though, and the meal had passed pleasantly enough while trivialities about the weather and the countryside had been exchanged.

Rodney had served the few courses silently and efficiently as was his wont, but had now left the room.

They were alone.

She raised her eyebrows at his question. "Yes, as a matter of fact, you may. I find I enjoy brandy now and again."

"I thought you might." Stephen poured the liquor and returned holding two goblets, one of which he passed to Ileana. He also seated himself next to her instead of across the small table where he'd partaken of his meal.

She nodded her thanks and sipped, letting the burn of the brandy slide pleasantly down her throat.

"What else do you enjoy?" His question was quiet, intimate almost.

"Learning about people. Let's take you, for example." She watched his face. "You are a traveler, Sir Stephen. And yet it would appear you have no destination in mind." She waved her hand at his attire. "Clearly it has been a long and perhaps hard road. Would you tell me how you ended up in this spot? We are not exactly on the turnpike to Brighton…"

He studied his glass, swirling the liquid slowly. Thinking, always thinking—and yet Ileana wondered if there was more to that abstract look than simple cogitation. He occasionally seemed to *listen*—to something other than what was being said.

"I'm a bastard, you know."

Short and to the point. "By birth or by nature?" Her lips quirked.

His smile answered her. "Some would say both. My father—and I use the word advisedly—knows that it's by birth. Perhaps that knowledge has led to my nature."

"It happens."

"But not to Lionel O'Mannion." In blunt and simple terms he told her of his father's desire for an heir and what finally happened when a true one was born.

"So your real father…"

"Was a gypsy, apparently. My mother made the mistake of leaving a diary detailing her affection for him. *Not* something Lionel took lightly."

"Thus you wander. For how long?"

"Months." He chuckled ruefully. "In truth, ma'am, I have scarcely sixpence to scratch with and no prospects whatsoever." He leaned back in his chair and spread his arms. "I am in your debt for the meal and the bath. Otherwise I'd have enjoyed neither for quite some time to come."

She ran a finger around the edge of the crystal, producing a slight sound as the glass resonated to her touch. "I may be in a position to assist you, Sir Stephen."

"Really?" He stared at her, but she could not read his intent.

"I need…"

"What? What do you *need*, Ileana?"

And in that moment, as he used her given name, the air changed around them from polite to heated. A bolt of desire shot up into Ileana's throat and she had to swallow several times to quell the shivers it produced.

"I need a man."

Gratified, she couldn't help but notice how his cock leaped beneath his breeches. Just thinking of that fine male instrument, remembering how it had looked after his bath, and the shivers returned in full force.

Carefully she put down the glass. "I see I must tell you something of myself. 'Tis as ugly a tale as yours, I fear." She gulped. "I am a whore, Sir Stephen. Mother of a bastard child, myself. So you can see that naught you have told me has shocked me."

He tipped his head to one side. "You may be many things, Ileana, but *whore*—I doubt that. I doubt that most strongly."

She looked away. "What else would you call a woman who gives herself before marriage to an unsuitable man who leaves her with child?"

"Unlucky?" He grinned. "Oh, and I'd gladly shoot the miserable swine who deserted you if you'd like."

She couldn't help her answering smile. "That will not be necessary, but thank you for the offer." She rose, putting her glass on the table and pacing to the fireplace. "I live here on sufferance. 'T'was a distant aunt's estate—she permitted me residence until a certain time and under certain conditions."

"Tell me?" He'd risen too and was standing casually, arms folded, resting his buttocks on the table as he watched her.

"I was rushed from the bosom of my disapproving family and interred in this—this place—seven years ago. At that time, my aunt was living, but upon her death her will laid out conditions quite clearly. If my son reached the age of six and I had not found a man willing to be his father, then I was to leave and receive nothing more from her—ever." She paused. "Unfortunately, she also spread word that I was, indeed, a whore. No man hereabouts will pass the time of day with me. Except for one or two—"

"Who would like to test the veracity of that rumor."

"Exactly." He'd hit the nail on the head. She'd turned away the drunken louts who'd assumed she would spread her legs and lift her skirts for a few coins. One of them had left with a load of pellets in his backside and the tales *he'd* spread around hadn't exactly helped matters along.

Stephen closed the distance between them, his boots making soft sounds on the worn carpet. "Has there been nobody, Ileana?"

"Nobody I could accept. Nobody who could call to my heart. And I will not settle for less." She turned. "I care not if it means my son and I will have to leave here and wander the world. My son's father was a gypsy and I loved him, worthless though he was. Wandering is not an alien concept nor is it something I'm afraid of."

"But…"

"But I *must* consider Ben. He may not take to life on the road. He does not know what it will mean. The ostracism, the slights and slurs. He has a birthright, here in this house. He should be permitted to claim it. He's only six, Stephen—so young to learn that hate is still out there. Too young to face it."

Stephen was silent after her outburst and she wondered if he was trying to find a way to excuse himself and leave. After all, who would want an unmarried woman with a bastard son who was half-gypsy to boot? The house was decaying, there were little or no funds to go along with it—truthfully, there was no solid incentive for him to stay.

"I'll stay." His gaze locked with hers. "Under one condition."

"What's that?" Mesmerized by the heat in his eyes, her heart thudded.

"Let me spend this night with you. In your bed. Let us explore each other and learn about each other in something other than words. Let us find out if we can tolerate each other's touch, each other's body. If there is pleasure to be had, let us take it. If not, then you can throw me out and I shall never speak of it, or you, ever."

"And you? What if you find no pleasure in this...this night of ours?"

"I'm not worried about that. You see, you have already called to my heart. It just took me rather a long time to hear you."

He moved close and lifted her chin with his fingertips. "What do you say, Ileana? Will you come to bed with me this night?"

He kissed away her answer with lips that singed hers, perhaps knowing that even as she breathed the word "yes", it was unnecessary.

She couldn't *wait*.

* * * * *

They saw no one on their way through the darkened passageways, Stephen's hand clasped firmly in Ileana's. He allowed her to lead, following where she hurried with as much impatience as he had experienced in a long time.

He was glad there were no servants. His cock was solid and swollen beneath his breeches and he'd have been hard pressed to hide the evidence of his need from curious eyes.

She'd captured him with her honesty and her story had the ring of truth about it. She was lovely enough to have been claimed by some unscrupulous man, but why he'd left her, Stephen couldn't fathom. Had it been *his* child she'd conceived, it would know its father and probably have several brothers and sisters by now.

The thought of getting a child on Ileana nearly knocked him off his feet and he stumbled a little as she pulled him through a door and into her chamber.

It was *familiar* — the mirror standing off to one side.

It *had* been Ileana he'd watched in the crystal ball. Ileana that he'd seen with his heart, not his eyes. Now he could sate both.

He did just that as she turned and reached behind her for her laces.

"No, let me." Stephen led her to the mirror. "Just watch, Ileana." *Like you did before.* He kept the words to himself, noting the flash of awareness in her eyes. He unfastened her gown rapidly and tugged it down over her body, leaving her in a short chemise and stockings that ended in garters just above her knees.

She was truly a work of art. One that he felt he'd seen in his soul or his dreams for so long that it was like coming home to touch her at last. He pressed himself against her and pulled her chemise off her shoulders, slowly revealing her breasts as the ribbons came undone and the two halves parted around the womanly curves.

"Beautiful. So beautiful."

Her eyes followed his hands as they crept around her and cupped the warm swells, toying gently with her nipples as he'd seen her do when alone. The contrast of his dark clothing against her pale skin and lacy undergarments was a visual arousal for both of them and she sighed, leaning against him, pushing her backside into his groin, searching for his cock.

Releasing one breast, he quickly undid his breeches and let them drop, kicking them free of his boots with a muttered curse. Then he returned, naked from his waist to his shins, his heat unfettered and thrusting against her. Somehow, their partial nudity was even more erotic than if they'd both been bare—the glancing touch of wool and silk against hard muscle and soft skin emphasizing the places where body rubbed against body.

She moaned, eyelids drooping with desire, lips parted, tongue flicking out to moisten the dryness her rapid breaths brought to them. "More. Please more."

"All right." Stephen pulled away and stripped, tugging off his boots impatiently and never taking his eyes off Ileana as she shrugged her chemise to the floor and reached for her garters. "No, leave them. Please. It's...they're...*exciting*."

Blushing, Ileana smiled. "If you wish."

"I wish." He turned her back to the mirror and pulled her hard against him, his cock squashing between them into the crack of her arse and coming to rest against her sensitive muscles.

He felt them twitch, a movement that sent shudders through his balls. "I want you. Any way, any position—tell me what you want..." He shifted, rubbing his cock between her cheeks, loving the way her nipples had hardened to peaks and her pulse throbbed at the base of her neck.

"I just want *you*. That's all." She breathed the words so softly he would have missed them if he hadn't been nipping her neck at the time. He brushed his moustache over her shoulder and slid his hands downwards past her belly to her mound. Imitating her earlier moves, he tugged on the soft curls, just enough to get her attention.

"Oh...oh..." Her hips moved as he touched her. Yes...he'd managed to get her attention, all right. And as he delved lower, his hands grew wet from the honey dripping onto them. Her folds were hot and puffy, shining pinkly in the reflection as he parted the delicate skin to seek the treasures within.

Her clit was hard, gleaming with moisture, ready for him to caress with the lightest of loving attention. Gently he did so, strumming it then retreating only to return once more and stroke the heart of her arousal.

"*Stephen...*" She cried out as he found her, found the rhythm and the places that drove her higher into the insanity of desire. Her hips ground against him, abrading his cock and pushing herself into him, begging...needing...

She reached for her breasts, finding her nipples and tugging on them, hard now as he whipped up a frenzy of passion within her body. His balls chose that moment to remind him he was doing a pretty good job of arousing his own needs as well as hers.

He turned Ileana, the mirror to her side now, reflecting both of them. "I'm going to fuck you, sweetheart. I want to be inside you the first time you come."

She nodded, her throat working to produce words, her fingers scrabbling at his shoulders, her legs parting in welcome.

His hands cupped her buttocks and he lifted her, pulling her into the right position for his possession. Her thighs opened wide, a natural move that allowed him to step closer and lower her—slowly, oh so slowly—down onto his cock.

They both gasped as Stephen claimed her and came to rest with her body flush against his. He filled her cunt, her slick heat cradling him like a glove custom-designed for his cock.

"Look. Look at us, Ileana." He tilted his head towards the mirror as she glanced at their reflection. Two bodies, linked together, twined around each other, breast to chest. An image that Stephen knew would be branded on his soul forever.

He stayed still, buried to the hilt within her, and instead of moving his body, he moved his head. He found her mouth and kissed her savagely, eating at her lips—her tongue, devouring her again and again.

"Come for me." His command was rough, harsh with lust and passion, as he continued to kiss her with all the skill he possessed. His tongue dueled with hers, learning her, teasing her, finding her once more as it darted in and out—a prelude to what lay ahead.

She tore her lips from his. "I can't...you must *move*..."

"Not yet." He grasped her as tightly as possible with one arm and freed the other to slide a hand between their bodies. Ileana was a woman with unimagined heights of passion locked within her. Stephen was about to find the key.

Even as his mouth took hers once more, his fingers found her clit and pressed it—hard.

She screamed, a savage cry of release as she shattered around him. He swallowed her pleasure, rode her spasms and held back his own climax by the skin of his teeth. This one was for her. And perhaps the second one would be too.

Eventually, it would be for them both.

In the meantime she shuddered around him, an armful of shaking, roiling heat. Her cunt gripped him fiercely and he clenched his teeth, hanging on to his sanity by a thread.

As she eased he separated them, quickly tumbling them both on the bed. His shoulders were shaking from the strain and it was a relief to lie down, to let the mattress take her weight and to cover her with his body.

He slid downwards, pushing her thighs apart and revealing her still-throbbing pussy. "*Stephen…*"

He loved the way she moaned out his name. Carefully he inserted a finger into her cunt, feeling the remnants of her orgasm caressing it. "So good. So beautiful, Ileana."

"I…*what*…"

She stuttered in shock as he put his mouth on her.

Chapter Five

ಬ

Ileana's world had ended—vaporized at the hands of Stephen O'Mannion. Disintegrated with the touch of his fingers to her breasts, evaporated with the feel of his cock inside her and now was threatening to completely explode as she felt his tongue probing the sensitive flesh that still quivered.

"Again, love. Come *again*."

He was asking her something—she moved her head restlessly, unable to make sense of his words. All she could feel was his mouth, his lips—his heat driving her to someplace she'd never imagined.

Delicately he drew her back into the maelstrom of desire, not waiting for her to recover, but building on what had gone before to send her to new heights. His skill was beyond belief, taking Ileana's breath away.

Once more the savage ache gathered in her cunt, the tingle at the base of her spine more pronounced than ever. This was—incredible, unbelievable, and Ileana knew not what to think.

Then she stopped thinking about anything at all as his tongue replaced his finger inside her.

The unique sensation shot from her cunt to her breasts and back down to her clit. The softer and more malleable texture was a counterpoint to the hardness and velvet steel of his cock, a delicate teasing of aroused and swollen folds both without and within.

She scrabbled for his head, finally grabbing handfuls of his hair. Tugging, she drew him away from her pussy, loving the gleam of her juices that soaked his moustache and the deep color that flooded his cheeks. "Please. Together this time. *Please…*"

He paused, dark eyes burning, chest heaving with his suppressed desires. "All right."

He rose over her, taking his weight on his arms and unerringly finding the heat between her thighs with the head of his cock. Muscles flexed and twisted as he thrust himself into her with a groan of pleasure.

She groaned too, just the feel of him enough to begin her orgasm anew. He pushed deep then withdrew only to plunge again and again, taking her, claiming her as his own.

Cries of sharp delight strangled in her throat, lights exploded behind her eyes and she surrendered, leaping off a mighty peak into a void that contained nothing but exquisite ecstasy.

She vaguely heard his own guttural shout as he buried himself inside her and erupted, hot jets of his come fueling the fire that was raging inside her cunt. It went on for a trembling pulsating eternity, a voyage into a universe with only two inhabitants.

Ileana's mind whirled, trying to grasp the reality yet unwilling to leave the magic that they'd both created together. Her body was clenched around his cock, her hands grasping his arms and her legs locked behind his thighs as she held him so deeply within.

As the shudders subsided and the world righted itself, Ileana accepted the inevitable. Stephen had not only fucked her body—he'd touched her soul. As she'd known he would when she'd seen his face behind her in the mirror.

It was destiny.

Finally they separated and tumbled together into a panting heap of quivering muscles and sated desires. Stephen pulled her close, tucking her head into his shoulder.

Neither spoke for long moments—Ileana because she simply couldn't think of a thing to say. They'd let their bodies speak for them. It was more than enough.

Stephen was the first to break the silence. "If you still want me to stay, I will stay."

"Yes. I want you to stay." She rasped the words from a throat still hoarse from her screams of pleasure. "I want you. Here, in my bed. Here in my life. Beside me."

"You have me. Always." He turned his head. "You had me from the first moment I saw you in that crystal ball."

She blinked. "It *was* you in the mirror, wasn't it?"

"You saw *me*?" Stephen looked at her. "I ended up in a fortune teller's tent this afternoon. She had a crystal ball. I looked into it — and saw you." He grinned. "And your mirror."

Ileana, amazingly, found she still had the strength to blush. "Ah." She cleared her throat. "You do have the *sight*, it seems."

"Indeed I do. I've ignored it most of the time, but now and again…" He brushed a kiss on her head. "I wondered if I'd see my fortune in that crystal, Ileana. I wondered if I had any future to see at all. And then I saw you."

"So t'would seem I am to be your fortune, then, sir." She giggled.

"I do hope so. And I hope your son will approve."

"He will." Ileana smiled. Ben would like Stephen. They were kindred spirits — both sharing that dark gypsy smile.

"Let's hope he enjoys having brothers and sisters too."

"I'm not so sure about that, but I can tell you his mother will enjoy making them." Ileana turned and dropped kisses on Stephen's chest in her turn.

Stephen yawned. "In a little while, you must show me that — toy of yours. You know…" His fingers traced their way down her spine to her arse. "The one that disappeared somewhere around here…"

Ileana sighed with pleasure. She would show Stephen anything he desired. Give him anything he desired. Maybe even tell him that she was probably falling in love with him. When he was ready to hear it. "Perhaps." She paused. "Stephen, I have little to offer you. Have you truly thought this through?"

Strong arms banded around her. "I have even less to offer you. All I have is my heart. It's yours, Ileana."

For Ileana, that was more than enough.

Epilogue

ଧ

Summertime at Mannion House was always a busy one. The gypsy encampment had filled half of one fallow field and the comings and goings made for a merry few weeks.

At first uncertain, the local residents had come to accept these wanderers in their colorful caravans, appreciating their food, their crafts, their music and their dancing. It had taken a couple of years of leaving subtle signs on their property for Stephen and Ileana to persuade the gypsies that they were welcome, since there were many places that greeted them with silence, distrust and sometimes outright hatred.

But here, on the newly designated Mannion grounds, they found a home. There was fresh water, fuel aplenty, and the chance to trade for supplies. If a chicken went missing from a local farmer's coop, odds were pretty good that something useful would be left in its place, and for several seasons now the gypsies had wandered here to stay for a while.

There were no more welcome visitors to the camp than Sir Stephen and his lovely wife, the Lady Ileana. Few bothered to recall the rumors about her past, or the fact that he had some possible ties to the O'Mannion family in Ireland. They had slowly restored the house to its former beauty, and if they were not rich—at least they were caring.

Anybody in need could find a helping hand at Mannion House. And with the addition of the gypsies, it was a rather bohemian community that centered around Sir Stephen and his lady. For their part, they cared not one whit. When there was a feast to be enjoyed, they shared it. When there was music to be played, they danced to it.

The Romany elders looked at each other and shook their heads, whispering the old phrase "*Jek dilo kerel but dile hai but dile keren dilimata*". One madman makes many madmen, and many madmen make madness.

Yes, it was madness...but madness of the best kind, a madness born of sadness and pain that had become a deep appreciation of life, joy and love. A madness shared by Stephen and Ileana, not to mention Ben and his two brothers Nicholas and Simon. Young Susanna was not quite ready to share anything yet, but bid fair to become a stunning beauty in her own right.

As the sun set and the fire was stoked in the clearing, Stephen drew Ileana into the shadows between two caravans. "Dance with me tonight?"

She laughed. "Of course. Try to stop me."

"Never. You're a whirlwind on two feet when those violins begin to play."

Ileana leaned back against her husband and watched the first stars emerge. "I'm so..."

"So what, my love?"

"So blessed. To have found you. To be here now, and be so happy."

"We're both blessed." He gazed around. "'T'would seem that we *both* have found our fortune. And it's very good indeed."

Then the music began and lured them both back into the present. Sir Stephen had been right—it *was* a very good fortune indeed.

The End

Also by Sahara Kelly

80

A Kink in Her Tails

All Night Video: For Research Purposes Only

All Night Video: At Cross Purposes

Beating Level Nine

Detour (with S.L. Carpenter)

Ellora's Cavemen: Legendary Tails III (*anthology*)

Ellora's Cavemen: Tales From the Temple I (*anthology*)

Flame of Shadows

Georgie and Her Dragon

The Glass Stripper

Guardians of Time 1: Alana's Magic Lamp

Guardians of Time 2: Finding the Zero-G Spot

The Gypsy Lovers

Hansell and Gretty

Haunting Love Alley (with S.L. Carpenter)

Irish Enchantment (*anthology*)

The Knights Elemental

Lyndhurst and Lydia

Madam Charlie

Magnus Ravynne and Mistress Swann

Mesmerized (*anthology*)

Mystic Visions (*anthology*)

Partners in Passion 1: Justin and Eleanor (with S.L. Carpenter)

Partners in Passion 2: No Limits (with S.L. Carpenter)

Persephone's Wings

Peta and the Wolfe

About the Author

ಐ

Sahara Kelly was transplanted from old England to New England where she now lives with her husband and teenage son. Making the transition from her historical regency novels to Romantica™ has been surprisingly easy, and now Sahara can't imagine writing anything else. She is dedicated to the premise that everybody should have fantasies.

Sahara welcomes comments from readers. You can find her website and email address on her author bio page at www.ellorascave.com.

Why an electronic book?

We live in the Information Age—an exciting time in the history of human civilization, in which technology rules supreme and continues to progress in leaps and bounds every minute of every day. For a multitude of reasons, more and more avid literary fans are opting to purchase e-books instead of paper books. The question from those not yet initiated into the world of electronic reading is simply: *Why?*

1. *Price.* An electronic title at Ellora's Cave Publishing and Cerridwen Press runs anywhere from 40% to 75% less than the cover price of the exact same title in paperback format. Why? Basic mathematics and cost. It is less expensive to publish an e-book (no paper and printing, no warehousing and shipping) than it is to publish a paperback, so the savings are passed along to the consumer.

2. *Space.* Running out of room in your house for your books? That is one worry you will never have with electronic books. For a low one-time cost, you can purchase a handheld device specifically designed for e-reading. Many e-readers have large, convenient screens for viewing. Better yet, hundreds of titles can be stored within your new library—on a single microchip. There are a variety of e-readers from different manufacturers. You can also read e-books on your PC or laptop computer. (Please note that Ellora's Cave does not endorse any specific brands. You can check our websites at www.ellorascave.com or

www.cerridwenpress.com for information we make available to new consumers.)

3. *Mobility.* Because your new e-library consists of only a microchip within a small, easily transportable e-reader, your entire cache of books can be taken with you wherever you go.

4. ***Personal Viewing Preferences.*** Are the words you are currently reading too small? Too large? Too... ANNOYING? Paperback books cannot be modified according to personal preferences, but e-books can.

5. ***Instant Gratification.*** Is it the middle of the night and all the bookstores near you are closed? Are you tired of waiting days, sometimes weeks, for bookstores to ship the novels you bought? Ellora's Cave Publishing sells instantaneous downloads twenty-four hours a day, seven days a week, every day of the year. Our webstore is never closed. Our e-book delivery system is 100% automated, meaning your order is filled as soon as you pay for it.

Those are a few of the top reasons why electronic books are replacing paperbacks for many avid readers.

As always, Ellora's Cave and Cerridwen Press welcome your questions and comments. We invite you to email us at Comments@ellorascave.com or write to us directly at Ellora's Cave Publishing Inc., 1056 Home Avenue, Akron, OH 44310-3502.

THE
☥ ELLORA'S CAVE ☥
LIBRARY

Stay up to date with Ellora's Cave Titles in
Print with our Quarterly Catalog.

TO RECIEVE A CATALOG,
SEND AN EMAIL WITH YOUR NAME
AND MAILING ADDRESS TO:

CATALOG@ELLORASCAVE.COM

OR SEND A LETTER OR POSTCARD
WITH YOUR MAILING ADDRESS TO:

CATALOG REQUEST
c/o ELLORA'S CAVE PUBLISHING, INC.
1056 HOME AVENUE
AKRON, OHIO 44310-3502

erridwen, the Celtic Goddess of wisdom, was the muse who brought inspiration to storytellers and those in the creative arts. Cerridwen Press encompasses the best and most innovative stories in all genres of today's fiction. Visit our site and discover the newest titles by talented authors who still get inspired - much like the ancient storytellers did, once upon a time.

Discover for yourself why readers can't get enough of the multiple award-winning publisher

Ellora's Cave.

Whether you prefer e-books or paperbacks,

be sure to visit EC on the web at
www.ellorascave.com

for an erotic reading experience that will leave you breathless.